SNOWDRIFTS

Dear Carol-Ann
I hope you
enjoy my novel.

Live what
you love
Kathi Nidd

a novel by

KATHI NIDD

Snowdrifts
Copyright © 2016 by Kathi Nidd

Library and Archives Canada Cataloguing in Publication

Nidd, Kathi, 1964-, author
Snowdrifts / Kathi Nidd.

Issued in print and electronic formats.
ISBN 978-1-77302-097-6 (paperback).
ISBN 978-1-77302-096-9 (html).

     I. Title.

PS8627.I4S66 2016   C813'.6
C2016-905570-1
C2016-905571-X

Tellwell Talent
www.tellwell.ca

ISBN
978-1-77302-097-6 (Paperback)
978-1-77302-096-9 (eBook)

To Jeff,
because everything
is possible when we are
hand in hand.

Elephant Shoes.

Acknowledgements

A novel grows from inspiration to finished manuscript through creativity, hard work, self-belief and amazing support. It has been many years since the whistle of a fierce winter storm nudged an idea into my mind and many people have stood beside me through the process.

I am forever grateful to my husband and best friend, Jeff. His ongoing love and support not only makes anything seem possible but has proven, in so many aspects of our lives, that the possible is often more brilliant than I can imagine.

I want to thank my parents: Mom for believing I could accomplish whatever I set my mind to, and Dad for reminding me to do what makes me happy. I wish you were here to celebrate with us.

Thank you to my sisters, Diane and Judy, for being such dear friends and for your unwavering willingness to read random scenes sent in the heat of writer's passion. You both provide me with a safe haven to share my work as well as honest, insightful feedback, each in your own unique way. Thanks Judy for helping to piece it all together and Diane for being the first full end-to-end reader.

To my dear best girlfriend, Mary, who saw me as an author from the first day I admitted my dream to her. I think I have finally figured out what I want to be when I grow up! And to Snowdrifts' greatest fans, Heidi and Sandy, for the many long days and nights of "Book Club" and your ability to know my characters so well.

To my family of fellow authors: Kit Flynn for her enormous heart and willingness to hear my latest words despite ever-changing character names, thank you for letting me share your dragonflies. To Coralee Boileau who taught me to hold out for the perfect phrase and cherish it like a ladybug in February, thank you for keeping me in your contact list as "Writer Lady". To my amazing writing mentor, Susan Jennings, who listened to my firstborn words and helped me nurture them. Susan's guidance gave me the confidence to re-embrace writing and the methods to complete a full novel. To "The Ottawa Story Spinners": Barry Alder, Chantal Frobel, Rita Myres, Tony Myres and Audrey Starkes for your extraordinary insight and advice. Special thanks to my lovely fellow "spinner" and dear friend, Anne Raina, for your constant encouragement and willingness to read my words.

I have heard that when a first draft is done, that's when the real works starts. Nothing could be more true. I was blessed that my first draft was entrusted to my editor, Mark McGahey. Mark not only knows where the commas go, but cradles my sentences with fresh and caring eyes, questioning what needs to be questioned and gently nudging me to "author it up", often in the exact places I already knew needed attention.

If you ever doubt the enormity of support around you, just mention that you are writing a book: To my other incredible family members and friends who have provided everything from proofreading to feedback, ideas to encouragement, my heartfelt thanks.

Finally, I thank my best furry friend, Brooklynn, who patiently waits on her blanket when I am lost in a flow of ideas. And, more importantly, when the words won't come, she reminds me of the solution to many of life's problems—a long walk in the park to clear your head.

Trust dies but mistrust blossoms.

— Sophocles

CHAPTER 1

SIPPING THE AIR LIKE AN INFANT, for any real breath felt like a knife twisting in his ribs, Joe leaned forward and moaned. All that remained was darkness. The last pinpoints of light in the windshield had been extinguished under an ever-thickening blanket of snow. He stroked the remnants of the limp airbag between his fingers while a salty tear crept onto his lips.

He'd count to three, and then try again. Try again for the umpteenth time to smash the window. This time he'd ignore the pain from the snarled metal that gripped his leg. He'd pull up his buttocks, release his leg and push, push with all his might. Turning to look to his right, he snapped into action.

One. Two. Three. Push! He hurled himself up, straightening his bloodied knee for leverage and holding his elbow like a pointed weapon to smash the glass. He heard a pop and it felt like his hip was ripping from its socket.

Nausea returned. The window remained intact.

"God dammit!" he yelled, and then winced as the outburst caused his broken ribs to grind against each other. He knew it was hard to break a car window without a tool to weaken the glass, but why on earth hadn't it broken on its own? The door was already smashed from top to bottom from the second flip to solid ground

1

as it tumbled down the embankment, so why no broken window like on the passenger side? Cold air and moisture flooded in from that side, but he couldn't climb over there. There was no way. And why hadn't the windshield shattered? He could hear his shallow gasps and a flutter in his chest as he laughed sickly at the irony: the BMW's windows were too well made.

Darkness. The electrical system had shut down seconds after the car had stopped rolling. And with the whole car now buried in snow, Joe lost sight of the hope-giving headlights on the cars of the unknowing drivers passing above. He thought of them up there, driving along the highway unaware that his car had fishtailed on ice, and that as he'd attempted a recovering turn to the left to avoid the guardrail, the car had become airborne. Those above, if any, had missed the car soaring, hawk-like, then landing right side up twenty-five feet below on the only moderately flat patch of ground on the otherwise steep slope below the road. No one witnessed it hesitate there for a brief moment of hope before regaining momentum and losing grip with the earth again to fall another thirty feet. No one above, nor below at the river's edge, saw the car rolling over before finally stopping again right side up in the middle of nowhere. Above, they drove through the storm, home to their families, not noticing the damaged guardrail, unaware of the accident below.

Joe licked his lips and swirled the taste of acid and blood again on his tongue. He wondered what time it was; the car's clock display was now stuck in a dull, stunned 88:88. He felt around on the dashboard for his discarded smart phone and stroked the smashed face to feel the roughness on his fingertips, then tried once again to turn it on to find some light, or better yet a signal. Dead.

He had to get out of there. Although he knew the highway was a mere fifty or sixty feet above and behind him, ascending the steep rocky cliffs beneath Old Country's Edge Highway was impossible. The other option was to walk, or perhaps crawl, towards the river-front. Familiar with the landscape, he thought he might be able to figure out his location and find a house or cottage somewhere down below, but, in his condition, he was far from safety. Although everything was dead silent now but for the tapping of ice pellets against the car hood, he played the crunching and crashing noises over again in his mind, those few moments that seemed like they lasted hours, careening down and knowing his life might end that night.

Joe reached down and touched his pant leg. Uncertain if he was wincing from pain or fear, he ran his finger up from his shin towards his hip, patting slightly to evaluate his injuries. Just below his knee, some piece of the car's interior seemed to clench him like a claw, preventing movement without excruciating spasm. He continued his fingers' journey upward, ignoring the warm, wet blood that had soaked through the fabric. Then, in the upper part of his thigh, he felt something hard and cold protruding outward. Horrified, he gently touched its ridged edge, recoiling from pain at the slightest movement of the foreign object, and cried out as realization slid into his consciousness. It was the screwdriver. Earlier today he'd carelessly tossed the Phillips into the car. Now the metal rod with its crossed point was completely lodged in his flesh and only the grip of the handle remained exposed. He gagged, losing control of his gut for a moment, and then inhaled deeply to focus.

The screwdriver could break the window, but what had he learned about impaled objects in first aid classes long ago? NEVER remove them! But he needed the screwdriver to smash the window and he needed to release his lower leg from the jaw that held him captive. Panting, he gripped the handle and gritted his teeth, then cried as his instincts prevented him from pulling it out on his first try; just the movement of his hand on the handle caused intense pain and dread. He sat a moment, trying to think of another way, and then tried twice more, failing both times. Then, as though something stronger than him took over, he reached down again, closed his eyes, yanked, and yelled, collapsing into sobs but triumphantly holding the bloody screwdriver.

Now it was time to release his body. He removed his necktie and tied it around his leg as a bandage, feeling a nub of shattered bone under his thumb as he tied it. Adrenaline surged and he inhaled as hard as he could, mustering everything he had to push on. In one swooping motion, he lifted his buttocks, twisted and hoisted himself up, releasing his leg. In the darkness he touched the familiar ridges of the screwdriver for a single moment, remembering.

Then, with all his might he drove the screwdriver and his fist through the window. Exhilarated by the sound of the smashing glass and the chill of the air that blew fiercely against his face, he yelled like a feral animal, letting the wet snow that had accumulated beside the buried car fall on top of him until his suit jacket was covered. Sobs escape his mouth into the unsympathetic night air.

He twisted and heaved himself halfway out the window then hung there a while in an inverted vee, sobbing at the accomplishment and noticing the pressure of the door against his ribs was creating an almost pleasurable traction. Then he braced himself one last time and forged on. Using every bit of core strength he had left, he pulled inch by inch until he was able to slide out onto the snow and arch his chest to breathe, despite the stabbing in his ribs. He looked down towards where he imagined the banks of the Argent River began, trying to make out where he was in relation to the city he knew so well. He knew this was the worst possible area, the most remote section beneath Old Country's Edge Highway. The section that provided the most enchanting and barren views from above. He dragged his dead weight lower half like a lizard, feeling as though every nerve from his ankle to his hip had been ripped to shreds. He moaned and grimaced, then shivered and slid painfully around the back of the car, pausing to look at the trunk and realizing the back end was so compressed that opening it was impossible. Tiny ice crystals prickled his face. A full moon sliced through two sections of cloud, briefly providing a taunting light then vanishing again. He tried to calculate what time it was and how many hours of darkness lay ahead.

He crept along the side of the car, pulling his overcoat out through the smashed back window then finally reaching the broken passenger window. He reached through the shattered glass and a wave of sorrow gripped his chest. A pain that far outweighed any injury the accident had created.

"If you can hear me ..." he gasped. "If you can hear me, I'm going for help."

CHAPTER 2

"Where ARE you?" Scalding tears rolled down her cheeks. Andrea turned back to the clock on the bedside table for the hundredth time, 2:41 AM. One minute later than the last time she'd looked. Lashing the bedcovers off and standing to look out the window, she paused as anger and fear fenced with sharpened swords. She whipped the long, billowing curtain in annoyance then grasped it back, clenching the fabric in her fist. Outside the window, the street slept, languishing in a lull from the day-long blizzard. Snow swirled into meringue tops at the edge of her walkway while on the road a plow ground its way forward and back, its unforgiving blade creating a sharp wall of snow.

"Damn it." She reached for her smart phone and, once again, looked at her last six text messages to Joe, starting with, "Hey, are you almost here?" "Hello? Are you on your way?" "Where are you?" "I'm getting worried, please call me." Up to the latest: "Joe, I'm losing my mind. CALL ME." She jumped as the fierce wind tossed some remnant ice pellets into the glass as though Mother Nature herself was spitting in her face. "Christ!" She let her thumb hover over his number, and then pressed it to dial. It immediately went to voice mail.

"Hi, you've reached Joe Sinclair of Forester & Sinclair, I can't take your ..."

"DAMN IT JOE!" she threw the phone down to land on the soft bedcovers as her diamond ring caught the light. Taking her left hand in her right, she ran a fingertip along the platinum band, imagining the days that lay ahead. *Okay Andrea, get it together,* she thought. *Think logically. There was a bad storm today, maybe he slept at the office. No, then he would have answered the office phone. Maybe the phone lines are out. But why isn't he answering his cell? And why would he not come over? My house is only a two-minute drive from the office. He could have walked for fuck's sake!*

"Oh, God, where are you Joe? What's happened?" she whimpered aloud as tears began to flow again. Sitting back down on the bed, she buried her head into her pillow, sobbing loudly, then catching her breath so as not to wake up Meg.

"Just breathe," she coaxed herself. "This will all make sense in the morning. He'll come strolling in here with some logical explanation and I'll feel like a fool. But seriously, he knew how important it was for him to come over tonight to meet Meg. Something awful must have happened. Oh God!" She buried her head again, scrunching the corner of her blanket under her chin and dreaming of Joe.

In just three weeks they'd be walking down the aisle together. She imagined Joe in his black tuxedo, dark green cummerbund and deep red rose boutonniere. He would reach for her hand while she stood in the glittering white ball gown she'd dreamed of since she was a little girl. Their wedding, on New Year's Eve, would be a glamorous and festive affair. Capturing the deep reds, greens and golds of the season, the main dining room of the Millerton Yacht Club would become a shimmering and magical place of fairy tales. At midnight, guests would raise their champagne glasses to Joe and Andrea while outside the wide French doors the Argent River would light up with fireworks. Andrea felt her heartbeat slowing down and calmness overtook her while she pictured every feature of the glorious night. Thinking through the details, her mind finally relaxed and she fell asleep.

She woke with a jolt.

"Joe?" She listened to the familiar creaks of the townhouse and heard neither footsteps nor the voice she so anxiously awaited. She looked at her phone again and found its screen blank but for the background photo of her and Joe from the office barbeque party. It was 4:56. *I need Meg. I should go wake her up. Oh God, then we'll both be worried sick, and she was so exhausted. Oh, I need her.* She sat up, disgusted that her soaking wet T-shirt was clinging to her body. Taking one last look at the phone and then gathering it up in her hand, she headed for the guest bedroom and nudged her sister awake.

"Andrea? What's wrong? What time is it?" Meg lifted her head from the pillow.

"Five. Meggie, I'm so sorry to wake you but I'm completely losing it." Andrea heard her own voice cracking.

"What's wrong?" Her sister sat up and leaned forward to where Andrea sat on the bed. Her older sister's face was flushed and wet with tears, and disheveled blonde curls fell onto her shoulders. "Did Joe never come?"

Andrea collapsed into sobs, shaking her head. "Something's happened. I just know it. He wouldn't have missed meeting you on your first night home. He wouldn't miss meeting his future sister-in-law."

"Gosh, Andrea, I had no idea you were up and worrying. I just flaked out so hard." Meg sighed, still gathering her thoughts from the sudden awakening. "Have you tried calling him?"

"Of course! And email and text and the office phone!" Andrea snapped and Meg turned her eyelids downward. "Sorry Nugget, I'm just tired and worried. I'm so sorry to wake you. I know how tired you were from the trip and all the flight delays with the weather."

"It's okay." Meg pulled her legs over the side of the bed and switched on the lamp. "I'm sorry I crashed on you last night. All that circling in the air, plus the time change, just did me in. I was planning to get up again though, once Joe got here, so we could meet."

She paused a moment, pulling down her long white nightgown and looking towards the window. "Has the storm let up?"

Andrea nodded, "Seems to be, for now. The plows are out." She reached for a Kleenex and blew her nose with a honk.

"Maybe he got stuck somewhere? It was pretty bad. I mean getting here from the airport took me hours."

"His office is only six blocks from here. He could've walked!"

Meg rubbed her eyes, contemplating the situation. "Did you try calling the ..." She stopped, debating. "Hospitals? Or the police?"

"I was thinking about it. Do you think I should? I'm so scared, Nugget."

"Well, I don't know. I mean. I don't know Joe—only what you've told me. Is it like him to not show up? To not call? You've told me how he works really hard and sometimes gets caught up in it."

Andrea pulled her knees into her chest, looking down at her engagement ring and shook her head. "He'd be here. He knew how badly I wanted him to meet you. And you are only here a few days. And the next time you come it's the wedding and we won't have a lot of time, you know, for him to really get to know you. I can't believe he didn't come. Something is wrong."

"Let me call the hospitals, and maybe the police. I mean, he's not missing but maybe they'll know." She paused. "I mean, if there's been an accident or something." She reached for her thick sweatshirt at the bottom of the bed where she'd discared it the night before and pulled it over her head.

Andrea stared at Meg in horror.

"At least you'd know then. And if they don't know anything that's a good sign, right?" Meg stood up and led her sister downstairs to the kitchen, guiding her to sit in front of the laptop at the counter bar stool. "Look up Highlands Hospital's number. I'll try the police. What kind of car is it?" She pushed two dirty plates and one clean one out of her way, surprised her sister hadn't cleared off the table from the night before.

Andrea sighed, tapping at the mouse, her face illuminated by the screen. "What? Oh, his car? It's a BMW, the 760Li. Oh God, I can't even concentrate!" She tapped hard on the keyboard. "White."

"Okay, don't worry," Meg whispered, listening for an answer, her neck crooked into the phone while she opened cupboards in search of tea bags.

A while later the sisters sat sipping camomile tea, facing each other on matching loveseats. There were no reports of a Joe Sinclair at the hospital and no unidentified patients. The police reported that there'd been numerous accidents overnight, but none involving a BMW. Satisfied that Joe was safe, Andrea had calmed down enough to sit quietly and Meg saw her sister's mood elevating.

Meg looked around the room with its modern decor and huge floor-to-ceiling grey stone fireplace against crisp blue walls. "Your townhouse is great. I didn't really take it all in last night."

"Thanks."

"Will Joe move in here then, after the wedding, or before?"

"Yes. He's selling his house. It's way too big. Over the top, if you ask me. And so far out of town. It's a long drive. I really don't know what he was thinking, buying and restoring that wreck of an old farm house."

Meg nodded. "This place is so nice and new. And so close to everything. It was a great find. Six blocks from Joe's office, you said? That's great. His office is on Argent Street?"

"Just off it, on Knoll. That tall building, you know the kind of orangey brick one."

Meg nodded, remembering the small city she'd grown up in, picturing every inch of the main street with its quaint shops. It was a long way from Vancouver—where she'd moved at age eighteen—in so many ways. "Yes, the Frosst Building; still the tallest in Millerton, I suppose. And what about you? Are you looking for a new job?"

Andrea dropped her tea mug hard onto the glass topped coffee table. "Seriously? Seriously Meg, you think I have time to look for a job? With the wedding and everything else that went on?"

A familiar strain caused Meg to look away and take a deep breath before answering. "I suppose not. I was just wondering if you had any plans. I, I still don't really understand what happened. You seemed so happy working at Joe's firm. I mean, you said you liked the work and you two fell in love there. How'd everything get so nasty so fast?"

"I don't want to talk about it. They're awful there. I can't wait for Joe to realize it and go out on his own." She looked at Meg's curious expression. "What?"

"Well, you have this new townhouse and all the wedding costs. I was just ..." She looked at Andrea's deep blue eyes carving into her the way she'd done since they were girls. "Never mind. I was just thinking out loud." Meg smiled.

"Well, I have money. And Joe's a lawyer. He does well."

"I know. Of course. Forget it. Your house is great. A far cry from Ruston Street." She changed the subject. "So, here I am for three whole days. We need to think about what we have to do for the wedding. First, we have to figure out my dress."

"Right. Yes. So glad you are here, Nugget, and so happy you've agreed to be my maid of honour. You still okay with the dark green?"

"Of course." Meg nodded.

"Great, well I put two dresses aside for you at Timeless Lace. Do you remember that store? I'm sure it was there before you left." Meg nodded. "I hope you like them. I think they are both amazing. They'll both suit your tiny frame. If not, we can keep looking. The green will go so nice with your dark hair. Of course, we'll have to figure out what to do with it. Do you think it's long enough for an up do?"

"Probably not." Meg tugged at the ends of the dark brown wisps on her neck.

"Hmm, that's too bad."

Meg lowered her eyelids. "What else do we need to do while I am here? You wanted to talk about the cake?"

"Oh yes, the cake. I want lemon. We'll pop over to Grady's so you can taste the one I chose."

"Okay, I was also going to try to grab a couple of hours to meet up with some school friends. You remember the Blacks?"

Andrea shook her head and Meg took a deep breath.

"Well, there were two sisters and I was really good friends with both of them. Jen and Julie Black?" Her sister stared blankly. "Anyway, I was going to try to grab a coffee or maybe lunch with them while I'm here."

"I don't remember them."

Meg bit her lip. "And, uh, well, I was going to go and see Mom."

"And Joe, of course. You have to meet Joe."

"Of course, Andrea. That's why I'm here, to meet Joe. But I also just wanted you to know that I was going to go and visit Mom while I am in town."

"He must have fallen asleep at the office. It's the only explanation that makes sense. He works too hard and he probably got caught up with something. He's not hearing the office phone. I should try again now that it's getting lighter out."

Meg gave up. "Good idea."

"Maybe I'll leave a message at his office too, for Margot. She's the secretary. She can be nasty but I'm sure if it's about Joe, she'll be nice. I'm sure she'll return my call. She's always in by 7:30 and it's almost 6:30 now." She dialed the number and left the message, then tossed her phone on the cushion. "Or you know what? Maybe I'll just go over there. I'll go take a shower and then just walk over. I bet you anything he'll be crashed out asleep on that ugly sofa in his office."

"Probably. But I'm sure—Margot was it?—she'll call back soon. Why don't you just wait until she gets in? Plus, it's morning now, so if he did fall asleep he'll be waking up." Meg frowned.

"No, I should go over there. I need to see him in person."

"But, if he's not there, the office will be closed and then you'll worry even more."

"No." She shook her head. "I need to see if he's there. And if he's not, maybe I'll find some clue of where he is. And being closed doesn't matter."

Meg watched Andrea take in a gulp of air. Suddenly, Andrea's expression softened into a grin. "I still have a key!"

CHAPTER 3

JOE HAD ALWAYS FELT a special connection with snow. He'd heard the story a dozen times about how, during the big storm of 1982, his father had dug a path to the car for his mother just minutes before her water broke. Then, two years later while the city recovered from a late March storm, his younger brother Dan had seemed to magically arrive. At age sixteen, a phone call from Doug Forester during 1998's late February blizzard had turned Joe's worst nightmare into shimmering white absolution. Most importantly, snow had fallen as Joe had fallen in love under a streetlamp during a memorable Christmastime snowstorm in 2009. Now, another extraordinary snowfall had come to Millerton.

He removed his gloves and stretched his arms above his head to keep the blood flowing. Scooping some snow into his hand to wet his mouth, he then pulled himself up to stand on his good leg and scanned 360 degrees to orient himself in the dawn light. Recalling the adage that when one dies, their life flashes before them, he considered the idea that he was dying. But instead of his whole life flashing, only yesterday played out in front of him like a flickering, antique projector show.

In the morning, on the way back to the office, gentle snowflakes had danced and dived across his windshield, causing Joe's mind to escape to carefree childhood snow days. He'd relished the icy blade of the wind as he walked to the office. The intensity of the storm, and people's reactions to it, had amused him. Colleagues had popped by his office "because it has the best view" and lingered, transfixed by the blender blizzard like wide-eyed children awaiting a school bus cancellation. An onslaught of emails from Weather Alert had nagged him repeatedly. Was it really that bad, or had this era of information reached the saturation point?

He remembered her voice too, "Perhaps you should just sleep at the office?" and his review of the suggestion. Everyone had been caught up in the weather while Joe was, instead, caught up in Chase McGill.

Today would have been Day 1 of Chase's murder trial. The fate of the nineteen-year-old lay in piles of navy blue file folders and notes scrawled on lined yellow pads. Chase was finally ready; practiced, polished. He'd even made jokes when leaving Joe's office yesterday. It was time for the chaos to be over. In the afternoon, Joe had worked meticulously, dotting and crossing every detail to the fine point of unwavering confidence, without consideration for the weather, without heeding the departure of the rest of the law office's staff, and without noticing the arrival of an unexpected visitor.

But outside his window, as the day moved into late afternoon, this "storm of the decade" had picked up intensity and spun the unprepared city on its axis, disrupting everything in its path. For although quaint Millerton had been warned of impending bad weather, no one knew the main body of the storm would change course so suddenly and plow into the city like a freight train. More snow had been dumped on the city in the past six hours than over the entire previous winter. Removal crews stood helpless, gathering to shake their heads and tell tales of past storms, perching their gloved hands on their shovels. Then the rain began, freezing on contact into a thick coat of ice, pulling down power lines and shellacking every rooftop, car, and tree branch. Finally, as evening fell, the heavy snow returned, trapped in a walloping wind that writhed with uncertainty.

Later, with each passing mile on Old Country's Edge Highway, Joe's headlights had illuminated a moving picture of swirling acrobats as he wove his way past peaking snowdrifts. Oddly, the highway hadn't been slippery at all. In fact, while there was snow in some areas, other spots were bare pavement, but Joe had been driving in the northern climate long enough to know about black ice. When the rear of the car started to slip, he'd recalled everything he should do without having to think—don't touch the brakes, ease off the gas and steer in the direction the back end is going. He'd done that. He knew he'd done that. But as the movie played over and over in his mind, it became clearer and clearer that the steering had failed him.

He recalled that when he had first pulled out of the parking lot he had noticed it was a bit off and commented that it was looser than usual. He'd even mentioned bringing it in to get it checked if time permitted during the trial. Why the hell hadn't he just pulled over when he first noticed it? What was he thinking? He cursed himself for being so eager to get to the house, for taking that particular route home, for so many things.

And now he questioned his latest decision, to abandon the car and leave her behind. At some point during the crash her head had hit the window or door frame causing blood to pour down the side of her face as she'd sat unconscious. He'd felt her breath against the back of his hand and her faint pulse beat against his fingertips but no amount of gentle nudging nor yelling had brought her back. Joe cursed, wishing it was him who lay unconscious in the car against the rocky cliff. Would he have been better off staying in the shelter of the wrecked car, using his body warmth to save her, attempting to build a fire to alert those above? Instead, instinctively, he'd covered her with his suit jacket and left to find help. But staring at the endless snow-covered ground he'd painfully traversed and the thick tangle of trees that lay ahead between him and the river, he wasn't sure. And now that dawn had broken, would someone above possibly see a glint of the white metal against the snow? Had she awoken? Was she dead?

He zeroed in on the direction of the river and tried his best to recall the area. As far as he could tell, he was near an area where he and Dan had gone to a camp as kids. If he could figure out where that was, there'd probably be people nearby. He recalled that there were a number of farms in the area—but which way to go? He tried again to put his weight on his bad leg and grimaced at the familiar pain. He wanted to remain upright now, so he'd have to drag it somehow, like an injured animal.

He looked at the glistening tree branches as he pulled himself along, eventually finding one that had obviously met its demise before the storm. Picking it up, he assessed that it was the right length and pushed it flat against his leg, then retied his necktie around his shin and his coat belt around his thigh as a splint. He pulled his overcoat tightly around his ribcage, pressing into it with his forearm to alleviate the pain he was trying to learn to ignore and looked back in the direction he'd come. Having managed to descend to flatter ground, he marvelled that he hadn't fallen completely over in his attempt to proceed downward. He peered up to where the car was; a barely visible white patch against the snow-painted rock face. He should have put something on top of it, a marker that someone could see from the air. He should have taken off his shirt and used it as a flag. He berated himself, feeling helplessness taking over. Should he go back? How long it had taken just to get here? He stared to the right then left, and for a split second thought he saw something black bob up and down. Was it a person?

CHAPTER 4

MARGOT NUDGED CHARLIE with the toe of her boot, coaxing the elderly cocker spaniel to relieve himself after the long night. Reluctantly, Charlie sniffed and evaluated every inch of the yard, looking for the perfect spot, much to Margot's dismay as she was already late. It seemed like no matter what she did today, she was behind. First, it seemed to take an unusually long time to get Mom bathed. And then no matter what outfit Margot held up, her mother shook her head and spat, until finally Margot had just picked one, then melted with regret at the pain she saw in her mother's eyes. Feeling terrible, she had reinforced to Mom how pretty she looked once she'd gotten her dressed. She even took the time to apply Crimson Blush lipstick to her mother's sagging lips, reminding her mother that it had been her favourite and sitting with her a moment longer than usual, putting her even further behind schedule.

Then Dalia, the latest agency nurse, had arrived late, blaming yesterday's storm and some long-winded tale about the bus turning the wrong direction. Now Charlie, urinating according to his own leisurely schedule, caused heat to rise in her cheeks.

Margot liked to get in to Forester & Sinclair promptly at 7:30, long before any of the other office staff arrived, and typically an hour or two before Joe and Doug arrived. It gave her time to ease into the day, away from the pressures and loneliness of home. She would sit at her desk outside Joe's office and sip her vanilla swirl coffee while combing through the morning paper. By eight, still a good hour before the rest of the staff arrived, she'd sign into her computer and catch up on emails, planning the day and making sure everything Joe needed for his day was organized and prepared.

Margot had been an administrative assistant at Doug Forester's law firm since his first case over nineteen years ago. Back then it was just the two of them, making do in the shabby basement office of a rather dilapidated three-story building off Millerton's main thoroughfare. As Doug's reputation grew, so did his firm, and while life took its twists and turns, Margot had remained his most loyal ally.

For the past six years, Margot had formally worked directly for Joe Sinclair, Doug's young protégé and recently-named partner. Wanting to give Joe the best start possible, Doug had assigned him the best assistant possible. But in her heart, and in everyone else's eyes, she still worked for both of them and pretty much ran the entire firm, especially since Doug hadn't predicted the long line of inadequate assistants he'd end up with in an effort to replace her, and his constant need to pull Margot back into anything that required special attention. Neither lawyer could imagine getting through a week without Margot's guiding touch and loving diligence. And Margot couldn't imagine a day not devoted to her Doug and her Joe.

It was already close to eight when Margot smiled and patted Charlie on the head as he finally finished his business. She popped him back into the house and gathered her oversized quilted handbag, pausing only a moment to kiss the tips of her fingers then run them along the frame of the photo in the front hall. The soldier stared ahead, as always, pride with a mix of loving mischief. She took a quick last look in the hall mirror, tousling her mass of red curls that headed in every direction, then headed outside.

Testing the driveway again with her boot to ensure it wasn't too slippery, she gingerly made her way towards the street. On a good day, it was a fifteen-minute walk to the office, today it would be more like twenty on the still-buried sidewalks.

Convincing herself that staying upright was more important than punctuality, she made her way very slowly from her home towards Argent Street, the main street in Millerton's newly-revived neighbourhood of Riverwalk, where store owners were beginning to open doors and clear off their walkways. Across the street from where she walked, Mr. Greeley, the long-time owner of FreshMart, stood holding a shovel, red-faced and wiping his forehead with his scarf. Margot considered crossing over to tell him to be careful for his health, but chose instead to wave and nod. Her attention then focused on the store window at Quills, where all the latest best sellers were stacked amid red ribbons and holly. She made a mental note to come back when the weather was better and buy herself a nice Christmas gift. Since her husband's death overseas fourteen years earlier, she'd made it a tradition to buy herself some new books, as he'd always done for her at Christmas. Somehow, reading them on cold winter afternoons made her feel like he was nearby.

Passing the Rising Bean, she paused, debating picking up another bag of coffee for the office and arriving even later. It wouldn't matter. After all, Joe was in court this morning. And lately Doug had been arriving later and later. If anything, both of them would be the first to tell her to take her time. Still, she hated to take advantage.

Twenty minutes later, brown paper coffee bag in hand, Margot ascended the wide staircase of the high rise office building, mentally noting that she'd have to call maintenance to come and clear off the steps before clients arrived. For, despite the building having numerous tenants, including the administrative offices of its founder, Frosst Toothpaste, it seemed Margot had to run the show. She rode the elevator up to the twelfth floor, then pushed her key into the lock of the wide double doors, surprised to feel the door push open before she had a chance to turn the key. Margot shouted out as she used her heel to pull off one wet, fur-lined boot and then her hand to pull off the other. Calling out again, she scanned the main foyer and peered down the hallway to the right, where most of the associates and clerks worked, but neither heard nor saw anyone. Moving to the left, she made her way past the entrance to Doug's outer office where his latest assistant, Amber, resided and found it empty as well. Finally, she continued on to her own office and jumped in alarm.

"Andrea! Oh my God, you scared me to death! How did you get in here?"

"I still have a key." Andrea flipped a key ring around her index finger. She was seated atop Margot's large metal desk wrapped in her oversized coat with a lavish fur-lined hood and lapels.

Margot frowned. "Well, you shouldn't! I didn't even know you ever had one at all. Uh, why are you here?" She noted Andrea's flushed cheeks and tearful eyes.

"Oh, Margot," Andrea hopped off the desk and rushed towards her as Margot recoiled, unbuttoning her coat and setting her handbag and the coffee down on a chair. "Joe's missing, Margot!"

"Andrea, I really don't think you should be here. Joe's not here. Wait, what do you mean, missing?"

"I've been trying to reach him all night. He was supposed to come over last night, for dinner, but he never showed. He hasn't answered his cell or his office line. "Have you talked to him?"

"No." Margot walked around her desk to pop her bag into the large cabinet that, oddly, stood on a wide step left over from the building's original design. Remaining on the step, she leaned back against the cabinet, bringing the two women to the same height, "But he doesn't always check in when he has court. He has a trial starting today." She hesitated. "I'll give him the message that you were here." Margot paused and absorbed Andrea's words. "He was going to your place for dinner?" She looked at the tall blonde, amazed at how much she'd changed in the three months since Doug had escorted her out the front door, holding her elbow firmly and tossing her briefcase and purse out into the hallway after her. The previously well put together woman appeared worn and tired.

"Margot. Please help me. I'm just sick inside. He never showed up and I can't reach him. We tried the hospitals and even the police."

"We?"

"Me and my sister. She's in town. Margot, are you listening to me?"

"Well, he's due in court at nine and he wasn't planning to come here first. I'm sure he's fine." She felt herself softening as a small tinge of concern rose in her own heart.

"Is it possible he slept here? You know, with the snowstorm and all? I don't have a key to his office and I, well, I couldn't find one in your desk."

Margot returned to her desk and began to speak but bit her tongue. She cast a glance at the tall, metallic wall clock. "Well, I'm sure if he was here, he'd hear us talking and come out," she said. "Besides, he'd be at the courthouse by now. He likes to be early in case the client needs anything. If he checks in I will tell him to call you." Matter-of-factly, Margot began straightening folders on her desk, silently hoping Andrea would leave.

"I ... I ..." Andrea's voice cracked and Margot leaned forward as the curvy woman reached for the wall as though suddenly dizzy. Her long plum-coloured fingernails appeared almost black against the white doorframe.

Margot pulled a chair forward. "Oh my God. Sit down, let me get you some water." She fumbled towards the water cooler. "Or coffee?"

Andrea pulled a tissue from her pocket and dabbed her eyes. "No thanks. I'm just worried sick, Margot. He always calls and he didn't." Margot flinched and Andrea continued. "Yesterday morning we chatted about the storm. Then he said he was tied up with work yesterday afternoon. Then no word and he didn't show up for dinner." She glared at Margot. "I even tried calling you this morning, but there was no answer."

Margot's face flushed slightly. "Well, I took advantage of a court day and came in a little late. I had some things to do. I figured Joe wouldn't mind, but did you leave me a message?"

Andrea nodded her head as Margot pulled a second chair up beside her.

"Okay, well, you said you called the police? What did they say?"

"Nothing—no accidents for a car like his."

"Okay, well that's good! Look, maybe he left me a message too. Let's listen and if he hasn't called in I'll call the courthouse. He should be there already." She slid across Andrea to grab her office phone by the cord and pull it forward. She hit the lit up "Messages" button then punched in a code and put the phone on speaker.

The first two messages were from clients. Margot punched in the number to skip over them. The third message was Andrea's. Despite knowing what it said, Margot listened, feeling increasing guilt at arriving later than usual despite there being no expected need. Then came a fourth beep for which the machine indicated the message had been left just ten minutes earlier, followed by a gruff yet nervous voice.

"Joe, eh, Mr. Sinclair? Hey, it's Chase. Chase McGill. Uh, I called your cell but I guess you got held up or something? I'm at the courthouse early, like you said, so we could go over everything again. I'm outside the room you said, uh B110? Hey, can you call me back man? I'm freaking out a little here."

The message ended and Margot returned the receiver to the cradle. "Oh dear!" She hit the "On" button on her desktop and waited for the musical chimes of it starting up to end, then clicked open her email and muttered, "Nothing." She glanced at the clock again. "Well listen, Andrea, perhaps you should just head home. I'll call you if I hear anything." She couldn't deny the worry brewing inside of her.

Andrea scrunched her face. "Will you?" she questioned.

"I promise," Margot said, watching Andrea's distrust. "Look, Andrea. We both know how things have been. But I can see you are worried, so I promise. I will call you as soon as I hear from him."

Unconvinced, Andrea stood, scooping up her large, shimmering handbag, and turned towards the door mumbling a thank you. Then she pivoted on her burgundy leather boot heal. "No. No, I don't want to go. I need to know what is going on."

Margot lifted her cell phone from her desk and tapped on the screen, holding her hand out towards Andrea as if to begrudgingly say, "Okay, I'll try him." The two listened again to four rings followed by Joe's professional voicemail they both knew so well.

"What about his office? Can you let me in to his office?"

"Oh, I don't think so." Margot looked towards the office's double doors as Andrea sighed and rolled her eyes. "Okay, just a second." She headed towards the office as Andrea crowded her so closely from behind that the two women ended up entering at the same time.

"What is that stink?" Andrea threw her handbag down on the sofa and headed towards Joe's desk. "*Ugh!* What a mess!" She looked at the coffee table covered with open containers of small paper cartons, each partially filled with room temperature Chinese food. Two paper plates, one emptied but stained with red sauce and a few random lost kernels of rice, the other half-clean and half piled with peppers and bean sprouts. She lifted a red-stained clear plastic cup to her nose. "Wine?" she said with a snorting noise then tossed the glass back down before picking up the wine bottle and holding it up to the light. "This is empty. What the hell? Did he have a party here last night?"

"I don't ... I'm not ..."

"Margot! This makes no sense! He should have left early because of the storm and come right to my house. Did he leave before you? Before Doug?"

"No, I left first." Margot strained to remember. "But he said he was heading right out once he finished up a few things for the trial. A bunch of the staff kept popping in here, you know, because of the view of the river and the storm. They kept interrupting him."

"What time did you leave?" Andrea stroked her forehead in frustration.

"Oh, around two-thirty. I was worried about my mom. The caregiver had called and said she wanted to get home early herself."

"And he said he was leaving right after? So this was lunch?"

"No, no." Margot's face was flushed as she struggled to remember. "I picked him up lunch from the coffee cart downstairs. Turkey bacon club." She paused, scratching beneath her ringlets. "Andrea, please. I really need you to head home before Doug gets here. We don't need a scene. Once Doug's here, I'll ask him. Maybe he talked to Joe after I left. I know Joe was eager to speak with him."

"How about *we* wait and then *we* go and speak to Doug?"

"Andrea, I know you are worried but ..."

"I know." Andrea's blue eyes flashed. "I know I'm not very popular around here." Her voice softened "Please? Can't I just sit here and wait with you?"

Margot seated Andrea in one of the client chairs across from her desk while she began her day. She felt her stomach leaping with nerves at the thought of a confrontation. Ignoring Andrea, she began organizing some files, glancing at the clock every couple of minutes. Finally, she looked up to see Doug approaching her doorway with a big smile.

"G'morning!" he said, then stopped in his tracks. "Andrea?"

"Hi Doug," Margot began just as Andrea interrupted.

"Hi Doug, long time no see."

He stepped inside and raised his arm. "What? Look, you need to go."

"Doug, Doug," Margot began, "just calm ..."

"Doug," Andrea interrupted, standing to meet his stare. "I know I may not be welcome here, but this is an emergency. I haven't heard from Joe since yesterday. Margot hasn't heard a word either."

"What?"

"It's true, Doug," Margot whispered. "I am a bit concerned also. His client called and left a message. He's waiting for him at the courthouse. And I can't reach his cell or his house." Doug's expression changed from annoyance to concern. He looked directly at Margot.

"I called the police," Andrea continued, "and there weren't any accidents or anything in the storm. I, well my sister and I, called the hospitals, nothing. Doug—his office is a mess! There's Chinese food everywhere and some glasses like he and someone else drank wine. There's an empty bottle. Do you know anything?"

Doug looked at her, confused. "No, I don't. I don't know anything. But I'm sure he's at the courthouse now."

Margot spoke up: "She's right, Doug. The office is all messy. It looks like he had dinner here, with someone else."

"And a bottle of wine," Andrea interrupted. "Why the hell would he drink a bottle of wine?"

"Just a second, just a second." Doug began removing his coat and rubbed his forehead. "Is his car in the parking lot? I didn't notice."

Margot paused to think then shook he head. "No, it wasn't there when I got here. No."

"What time did you leave yesterday, Doug?" Andrea interrupted them.

Turning to snap at her, he saw Margot's huge eyes begging for his answer. "I left early yesterday too, but straight from the courthouse. I was in court all day and left around four. Yes, it was four; I remember the news coming on as I pulled out of the courthouse parking lot." He lowered his head. "I remember you called me saying Joe wanted to speak with me, but with the storm, I just figured we'd chat this morning."

"He did want to talk to you. You don't have any emails from him, or texts?"

Doug checked his phone quickly, scrolling with his thumb and shaking his head.

"What was on his calendar yesterday?" he asked.

"He left in the morning and didn't say where he was going, then he had a meeting with a client later in the morning, the one that he's in court with today." Margot said. "In the afternoon he was working on the trial."

"What client was it?" Doug spoke quickly, then turned to Andrea.

Margot hesitated. "Oh, for God's sake just tell him. I know about the cases. Besides, I won't know one name from another."

"It was Chase McGill." Margot looked directly at Doug's eyes and watched them pierce her back with a twinge of concern and a deep sigh. "Shit, that's right!" He sat down in one of the chairs just as the office phone rang and Margot jumped, then looked at the call display.

"It's the courthouse." She picked it up while the other two listened to her side of the conversation. When she hung up she said. "That was Lori, the bailiff. Joe's not there and Judge Miles is fit to be tied. I also had a message from Chase. He's very upset."

"Get him on the line for me," he commanded Margot, then softened, "please. Then give me a few minutes in my office to speak with him. Meanwhile, has anyone contacted Taryn?"

"He wouldn't be with her," Andrea scowled, interrupting him, flicking the hair that constantly fell in front of her eyes back behind her ear. Margot brought her fisted hand to her chin then returned to her desk to get Chase's number. Andrea shook her head in disgust.

"Margot?" Doug whispered. "Just to be sure, please give Taryn a call." He turned to Andrea. "Please leave." Andrea crossed her arms and didn't budge.

"We'll call you if we hear anything." Margot assured her. Andrea rose slowly, walking past Doug without making eye contact and left the office.

CHAPTER 5

IF THE BLACK OBJECT bobbing near the car had been a person, they were long gone. In fact, Joe began to wonder if he'd seen anything at all. He'd managed to find himself on a worn path amid the trees and, using the toe of his boot, had dug down in the snow to reveal a bit of a dirt road. He paused a moment, pleased that his burning cold, wet left foot was now on a harder surface and wondering why his right foot wasn't really feeling cold at all. He wanted to take his shoes off to rub his toes but feared what he might find; wanted to rip open his pant leg at the tear and examine what he imagined was blood, bruising and swelling. At least it appeared that he had stopped bleeding from the point where he'd been impaled by the screwdriver and the protrusion of the broken bone; the last dribbles of blood against the snow were now many yards behind. *Is this a good thing?* he wondered, trying to remember details from articles he'd read about survivors.

He guessed that it must be midmorning by now. At some point, Margot and Doug would realize he was missing. He pictured what would happen at the courthouse, the familiar faces standing around and questioning how Chase McGill's lawyer could possibly be a no-show on this of all days. He imagined Chase's confused expression and a lump formed in his throat as he recalled the evening eighteen months earlier when Chase had sat in the dingy interview room and leapt to attention as Joe had pushed open the heavy metal door.

"I'm Joe Sinclair and I've been retained as your lawyer." Every time Joe heard his own introduction to a new client, he paused with pride. This time, he had done a double take. The wild-eyed, mussy-haired teenager met his gaze with fear and bewilderment. A limp handshake from a hand inked with a black spider lasted only a moment before Chase retreated, resuming his hooded-lump pose on the metal chair. "Your uncle sent me."

Chase nodded and placed his entwined hands on the cold table. Joe straightened his grey-striped tie, pulling it away from his neck and feeling, like always, that ties hindered his ability to move freely. He pulled a pad of paper from his bag and watched as a faint smile passed over Chase's face. Joe had been chided by Margot, many times, that his bag looked more like a hiking knapsack than a briefcase.

"I don't want you to say anything else to the police without me there," Joe stated. "Now, are you up to telling me what happened?"

Chase nodded but shrugged his shoulders at the same time, causing Joe to cringe. "Sure," Chase answered, dragging the 'sh' sound. "But honestly, I'm kinda messed up here. I have no idea what's going on." He pulled his hands down and rubbed them against his thighs.

Joe took a deep breath as an equally confused teenager sitting on the other side of a cold table nineteen years earlier emerged and caused him to gulp. He cleared his throat. "Well, let's start at the beginning."

Andrea wandered in circles around the kitchen island, straightening a few envelopes of mail into a tidy pile before her next lap. It was after ten now, and Margot and Doug hadn't called as promised. Despite the early hour, she pulled a crystal glass from the cabinet and filled it halfway with chardonnay, swigging it back and allowing the fruity essence to tease her tongue. She inhaled deeply then felt her jaw tense. Doug Forester was so unnecessarily mean, even after she'd explained why she was there. The past six months had been so full of misunderstandings. All she had done was take a job at the law firm as a clerk after finishing her legal assistant certificate. She'd done her best to do a good job and be noticed by the two partners. Then, this past summer, Joe Sinclair had taken an extra interest in her and they had fallen in love. There was nothing anyone could do about it. They were meant to be together. But Doug, and that Margot too, had been so incredibly rude, making up stories and accusing her of purposely messing up cases. They were so obsessed with Taryn, Joe's ex. They acted like she walked on water or something.

Startled by the chime of her smart phone text alert, she lurched across the counter, picked up the phone and groaned. Illuminated on her screen was a text bubble with the words, "Leaving today." She tossed the phone down, surprised by the loudness of the *thunk* it made on the granite counter top. Then she reluctantly picked it up again, using only one hand to text back a reply, punching in, "Go. Leave me ALONE." She hit "Send" and tossed the phone down again. She stood for a few minutes, staring at it, waiting for a response that never came. Gulping the last sip of wine, she jumped when the doorbell chimed, bringing her back to the present moment.

"Hey! Sorry, I didn't bring a key. I went ahead over to Timeless Lace. I mean it's so close by." Megan plowed through the doorway loaded with garment bags. "I texted you to see how things were going. When you didn't come right back and didn't answer, I figured you'd met up with Joe. And I figured after last night we were both tired that it might be nice to just look at them here without salespeople all over us. Is he okay?"

Andrea looked down at the garment bags in confusion. Meg continued, "They let me bring both dresses after I made a deposit. I'll just return whichever one you don't like. Oh, and I got shoes. I think you'll adore them. They match both dresses so either way!" Out of breath, Meg dumped the bags on the living room sofa. "Is Joe okay?"

Andrea shook her head.

"He wasn't at the office?" She unzipped one of the garment bags then turned to her sister, surprised to see her holding a wineglass, appearing hunched over and less tall than usual.

"I needed something to calm me down." Andrea sat down on the edge of the ottoman. "No, he hasn't been to the office. And he missed his court appearance this morning." She turned to the dresses. "Thank you. Thank you, Nugget, for going to get the dresses. It was very kind of you." She wept.

Meg sat opposite her sister and reached for her hand. Her usually glamorous older sister's fashionable haircut looked greasy and flat, her face unusually bland with minimal make up, her lips oddly colourless. "Oh, honey. What did they say at the office?"

Andrea recounted her visit to the office. Meg listened, concerned and offering suggestions. Finally, she bit her bottom lip in her "Meg" way.

"Andrea, you guys are good right? I mean everything is good? That Taryn is out of the picture?"

"Why does everyone keep mentioning her?" Andrea yelled, then looked at her younger sister's stricken expression. "Sorry. Sorry, it's just that Doug, you know Joe's partner, he was saying that he should call Taryn. It just bothers me that people would think he'd be with her. He left her ages ago. She wasn't the one for him, with all her going off to save the world. That wasn't a marriage. And her trying to get him back after what he and I found. I mean, marriages fail, it's not like this is something that's never happened before."

Meg smiled.

Andrea continued. "But it's not like him to miss court. Something horrible has happened. I just know it. At first I thought it was the snow—maybe an accident. But now I just don't know what to think."

"We'll figure it out. Maybe, oh I don't know, what about his clients? Maybe there was some kind of an emergency?"

"He's been pretty focused on this one case, but the guy he's defending, this Chase guy, he was one of the ones looking for Joe this morning too. He left a message from the courthouse, sounded as upset as we are."

"Chase McGill?"

"I guess. Yeah, that sounds right. What?"

Meg smiled in exasperation; her sister did not follow current events. "You act like you haven't heard of him. It must have been the biggest case going on when you worked there."

Andrea nodded, "Of course. Oh yes, I just didn't put two and two together. I'd forgotten his name. I was so flustered this morning."

"Pretty big case. He murdered that nurse over at Highlands hospital. He was stealing drugs."

"Yes, Meg, I know. Yes, of course I know the case. It wasn't one I worked with though. They only gave me boring stuff, and Joe keeps his clients pretty under wraps and he never, ever tells me the details of the cases. He works so hard. It's part of what I love about him. But you know, when he does talk in general about clients, he always thinks the best of them. That Chase guy, Joe said he was just a young kid who got caught up with the wrong people."

Meg nodded. "Maybe. Maybe Joe pissed someone off being his lawyer. I don't know? Maybe you should call the police again and tell them that."

Horrified and guilt ridden that she didn't know more about Joe's cases, Andrea stared at her sister in disbelief "You think someone's hurt him?" she exclaimed.

"No. Gosh no, Andrea, I'm sorry. Here, let me go try these on." She reached for the garment bags, folding them over her arm and heading towards the staircase, then turning back. "I'm just rambling. Ignore me. It's just a high profile case is all. I mean, I even heard about it in Vancouver. Biggest case in Millerton since, well, since Joe's I guess, but I barely remember that."

CHAPTER 6

THE SMELL OF OLD CHINESE FOOD caused a momentary gag in Doug's throat. He picked up the wine bottle, sniffing it unintentionally but happy for the change in scent. It was empty, but this likely wasn't enough to have intoxicated Joe, assuming he'd shared it with the other person. Joe would have been fine to drive last night. Walking over to the large mahogany desk, Doug placed his index finger on the edge and ran it along as he moved from front to back. Finally, he dropped down in Joe's tall-backed chair and swivelled around towards the wide window. Twelve floors below, a small sidewalk snowplow barreled along while pedestrians scattered like insects, climbing large, rough-edged snowbanks to safety. Its familiar grumble was muted by the distance and glass but Doug could recall the sound from years of living in this city that experienced its fair share of snowstorms. Cars struggled to pass one another despite reduced lane widths. From the distance, Doug felt as though he could pick them up like toys and place them where he wanted to, helping them get on with their travels.

Somewhere down there was Joe. With each passing hour, Doug's head and heart battled between the logic of Joe having taken off for his own unknown reason and the foreboding nag that his protégé had met harm. Now, as Joe's desk clock *tocked* over to ten-thirty, his heart dropped further into fear. Without a thought for privacy, he swiveled back and slid open the top drawer of Joe's desk, smiling and chuckling loudly when noticing the folded up Ramone's poster that lay beneath Joe's office supplies and thinking back to the days at the old office when Joe, fresh from law school, had taken over the small storage room in Doug's dingy office and propped the framed poster against the wall.

"This isn't a dorm, Joe." Doug had laughed as he watched the young new lawyer fumble his way through explaining that he was just "organizing his things". Now, nine years later, partners and running an office that shone with style and success, he'd had no idea that the poster still lurked inside their walls. Nothing else in the drawer was surprising. Office supplies, phone charger, a box of extra business cards, a leather-covered chequebook. Doug lifted out the chequebook, flipping through it and noting the blank top cheque's smoothness and the embossed heading "The Law Offices of Forester & Sinclair". Doug remembered the long discussions about the ampersand at O'Reilly's and Joe's determination that it be included. "Otherwise it sounds like one person's name! People will start calling me Forester!" They'd laughed, sketching various names on the moist napkins as the beers continued to flow. He'd always known, from the moment Joe had returned to him saying he wanted to go to law school, that he'd hire him and eventually make him a partner. Joe would carry on long after Doug was done, and make him proud.

And he had, joining the firm and bringing in more business and associates than Doug had ever imagined. Joe's sharp business skills and compassion for people had put them on the map as the biggest firm in Millerton, handling every type of litigation as Millerton itself grew and changed. Originally, a small factory town for the Frosst Toothpaste Company, the city grew along with Frosst as they expanded into an oral hygiene products empire. And as the population grew and other companies moved in, the beauty of the city's uneven terrain and enchanting riverfront turned Millerton into a tourist's delight. Now, Doug sat on the top floor of the original Frosst Building, gazing at the city below. Its growth had been so positive, yet along with the good came the ever-changing focus of their practice from typical small town cases—wills, real estate and divorces—to increasingly handling cases involving crime.

"*Ewww!*" Margot flew through the door carrying a white garbage bin lined in plastic. "Oh! Oh gosh, Doug I'm sorry, I didn't realize you were in here. No wonder the door was unlocked. Had me scared there a second, thinking I'd left it open after Andrea." She headed towards the coffee table and picked up the paper plates. "You okay?"

Doug shrugged and shook his head. "You?"

"Same as you, I guess." She slid onto the sofa, piling the two plastic wine glasses together then chucking them into the bin. "I've been managing calls all morning. Reporters who were covering the trial have been calling non-stop, trying to figure out where Joe is. A few of them were so pushy! One even asked if this was all some ploy to delay the whole thing." She looked back at the table. "Sorry for not getting this tidied up sooner. I just ..."

Doug scanned the Chinese food containers. "Wait, Margot."

"What?"

"Don't clean it up. Leave the glasses and plates."

"I, uh. It stinks."

"I know." He sighed, coming around the front of the desk and leaning on the back of the sofa. "I just wonder."

"Wonder what?"

"I don't know. Who knows what to think? He's only been gone what, eighteen hours? He's not a missing person by legal standards. But I've been thinking about calling Stuart Flannery."

"Oh Doug." She raised her hand to her mouth. "What, are you thinking this is evidence?"

"Maybe I'm just being paranoid."

"No, no, I get it. Oh God. Doug, I don't know what to do. I can't focus on work. Where could he be? Why did I leave early yesterday?"

Doug sighed again. "We all did. Joe was supposed to too. Everyone was cancelling appointments and you had to get home to your mom." He stood and walked over to join her on the sofa.

She shook her head. "Something's wrong." Her eyes became glossy.

"There's nothing you should have done differently." He watched as a tear escaped her eye. "You don't remember anything else he said?"

She shook her head. "In all my years here, nine working for him directly, neither of you have ever not told me where you were. And the trial today, Doug. He'd never leave that young man hanging, waiting."

Doug nodded and frowned. "I know. I've tried his house, his cell, email."

"Me too. Did you reach Chase McGill?"

"Yes, he sounds terrified. He's coming in this afternoon to see me."

Margot nodded. "What about Taryn?"

"She's not picking up either. I've tried about every fifteen minutes. It doesn't even go to voicemail."

"I think she's probably out of the country." Margot began nibbling on her index finger nail. "And obviously Andrea's not heard anything. And what the hell is going on there?"

Doug shook his head. "I was as surprised as you."

"She said that Joe was to come to her house for dinner!" They sat in bewildered silence. "We've really lost touch with what's going on with him this past while." She lowered her head. "Should we try his brothers? Parents?"

Doug scrunched up his face. "I don't want to worry them, especially Dorothy."

"His brothers then, Dan? It'll be all over the news soon, as pushy as these reporters are."

Doug nodded and reached in his pocket for his phone while Margot waited anxiously while he found the number and connected. After a few minutes of hearing only one side of the conversation, she shrugged further down on the couch. "Nothing?"

"Hasn't heard a thing. " He placed his hand on top of hers. "Said to call him if we do."

She paused and looked at her long-time boss and friend then turned her eyes to the floor. After a few minutes, she rose with intention. "Enough!" She stood up and brushed a stray grain of rice from her pant leg. "I'm going over to the house. I'll go home and get my car. Amber's here to answer the phones. I can't stand this."

Doug nodded. "No, we can take my car. I'll come with you. And if nothing turns up, then when we get back let's call Flannery. With the trial, the police will pay attention."

"Oh, my," Margot sighed.

They left Joe's office and headed out into the foyer just as Amber came rushing in, arms full of files and almost walking right into them. "Oh, sorry." She hesitated. "Doug, I need to speak with you."

"We're just heading out, Amber. Heading over to Joe's" He saw her shaking her head as soon as he spoke. "What is it?"

"It's, can we talk in your office?"

The three headed into Doug's office opposite the double doors of Margot and Joe's area. There was no question that Margot was invited. Everyone at Forester & Sinclair knew that Margot was in the know about everything, and no one questioned it. When they got inside, Amber dumped the folders on a side table then turned back to her boss.

Surprised that he wasn't sitting down, she stumbled over her words, "Well, it's Tammy from payroll. I mean, today is Tuesday, and they have to do the pay run so it processes for Thursday."

"Uh huh."

"Well, Tammy came in here just now. She's very upset. She was doing the testing, before she sends the file, you know, to move the money over to people's accounts." Every sentence Amber spoke ended with an upbeat tone, as though she was asking a question.

"Okay?"

"Well," she cleared her throat, "Doug, there's not enough money to make the deposits this time."

Doug wrinkled his face, causing his deep set eyes to appear even deeper. He paused a moment, then answered. "Amber, I'm sure it's just a glitch, a mix up. I'll deal with it when we get back."

"She's pretty upset, Doug. I mean, you know Tammy. She worries about everything. She said she did some checking and the payroll account is actually really low." She lowered her eyes then looked back up at Margot, afraid Doug's reaction would show something she didn't want to see.

"It's fine Amber. It must just be a mistake." He noted she was still avoiding his eyes. "Amber?"

She turned back towards him, red faced.

"Amber," Doug repeated, "there's no problem with money if that's what you are afraid of. We're doing great."

"Well, you know a lot of time and money have gone into the McGill trial for free," she commented then turned her eyes downward. "I'm sorry, it's none of my business."

"And we knew that going in, Amber. We are fine. There's nothing wrong with the finances. Whatever is causing the payroll account to be low is a glitch or an accounting mistake. Margot and I will be back in a couple of hours. Set up a meeting at two with Tammy, and the four of us will go over everything then."

Amber scribbled a note on a Post-it and said she would go speak with Tammy. Looking back at her boss and Margot, she could see their eagerness to find Joe was trumping anything she said.

CHAPTER 7

JOE GRITTED HIS TEETH and allowed his body to freefall as he attempted to sit down on the thick log at the base of a tree, which must have been completely uprooted at some point last summer. Coated in snow, the ball of twisted roots looked like one of the sculptures at Millerton Gallery. Relaxing for the first time in what seemed like hours, Joe paid attention to his grumbling stomach. He gulped his own saliva while, as if on cue, three chickadees appeared and landed on the roots. Joe smiled at their intensity, wishing he had some food to share with them and feeling pleased he was not yet at the point where they looked delicious. He watched them dance and flutter, unaware of him, as though he were invisible. Behind him he heard the faint crackling of ice, as tiny tree branches fought their way to freedom.

"The trees have a lot on their minds today." He heard his mother's voice as clearly as if she stood beside him. One of many random expressions she'd state to Joe's father and brothers at the oddest of times. "The trees have a lot on their minds today," she'd say, while washing dishes and staring out the kitchen window at the large property's tall maples and birches. "You should go see them." It was her way of convincing them to venture out, which didn't take much convincing at all. On drowsy, boundless summer days, the three boys would climb branches to high and exhilarating lookouts or swing endlessly on the old tire that hung on a rope from the largest elm. And on days when adults braced themselves against the cold, the Sinclair boys would lose themselves building snow forts and skating on makeshift hockey rinks that defied any thermometer. Joe smiled, thinking of the simplicity and stability of those days. Those days before Lauren.

April 1997

It didn't happen like his mom had talked about when he was little and shrugged in horror at the thought of girls. She said that one day he'd start noticing them gradually and sometimes when girls were nearby he'd start to feel butterflies in his stomach. For Joe it was more like being hit by a Mack truck. At fifteen years old, he was way more interested in hanging out at Donovan's Point and smoking hand rolled cigarettes and pot with Davey, Scott, and Scott's older brother, who they called "Slug", though no one was ever sure why.

Her name was Lauren Avery and, for Joe, it seemed as though one day she and other girls didn't even exist, then the next day nothing else mattered. It was early spring, on a year when spring too had arrived with an instantaneous clout. One week, she started smiling at him whenever he looked over towards her, with straight teeth against bubble gum pink lips that seemed to purse as though she was bursting to say something. Then she'd suddenly appear beside Joe and Scott's lockers with her gang of giggly friends; a cluster of pony tails and binders bejeweled with stickers and graffiti. They always looked like they understood something that Joe didn't.

The day after Easter long weekend was especially warm, as though the suddenness of spring had inspired summer to arrive early and just as forcefully. She stood outside the chemistry room, down the hall from him with her knee bent and foot against the wall. She was wearing tight jeans and a hot pink top with a silver edge. It looked like something a girl might put over a bathing suit at the beach and only covered one of her shoulders. Joe couldn't stop staring at the other one, the bare one where her skin looked so incredibly soft. She already had a bit of a tan line, a pale straight path leading down into uncharted areas. Over the covered shoulder, her long blonde sideways ponytail fell in cascades bound by a matching hot pink ribbon, interwoven with some kind of feminine magic. She caught Joe looking and cornered him as he walked by.

"Whatcha looking at Joey Sinclair?" she giggled and headed towards him, bolstered by an army of three girls.

Joe cleared his throat but heard the phlegm still present as he spoke. "It's Joe. No one's called me Joey since ..." He couldn't figure out what to say then. The truth was that people did still call him Joey, but he sure didn't want her to know that.

"Joe then." She stepped towards him and he darted his eyes away from that captivating tan line to her sapphire blue eyes as he felt his face flush. Her eyes were lined with a dark blue liner that made them appear catlike and her lashes fanned down slowly as she spoke. "Are you going to Mather's class?"

He thought it was a dumb question. Of course he was going there, it was starting in five minutes and he clearly had his math book stashed against his hip. But he wasn't going to point that out. He wanted her closer.

"I am," he stated and started forward, wondering why the process of walking like a normal human being was suddenly requiring so much concentration. "You can walk there with me if ya want," he said, surprised to hear the tinge of his voice, playing it cool while his guts wrenched inside in the hope that she'd appear to his left as he turned away.

She did.

Lauren Avery was the only daughter of Gary Avery, who had been the mayor of Millerton for more years than Joe could remember. That spring, while Millerton focused on the rising river and Mr. Avery spent every waking moment tending to his constituents' flooding basements, hand in hand with Lauren's Barbie Doll mother, Lauren spent every waking moment with Joe. He wasn't like the other boys; the ones her father approved of. Joe was the middle son of the hard working, sometimes harsh man who ran the print shop and his doting wife. He was edgy and rebellious and usually dressed all in black or T-shirts emblazoned with rock band logos and images. His looks were striking, with thick dark hair and jade eyes, but no one really paid attention to his looks since he cloaked himself in baggy clothes and a layer of self-consciousness. He hung out with Slug and the druggie crowd who liked to skip school and huddle in the outside stairwell near the parking lot. Friday mornings they'd load Slug's rusty pickup truck with beer and escape to Donovan's Point, spending the day in the sun, playing guitars and getting drunk and high.

Joe didn't win awards for marks in school like his older brother, Mark, and he wasn't an athlete like his younger brother, Dan. He was the other Sinclair boy, the one that didn't quite measure up. The one that made people wonder what Lauren, the A student with the model looks, was up to.

But Lauren came to learn over the next few months that Joe was just as smart as Mark and probably just as athletic as Dan. He was brilliant at writing music; his fingers and the strings of his guitar were like one instrument with a direct line to his deepest thoughts. He had a sense of humour that would creep up just when she needed it, and a way of listening that filled the void of attention she so needed. As spring rolled into the hot and hazy summer, Lauren's goal of finding the perfect boyfriend to piss her father off had turned into something surprisingly pleasing.

CHAPTER 8

FORTY-FIVE MINUTES AFTER LEAVING the office, Doug attempted to pull in to the circular driveway of Joe's gabled farmhouse but gave up near the roadway due to the deep snow. He and Margot paused a moment before getting out of the car. They both stared at the white panel siding and grey shutters, the welcoming wraparound porch and bright red double doors. Sensing Margot's mood, Doug leaned in to make eye contact and sighed.

"It's just such a shame." She shook her head, reaching for the door latch. Doug nodded in agreement, both of them knowing they were not speaking only of Joe's disappearance, but of the events of the past few months.

"I mean," Margot continued, "I always thought those two would make it. I guess you just never know. Oh, and the money and effort Joe and Taryn put in to renovating this place." She looked across the property, recalling the ramshackle appearance of the house's exterior and lawn just a few years earlier.

Doug's thoughts turned to the matter at hand. "No cars," he said, stating the obvious but pointing it out all the same as he stepped out of the car. He walked around the back of the car and met Margot on the passenger side. Once outside the car, the two stood looking down the length of the driveway and across the enormous property, the nearest house hidden far beyond a line of huge evergreen trees, dusted in snow and reaching to over fifty feet in height.

She shook her head. "I guess this means he didn't come home last night? Or he did and left again, but there are no tire tracks. And Taryn's car wouldn't be here." She looked down the driveway as though willing both cars to appear. Doug looked suddenly quizzical and she opened her eyes wide and continued, "Doug, she left him months ago."

He shrugged. "I know, I wasn't thinking. I forget sometimes."

"And not just Joe. I mean, they broke up months ago, but last I heard she was also planning on leaving Canada, probably taking that offer in Israel after all."

"Well, that part I didn't know," he said.

The two trudged slowly up the driveway through the deep snow, arriving at the front porch and noting that the morning paper still hung from the doorknob in a plastic bag. Despite this, Doug reached for the doorbell and pressed it hard, as though the extra pressure would make it louder, ensuring anyone inside would hear it. They both listened to its friendly chime, but no one appeared. After waiting a while, he then knocked hard against the door while Margot made her way across the porch to the huge bow window, trying her best to peer through a tiny gap between the curtains into the dining room.

"Anything?"

She shook her head. "No, lots of boxes."

Doug slid over behind her and peered along with her, the difference in their height allowing them both to look through the same opening. After a few seconds he backed up and looked at his long time friend. "So?"

"So." She smiled, lightening her sinking heart. "Should we break in?" She snickered and then felt immediate guilt at her levity which got worse when she saw Doug's frown.

"I think we should," he answered.

"I was kidding."

Doug raised his eyebrows and ran his hand along the back of his neck. "I don't know. We came all this way to figure out what is going on. Snow's pretty deep to think about walking around the back. Why not break in? No matter what, if Joe shows up, he'll just have a good laugh."

"I suppose," Margot agreed, then suddenly her face lit up. "There's a spare key, or at least there used to be. I just remembered, one time when Taryn and I went shopping, for the kitchenware, anyways it doesn't matter why we were shopping, but anyways, we came back and she realized she'd grabbed Joe's car keys and not her own ring that had the house key on it. This was before they'd finished the renos enough to move in. There was a spare key under one of the legs of that table." She pointed to a large, heavy table at the end of the porch. Carpeted by snow, the dark wood structure was almost invisible against the white railings. Margot stomped through the snow on the porch and lifted the table by each leg, freeing the snow in clumps as she felt under each one. After hoisting the third leg, she lifted the key triumphantly. "Got it!"

Doug smiled, taking the key from her hand and unlocking the door. The two called out for Joe with increasing intensity as they stepped inside, giving up with a sigh in unison at the overwhelming emptiness of the house.

Taryn and Joe Sinclair's renovated 19th century farmhouse always radiated warmth upon entering. Over the years, Margot, Doug, and Doug's wife Marlena had spent many cozy evenings engaged in great conversation, sumptuous cuisine and freely flowing wine. The main foyer was large and circular with dark inlaid hardwood floors and a breathtaking winding staircase. The home, completely modernized on the inside, was a welcoming display of warm reds and soft greys. Usually, every element, from the smell of cranberry scented candles to the dark, etched-chrome door handles, displayed Joe and Taryn's attention to detail and endless hours spent making this their dream home.

Now, Margot and Doug stood in the foyer and smelled only stale air. The once-inviting formal dining room on their left that they had seen through the window was a mass of clutter. The table was pushed against the wall and chairs were stacked upon each other. In the center of the room, stood two lines of packing boxes, stacked three high. Margot walked towards them and stood on her toes to read what was written in black marker on top.

"It says 'Storage'", she commented, walking towards the table and absently picking up a business card for a realtor, then passing it to Doug who turned in silence and headed back across the foyer to the double French doors. He paused a moment before opening them and Margot could see the shape of his tense shoulders, his head unusually hung forward. Doug opened the doors and stepped across the grey carpet of Joe's home office. On the wall facing him were three framed photos. In the first, Joe and Taryn stared back; he in dark bathing trunks and she in a bright sapphire bathing suit, covered by a sheer white shawl. Ocean waves were capped in white foam behind them as the two laughed uncontrollably at whoever was holding the camera. The second photo showed the couple again, this time with Taryn on the left. They were wearing high-necked red sweaters and linking wine glasses in front of the fireplace Doug recognized from the family room of the house. In the third photo, Joe sat in a clearing in the woods, with his legs outstretched and Taryn inside them. His arms surrounded her from behind as the two snuggled in thick hiking coats. Doug imagined the photo was likely taken on this very property, probably long before they'd begun restoring the house.

"It all just makes me so sad," Margot said, entering the room. "I don't understand what all went wrong. I mean, I understand her work would be challenging for a couple. But they knew that when they got married. And couples survive these things. Look at you and Marlena and how happy you are. And me and Sam, before." She paused. "Joe and Taryn, I never thought."

"I know." Doug sat down on the edge of the modern glass and chrome desk. "It's a shame. Honestly, I just assumed they'd make up. Joe's been so distant these days."

"He hasn't talked to you at all?"

Doug shook his head.

"Oh, I hoped he had. He hasn't been talking to me either, not for ages. I mean, other than work stuff." Margot faded into her thoughts. "I was so surprised this morning by Andrea's comments. I guess, well, I guess he's been carrying on with her."

She watched Doug close his eyes and his face fall. He spoke: "Yes, I know now that's probably *why* he hasn't been talking to me. Avoiding me I think."

"I can't imagine what he sees in her." Doug did not answer, his expression of distaste clear. The two stayed in silence for a few minutes.

"It won't last," she finally said.

"Andrea and Joe?"

"Well, if there is an Andrea and Joe, no it won't last. But I meant you and Joe. It won't last, him not talking to you about things. He loves you, Doug; you're like a father." She paused, lost in thought. "I guess with him and Taryn separating, he's just trying to figure it all out."

"I hope so. Anything here helping you figure out where he is?"

Margot shook her head as Doug stood and walked to the back of the desk then reached for the phone. Looking at the display screen on the front of it, he clicked a button and focused on the screen.

"What is it?" she asked.

"Nothing. Just wondered what the last number that called here was."

"And?"

"Doesn't say. Says 'Unknown Caller', 230-2808." He clicked another button "Yesterday morning, 0745".

Margot shrugged. "Local number? Probably a client. I'm going to the kitchen," she said, then noticed Doug smirk ever so slightly. "What?"

"Yeah, the area code is local. But, the last four digits, 2808, Marlena's birthday. August 28th."

"You mean after all these years of me having to remind you, you finally know when her birthday is?" she teased, and headed back through the foyer and down the long hall to the huge country kitchen. Again, boxes were stacked against the wall. Their normally open and friendly kitchen, decorated with dried flowers and bakery signs, now appeared empty and closed off. The marble countertop gleamed in the light from the triple patio doors, and Margot walked towards them, looking out over the old farmstead, an untouched, glistening blanket of white snow before her as far as she could see. Turning back to the kitchen, she walked around the old antique table towards the cabinets. She couldn't help but open them, finding only a few sparse piles of dishes in cabinets that used to overflow. Her eyes then looked across the room, in the direction of the small counter top that served as a computer desk and shelf previously piled with recipe books. On it lay a bright red picture frame, upside down, and on top of that, a passport.

Doug entered just as she investigated both objects. She looked up at him. "Well, she's not in Israel," Margot stated, flipping Taryn's passport open to the photo page and holding it out to him.

"What's the picture of?" he asked, pointing to the frame.

She turned it over and smiled, then watched Doug's face grin as well at her answer. "Gertrude!" The two gathered and looked at the photo of the chubby tortoise shell cat seated in the centre of a dark green lawn chair.

"Haven't thought of her for a while."

"Oh my," Margot added. "Remember how Joe didn't like her at all but pretended to when Taryn first moved in with him, back at his old apartment. Oh Lord, that cat!" Margot laughed, recalling Joe's antics, doing everything to convince Taryn he liked the cat.

"Eventually they became good pals though," she continued, and unconsciously stroked the frame, suddenly feeling a wave of sorrow. "Oh Doug, what the hell is going on?" She felt her eyes wet with tears. "Those two kids were so good together, and then what, some hard times and suddenly bang, it's gone. Then that Andrea shows up, and if they're together, she's ruining any chance of fixing it. And now Joe, missing! Doug, I can't stand it." She sobbed as he came towards her and wrapped his arm around her shoulders.

A few minutes later, calmer, they decided to ascend the grand staircase. Despite feeling intrusive, they figured that checking to see if Joe's bed was unmade might help them. Doug walked the long hallway to the master suite, leaving Margot, suddenly uncertain, behind.

"It's made. Everything looks normal," he called out after looking at the bed and closet. "Margot?"

She didn't respond so he left the bedroom to find her. She stood at the edge of a second bedroom; one that Doug had walked past only moments ago, with the door now open a crack. Together they stepped inside, both silent but for their breath, taking in the half-painted pink walls, step ladder, painting throws and brushes. A rocking chair sat in one corner and a white crib stood directly in front of them.

"Oh my God," Margot finally said.

He turned to her. "Did you know?"

She shook her head. "I wondered, back in the summer. But then they never mentioned anything." She walked towards the crib, placing her hand on the railing.

Suddenly, Doug's phone buzzed against his hip, startling them both. He looked at the number, smiled and answered. Margot listened, seating herself on the edge of the step ladder, watching Doug's face with puzzlement while she waited impatiently to be told what was going on. He thanked the caller, lowered his phone to his hip, and came towards her.

"Doug?"

"That was Stuart Flannery."

"Oh, you called him? When?"

"No, I didn't. Telepathy I guess." He smiled and went on to explain that Stuart had called to see if there was anything he could do, having heard about Joe's disappearance. "He's going to try to pop over later."

She nodded, thinking of the kind private detective who was so dear to them all. "Maybe he can make sense of this." She looked back at the crib, feeling sorrow deep in her chest.

"Thanks everyone. We thought it would be good to gather you all together this afternoon. I know there's a lot of questions and reporters, and I know everyone here is worried about Joe." Doug scanned the room, looking around at his loyal employees who stood wide eyed in small groups, hanging on his every word as their workday came to a close.

Several staff nodded with looks of sadness. Doug continued and explained what little he could, that Joe and his car were missing and it looked like he hadn't been home since the night before.

A timid law clerk shyly lifted her hand and caught Doug's eye. "What about the trial?" she asked almost inaudibly. "I mean all those reporters are asking what's happening. What are we supposed to say?"

Doug inhaled. "To the reporters? Nothing. As for us, business as usual. And, as for the trial, I have Chase McGill coming in shortly. Judge Miles is being very understanding. I spoke with her late this morning. Formally, she's delayed the trial by one day, but informally she says to just keep her posted and we'll do what we can. If Joe, ahem, if Joe doesn't turn up or if he does and he's not up to the trial, then we'll get it delayed while I catch up. Then I'll step in and take over."

Margot slipped away from the crowd, exiting the main office door to head to the ladies' room. She knew her eyes were rimmed with red and felt a splash of cold water would help her get through the rest of the day. Before her stood a tall and obese man with red cheeks and dishevelled hair. He held an unlit cigar in one hand, an iPad in the other and he leaned against the wall near the elevators. As she got closer she watched his face flood with recognition. It took her longer but soon she recalled the reporter's name and gruff personality from stories and encounters over the years.

About three feet from him she stopped. "You can't go in there," she said, her voice strong despite nervous energy flooding her body. Why wasn't the security guard monitoring who came up?

"Margot?" He nodded towards her. He stopped and smiled at her body language. Short in stature, she stood protective of her office, an unspoken but impenetrable barrier. "Okay, I get it. I'll go back downstairs with the rest of the lot. But *you'll* give me a statement, right? I mean, we go way back."

"I have nothing to say."

"Is Joe Sinclair's disappearance related to the McGill trial?"

"I don't know, George. Please. I have nothing to say. My office has no comment."

"Pretty inconvenient timing," he continued and stood up from his leaning position as if to walk towards her.

"George." She stopped him short, putting her hand up like a halting traffic cop. "Please. We don't want reporters here. I know it wasn't you, but all that nonsense with Joe back in the 90s. The press reporting his name despite his age."

"Some good folks paid dearly for that mistake." The reporter paused, reflecting a moment. "And like you said, that wasn't me."

"Still, George. Please, leave us alone."

Softening, the chubby reporter popped the cigar between his teeth. "Fine," he grumbled but his eyes sparkled at her spunk, a small smile forming on his lips. "I need to light this up anyway." He turned towards the elevator and she felt a flood of relief as he hit the down button. "It's crazy though." He turned back, shaking his head. "Those of us who've been around a while are sure intrigued. Joe Sinclair as a headline—again!"

CHAPTER 9

August 1997

JOE STEPPED OUT ONTO THE LARGE PORCH and reached in his pocket, lifting the joint to his lips and flicking his lighter. He adjusted the volume on his Discman, ensuring his favourite CD from The Clash would accompany his walk. Then he pulled his hood up around his head, blocking both the wind and any potential view his mom might have from inside the house. Inhaling slowly, he descended the steps and checked his jeans pocket for the condoms he'd stashed earlier. This was really happening. She'd as much as said so on the phone earlier when he called her from the print shop at lunchtime. "Yes," she'd said, almost in code, "that thing we talked about." He knew her parents were home so he didn't push her to say any more, but she'd been hinting for days.

Scott and Slug had gone away with their parents to stay with their grandma, who was sick. Their house would be empty and everyone in the gang knew the way in. *Go to the left of the back porch, the upper basement window never latched right and if you knew "the trick" it would give right away. Slide in feet first and you'd land on the sofa.* Everyone did it when Scott and Slug's parents were away, and those two used it to sneak out of their house on many occasions. Scott had even told Joe to go ahead: "The whole house to yourself," he'd said, winking at his virgin friend.

Unlike most nights when Joe picked Lauren up at her door, tonight she'd insisted on meeting him at their spot. He liked that. Facing Lauren's dad tonight would just make things worse. Mr. Avery already hated him, and Joe was sure he'd somehow manage to pick up on some signals of their plans for the upcoming night. He started walking down Kendal Street, silently counting his steps and smiling to himself. It was something she did, counting steps, and at one point over the summer she'd announced to him that she'd found their spot, the exact midpoint of steps between their houses. Their spot, it turned out, was in the middle of Bryan Park, just a bit beyond the playground. So, anytime they were heading out when Joe didn't walk over to the Avery house to pick her up, they'd meet at the spot. Sometimes she'd arrive first and hide behind the play structures, leaving brief messages or initials carved with a stick in sand long since abandoned by toddlers.

Two hundred fifty-six, two hundred fifty-seven, Joe took another draw on the joint, seeking the mellow courage he'd need to be cool, and entered the park. Dusk was approaching and Joe noted how surprisingly dark it was for the late August evening as he headed past the wooden benches, ignoring the large woman bending down to clean up after her poodle.

He had to think about something else. Staring down at his sneakers as he trampled the worn down entrance to the park, he took the last draw of the joint, holding the smoke in a bit longer than usual, then tossed the twisted end down onto a clump of clover. He reached in his front pocket again then pulled his hand out, as he noticed an old man on the parallel path staring towards him. He nodded and Joe nodded back without making eye contact, then returned his gaze to his feet. Three hundred and sixty-two steps had passed. It was four hundred and fifty to the playground. He could see it, the bright primary reds and blues were dimmed by the dusky August sky. The children had trickled home leaving the squeaky teeter-totter in muted still aftermath and only a slight summer breeze teased the swing set into slow, dissatisfying motion.

She'd be there. Alone. She usually waited on the far side of the weatherworn wooden picnic table. One leg would hang inside the table while the other she'd tuck up under her chin, staring forward, awaiting his arrival. He pictured her as she'd been last night, in worn, light blue denim shorts, cut off and rolled so high that another fold wasn't possible. He'd put his hand in her back pocket while they kissed there, both straddling the picnic table bench. A fresh rain scent from her loose hair wafted towards him as he'd kissed her soft lips and explored her warm, wet mouth with his tongue. Finally brave enough, he'd removed his hand from her pocket and slid it inside her shorts from behind. And then she, without any indication of misgiving, had slid her hand to the front of his jeans, pulling the zipper down slowly so that the unlocking of each tooth made a sizzle as he began to lose control.

"Soon," she'd whispered, lifting her hand from his pants and pulling back to entice him. "Not here," she'd said, grazing his lips with a wisp, "let's wait for tomorrow."

Joe knew to stop, no matter what your body wanted, and, in his heart, he also wanted to wait. He wanted his first time to be the following night, in the freedom of Scott and Slug's house. It was only one extra day to wait and an extra day to think about it.

And he'd thought about it. All day. He'd remembered the things Slug had said, and a couple of the stories he'd read from the magazines he'd smuggled in that Scott had picked up from his cousin. But all day, while trying to work at the copy shop, while eating lunch, and now, while walking to meet her at their spot, all he could imagine was that feeling, his first time, inside Lauren.

She wasn't there. The picnic table stood empty except for an abandoned peach juice box. Joe looked beyond the table towards the route where Lauren would appear. Oh God, had she changed her mind? They'd spoken on the phone just two hours ago. She'd sounded eager, excited. "Yes, Joe," she'd said in response to a question he hadn't asked. Her words and the tone of her voice had made him hard. *Please let her show up tonight*, he thought, even if she's changed her mind. I just want to see her. He looked down at his sports watch, 8:28. She wasn't late, he was early. He sat down on top of the picnic table then laid back, allowing the pot to move through his body as he gazed at the sky. It was still light out, but stars were pushing their way through, punching the canvas with promise. Maybe he should have saved part of the joint for her, although she never took part. Maybe tonight she would have.

He had to force his mind to stop thinking about it. Stop thinking about those stories in the magazine. Lauren wouldn't do those things. Not tonight. And he didn't care. He just wanted to touch her, if she hadn't changed her mind.

"It's way too late!" A shrill voice startled him from behind and he turned to see a tall woman in a long skirt yanking a boy of about seven. "I told you!" She twisted his arm under hers, dragging him reluctantly away from the playground, a golden retriever loosely attached to her other arm obediently walked alongside them. Amazed that he hadn't seen them coming, Joe sat up; he was too relaxed now. He watched their backs as they walked away towards the entrance where Lauren should appear: the entrance from the driveway behind the church hall. Perhaps Joe should start walking in that direction and meet her. Where was she? It was 8:37.

By 8:45, Joe was seated on the stone wall that marked the edge of the church property. He could still see the picnic table off to the left, in case she came in another way, but now he had an unobstructed view of the driveway, all the way to Drake street. He'd see her coming as soon as she turned on to Drake from her own street. He'd be able to watch her approaching for those three blocks.

Joe wondered if he should start walking up Drake. Maybe she thought they were meeting later? Maybe she'd changed her mind? Maybe Mr. Avery had got wind of what they were planning and had locked her in. She was only fifteen minutes late, but it seemed so much longer. His mind flashed back to the jean shorts. Oh God, please let her not have changed her mind.

Then, as he took one last glance towards the picnic table and playground he saw her. A girl—but not Lauren. She was around the same height, causing him to do a double take, but this girl was thinner, walking quickly away from him, almost running. Joe watched her for a second, questioning who she was. She did not look familiar and he knew most of the kids around here. Without another thought, he turned back to look for Lauren and then headed towards Drake Street, imagining himself heading towards her and her appearing, apologetically late. Then they'd head to Slug's house, break in and then ... He remembered her lips and tongue last night and began walking faster.

Past the church lane, he stepped up over the pile of lumber haphazardly piled next to the dumpster. This was the trash pile his mom had been complaining about at dinner the other night. As if anyone cared if some construction people were messy, but Mom had gone off over it. She didn't want them to build the new apartment building, something about it being too tall; Joe hadn't really been listening. Now that he saw the construction site and the big piles of garbage, he wondered if his mom had had a point. The blocked off area was huge and Mom's words about it overtaking the church roof infiltrated his more pressing thoughts of Lauren's raspberry lips, but only for a split second.

Passing a second dumpster, Joe turned his head away from his obsession with Drake street. The dumpster was overflowing, and wooden two-by-fours with nails protruding from them stuck out the top. Then, one of them lying on the ground next to the dumpster caught his eye. All the other two-by-fours were the colour of raw wood, but this one was covered in red paint.

Curious, Joe took five steps towards the dumpster and instinctively reached down, picking it up to throw it into the bin, then freezing as adrenaline shot waves up the back of his neck. Was that paint—or blood?

He dropped the beam back to the ground as though it burned his skin, the blood becoming clearer. But it wasn't just blood; there were clumps of something greyish beige. He felt himself gag at the realization, at the tangle of blonde hair.

"What the ...?" Joe took the last few steps and swallowed loudly. It was blood, and guts, and someone's hair. "OH GOD!" he yelled out loud, searching his view for someone, anyone. Where'd that girl go? Where'd that mother go? "HELP! Something's wrong here!" he yelled, looking over his shoulder. Turning back towards the church, Joe made a decision to go inside. Surely the church was open. He circled back around the dumpster to do so, then stopped dead.

"OH GOD NO!" He screamed in such a blood curdling voice that he did not recognize himself. In a pool of blood, twisted and contorted, beside the dark grey dumpster, lay Lauren. A gaping hole in her head next to her left eye made her appear as though her face was split in two; one side still his beautiful girlfriend, the other side unrecognizable. He screamed again then began to sob, kneeling down and leaning forward to pull her body up towards him as her blood dripped like thick paint down onto his shirt. He stroked the hair on the clean side of her head and lifted the silver pendant of the letter L she always wore, feeling it slip against his now blood wet fingers. "NOOOOO. NOOOO. Lauren? Lauren?" He heard his own voice, but it sounded miles away. "HELP! HELP!" he screamed. "Oh God, oh fuck. Oh God. Lauren, NO."

He pulled off his sweater and placed her head back down on top of it, then tried to stand but the world began to spin around him. Catching himself, he retched, then vomited on his shoes and stood bending forward, closing his eyes and hoping with each re-opening she'd be gone. Finally, he found the breath to scream for help again to the empty world, and then gathered enough strength to run towards the church, pounding his fists against the thick wooden doors.

CHAPTER 10

ANDREA WALKED PAST the green maid of honour dress, now hanging on the doorframe between the kitchen and living room. The two sisters had spent the past few hours selecting this one of the two dresses, for it had a sparkled bodice and fit more with the theme of a New Year's Eve wedding. The dress also accentuated Meg's tiny waist and made her appear as though she had curves when, in truth, her small body, fit from daily runs, was all but flat.

Approaching the front window, she watched as Meg attempted to pull her rental car out of the driveway to go visit the friends that Andrea couldn't recall. She saw her sister give up and exit the car and stand, hands on hips, with her back to her. The deep snow from the storm and the plow's attempts to clear the streets had left a small mountain of hard ice, barricading the car in. Cozy, in her long green sweater, Andrea was displeased at the thought of going outside to help, but knew she couldn't leave Meg stuck. Reluctantly, she dressed in her coat, boots, hat and mittens and headed out to the garage to find shovels.

"Thanks, it's pretty heavy. Maybe I should just walk down to the coffee shop," Meg panted, after lifting small chunks of snow with her shovel and giving an exasperated look at the remaining mound that did not appear to be depleting at all. She looked up at Andrea and couldn't help but smile. Her sister was doing her best to help but didn't at all look the part of a snow remover. Her fur-lined coat looked more suited to an evening outing and she slipped with each shovelful, groaning under her breath while sliding forward in her high-heeled boots. "We are a pair!" Meg laughed as they made little headway.

"We'll get you out." Andrea stated, not laughing at all.

"Andrea, do you want me to stay? I don't have to go meet those guys. I mean, if you'd rather—in case we hear something." Meg turned her back to her sister to focus on the snow on the far side of the laneway.

"No, go. I want you to enjoy yourself while you are home." Andrea swooped a huge chunk of ice up onto the snow bank, feeling heat rising in her body. Stopping a moment to lean against the shovel, she felt it being taken from her grip and turned to see Dominic. Meg turned at the same moment and saw a pudgy man smile and wave at her.

"Dominic. Hello." Andrea introduced him to Meg as her next door neighbour.

"So nice to meet you," he said with a slight accent Meg couldn't pin down but suspected was Spanish or something similar. He leaned forward to shake Meg's gloved hand and his left eye winked ever so slightly. "Another Vaillancourt girl. I had no idea. 'Dis is my lucky day." He leaned in towards her and she felt herself unintentionally back away. Even in the outdoor air, a wave of strong cologne wafted its way from the scruffy-bearded man. "Perhaps I should rescue you." He took the shovel from Andrea's hand and Meg watched as an odd expression passed between them.

Meg busied herself as Dominic began lifting large chunks of snow with intense speed. Soon the end of the laneway was clear enough for Meg's rental car to pass. She thanked Dominic and her sister and drove away to meet her friends.

"Nice girl," Dominic commented, keeping his eyes on her until the car was no longer in view.

Andrea smiled and nodded, also gazing down the street, her back to him. "So, the good neighbour act?" She spun on her heel to face him.

"It's not an act. I still like to help the two ladies in distress." He reached into his pocket, removing a package of cigarettes and a lighter. He opened the end of the package and pulled two cigarettes partially out and held the packet towards her.

She shook her head. "Seriously? Have I ever?"

Dominic laughed, more intensely than her comment warranted, throwing his head back. "I just thought you might need to relax with all the wedding plans."

"No, I'm good." She smiled.

"We have some things to clean up."

"Dominic, when I'm ready I'll be in touch." She pulled off her hat and flung her blonde curls away from her face.

"When *you're* ready? It's not up to you," he said, smirking. "You know, your fiancé really put it on thick yesterday. Is that the expression? 'Put it on thickly?'"

"I don't want to discuss it," she stated. "Please leave." With that, she opened the garage, threw her shovel inside, then pushed the button to have it close behind her.

CHAPTER 11

"I appreciate you meeting me here. I hope the reporters didn't give you any trouble." Doug escorted Chase McGill into his office.

"No, the cops brought me over."

"Great, it's just been a crazy day, plus I didn't really want to try to head out," Doug explained, leaving out the fact that he'd spent a good part of the afternoon at Joe's house. "You've been staying at your uncle's?"

"Yeah, since he posted my bail. It's fine. I don't mind coming here," Chase said, seating himself in the chair opposite. "Any news on Mr. Sinclair?"

"We don't know anything more than what they are reporting." Doug Forester leaned back against his leather chair, poising his yellow legal pad on his knee and staring at the thin nineteen-year-old in front of him. It was four in the afternoon on the day that should have been the start of Chase's trial, and Doug tried to imagine how it would feel to have prepared for such a day only to have the whole thing delayed. "So, Chase, I've been catching up on all of Joe's notes, plus what he'd already shared with me. But I do want to hear it all from you. I'd really like to hear the whole story."

Chase rubbed his pant leg, fidgeting and rocking ever so slightly back and forth. "Yeah, wuull, Mr. Sinclair, uh Joe, we went over and over it all a lot. He believed me. I was all ready for today, ya know. He made me practise. I can't believe he didn't show." Chase lowered his eyes to his shiny shoes.

"Well, we don't know where Joe is. Chase, I am very sorry. Please, on behalf of the firm. This is not like Joe, so of course we are all very worried." Doug tried to put the possibilities of the cause of Joe's disappearance out of his mind. "Now, I've spoken to the judge and she's awaiting word on when we can resume the trial. If it's soon and Joe's not back, then I'll take your case. I promise, we won't delay any longer than we have to. That's why I really want to hear your story today." Doug thought he caught a glimmer of moisture in the frightened eyes before him. "But I'm hoping he'll be back. I mean it's only since this morning that he's been missing."

"How can someone just disappear? I mean, why would he?" Chase said, yanking at the knot on his navy tie as though it had tightened into a noose.

"That's why we're concerned. But don't you worry, Chase. We'll be ready for trial. As partners, Joe and I share everything and often review our cases with one another. Yours was one we reviewed a lot so it's not like I'm in the dark here. But it's been a while, so I really just want to hear it all from you again, like what you practised. Better yet, not like you practised, just tell me your story as if I don't know it. Let's start with that."

"Sure." Chase lowered his eyes to his shoes again.

"How about you take that tie off." Doug smiled, remembering the other young man who'd sat across from him nineteen years earlier. "Why are you still dressed up?"

"Yeah, thanks." Chase slowly pulled the tie from his neck and unbuttoned his collar. "I wasn't sure what was happening."

Doug nodded, "Okay so, you were arrested seventeen months ago."

"Yeah." A slightly sarcastic smile formed on Chase's lips. "On my birthday! I spent my eighteenth birthday in jail." A *pffft* sound erupted from his lips: "They came right into my mom's house and hauled me out. I had no idea why but then when I got to the police station they said some nurse at Highlands had been stabbed."

"Gloria Barnes."

"Yeah, Gloria. I, I guess I knew her name was Gloria, or something like that back then. I'm all messed up now on when it was I first heard her name. I knew who she was though. She treated me a few times when I came in to the Emergency. I guess you read about that."

Doug nodded. "I'd still like to hear it from you."

Chase looked up and squinted his eyes from Doug's intense interest, resting his vision on the glass wolf carving on the desk. "Wuull, I admitted it to Mr. Sinclair, Joe. I was trying to get drugs. I'd fake a skateboarding fall or a wicked stomach ache, whatever."

"Anyways, Gloria—well I don't know if I knew her name then. Well, she was real nice to me and some others and, it's kinda like word got out, ya know?"

"Word got out that she was kind?"

"Yeah. Kind ... but more like easy to convince. So some people got in the habit of going 'cause if you could convince *her* you needed something, then she'd convince the doctors and sometimes they'd give you something."

"How many times did you go in?"

Chase shrugged.

"Two? Ten?" Doug glanced at the transcripts.

"More than two, less than ten. 'Course sometimes she wasn't there. I did the fake skateboard thing, that was the first time I saw her. She believed me about sayin' my shoulder was messed up even though the x-rays didn't show anything. It was a pain in the ass going in but, in the end, I scored some pills. A couple of times after that. Wuull, and then that last day." He looked back to Doug who nodded. "But even before that last day I guess, the time before that maybe? I guess they were on to me and had put some notes on my chart or whatever. Ya know, sayin' not to give me anything. She'd told me I should try to get help, which I have ya know."

"I know. Tell me about that day though; that last time you went."

"I did go hoping to see her plus hoping this one doctor, Doctor Wolfe, yeah." He nodded at the carving and smiled. "Yeah, Wolfe. Doctor Wolfe was a pushover. But, uh, well honestly man, that day I guess I was in bad shape. I don't remember much. I know I'd downed a lot of vodka that morning. At the time I didn't know how much, and who knew how much my mom had had. Anyways, there's some people at the hospital that said I was pretty bad. They said I threatened her, uh Gloria. I don't remember. I guess that's the bad part—not remembering."

"Doesn't help."

Chase smiled at the matter of fact voice of the grey haired man before him. "But I do remember later that night. I was more sober by then. People said they saw me at the hospital again and that's true. I was there and I did see Gloria come to her car, but I left. Everyone asks me why I was there and Joe kept asking me over and over. I told him the honest truth. I didn't know where to go. My mom was drunk too when I'd gotten home that afternoon from the hospital, lying in her own puke. Then our landlord came by and told me that if we didn't pay the rent by the next day we were out. Homeless. That's fuckin' nuts man. Anyways, I just got thinking and I thought maybe, maybe I should leave and go somewhere or maybe ask for help. Maybe ask Gloria for help. I don't know where the idea came from.

"One of the witnesses that Joe told me about, from earlier that day—that clerk with the big ..." he held his hands in front of him and Doug smiled.

"I forget her name. Big, uh chest. Anyways, she said that—that orderly guy had held me against a wall and told me to get help. I don't remember that but maybe, you know, maybe his words got stuck in my head—that I needed help—and that's why I went back that night. I saw my mom all messed up like that, on the night before my eighteenth birthday and, anyways, I did go back to the hospital but it wasn't to score and I wasn't anywhere near the parking garage. I took the bus and I was out front where there's those benches. I think maybe I saw that orderly guy again. I'm not sure. Anyways, I was wearing my jeans and my navy jacket and sneakers. They said the guy who stabbed Gloria at her car was dressed like that."

"So you returned to the hospital because you'd decided you needed help. It wasn't to get drugs."

Chase nodded. "Yeah, that time I wanted help. Things were out of hand at home."

"And you said you didn't go near the parking garage but you saw Gloria come to her car."

"Oh. Oh yeah?"

"Yes," Doug said, scanning his notes.

"Yeah."

"You just said you saw Gloria come to her car."

"No, I took the bus. I was over by the benches. I never went inside. I got scared."

"Chase, it's been a while since I've been over at Highlands Hospital but isn't the parking garage way off on the side?"

"Sorry man. I must be fu ... wuull jeez, sorry man. This morning's got me all fucked up."

"I don't remember reading that you said you'd seen her that evening in any of your statements."

"No." Chase ran his fingers through his hair, stopping his palm on his forehead. "I just got fucked up there Mr.?"

"Forester. Doug."

"Yeah, Mr. Forester. Look, I'm just a fuckin' mess. I've been waiting over a year for this trial and I was up all night panicking. Then I put on this fuckin' suit. Sorry, this suit."

"Go on."

"Well I get to the courthouse and no Mr. Sinclair. What the fuck kind of life?"

"It's unfortunate, Chase, I get that. But let's not forget where we were, okay?"

"Sorry, uh, I mean thanks for seeing me."

"Chase, did you see Gloria that evening or not?"

"No. I was just confused there, just now. I was thinking about earlier in the day when I went. I didn't see her that night."

"You sure?"

"Yeah. Yeah, I'm just messed up man. Today just really messed with my mind."

"You didn't see her go to her car? You were never in the parking garage?"

"No."

Doug inhaled slowly staring into the young man's eyes.

"Have you ever been in the parking garage?"

"Uh, in my life?"

"Yes."

"I don't know, maybe. I think I went there for some tests once. My mom might have parked there."

"Could you describe it. I mean, if you had to?"

"Uh," Chase smirked. "It looks like a parking garage."

Doug jotted something down on his pad. "So something, some mysterious reason—seeing your mom or realizing the next day was your birthday and you might be homeless, made you leave home and you wanted to go to Highlands to reach out for help?"

"Yeah, I dunno, I guess. I mean, I didn't know where to go and maybe that orderly had said for me to get help. And you know, those other times, Gloria had told me to also."

"Okay. Go on. Did you go inside?"

"No."

"Why not?"

"I dunno. I got there and it was just so, real, you know. So I just sat on the bench for a while, watching all the people coming and going. Then I went back home."

"Did you talk to anyone?"

"Isn't this all in the notes?"

"Yes, Chase. I told you I need to hear it from you. If we need to go to trial before Joe's back, I have to be ready too."

"I've told it so many times."

"I know. I'm sorry."

"Look, all I know is the next morning was my birthday. Mom was awake, sort of. I just got up and had some vodka and some Cheerios and then I went out and hung with some friends. I got home around two and the police came to the door. I had no idea what they were talking about or even who Gloria was right away. I spent the night in jail. They couldn't reach Mom and I didn't know anybody, lawyers or anything. They'd sent some chick, uh lady, and she was all up in my face and I hated it. The next day my Uncle Jack came by and he called Joe Sinclair. Uncle Jack bailed me out. He's a good enough guy I guess, but he doesn't speak to my mom, but I guess she'd called him or something. Joe was cool though." Chase paused. "Man, it's fuckin' crazy he's missing. Anyways, he came down to the jail and talked to me. He told me about him, ya know?"

Doug nodded.

"Told me he was charged with murder once too, when he was like fifteen."

"I was his lawyer."

"Oh, no shit. Wow." Chase let a moment pass. "He didn't do it, he said. He let me talk and understood, I guess. I guess he just believed in me. And he never asked if I'd done it."

"Some defence lawyers think it helps if they know if the client is guilty. I am one of those. I don't feel I can do a good job if I don't know the whole truth." Doug leaned in and paused, thinking of the witness accounts he'd read, the files outlining a story so different from what he'd just heard, and the press take that Gloria had refused to give him the drugs he so desperately needed. He watched the young man with his head down, faint red patches covering his neck. "Chase, is there something you're not telling me?"

CHAPTER 12

MARGOT TIED HER GREEN SCARF around her neck and flicked off the light, pausing a moment to look at her office in the dim light and re-thinking the events of the long day.

"Hey," Doug called out from across the hall. "You leaving?"

She met him halfway through his outer office. "I was just coming to see you to tell you I have to get home to Mom. I want to stay here, but I just can't, the agency nurse surprised me by staying as late as she did. It was kind of her, but I can't ask her for any more."

Doug nodded.

"How'd it go with Chase?"

"Just finished. Not great." He sat back on the edge of Amber's desk and closed his eyes. "I'll explain in the morning. I think we need to delay the whole thing."

"Sure." Margot made a mental note to follow up tomorrow. "Anything I can do for you tonight? Is Amber still here?"

"I think so", He looked down at his assistant's desk, still lit by a desk lamp and piled with haphazard stacks of files. As if on cue, the young woman strode into the office, holding her laptop closed against her chest like a school girl holding a binder.

"Oh thank goodness, Doug. I've been waiting for your meeting to end!" Amber said.

"You didn't have to stay," Doug stated.

"But I *did,* Doug, did you forget? Payroll? We were supposed to meet with Tammy hours ago."

"Shit," he muttered, looking at Margot, whose face radiated compassion for the stress he was under, while Amber stood like a puppy awaiting his next direction.

"It's not going to process, Doug. I've been over in accounting trying to calm Tammy down. Something's all messed up," Amber said.

Doug sighed, pushing against his forehead with his fingers and closing his eyes.

"We were going to go over everything? You said ..." Amber pushed.

"Yes, well not tonight." He felt himself shutting her out, unintentionally, then heard his own voice and regained control. "How short are we?" he asked calmly.

"To make payroll, we're short twenty-three K." Doug heard Margot make a soft gasp under her breath while Amber nodded. He turned away from them and headed into his office. On Margot's cue, the two women followed and watched their boss open his briefcase to pull out a chequebook. "Here," he said, scribbling to fill in the details. "Take it from my personal account. We'll deal with the paperwork later."

"But?" Amber started.

"Just take it," Margot whispered to the young assistant. "First thing in the morning, go and see Arnie at the bank personally and get him to transfer it in. Then payroll will file and we'll be fine." Amber nodded, slipping the cheque into her hand and exiting silently back to her desk. They heard her open her desk drawer and closet, preparing to leave.

Doug turned to Margot. "Go home. I think I will hang out here."

She smiled, "Well, call me? Oh my, Doug, we need some good news soon."

Amber long gone, Doug walked Margot out to the main hall and waited until her elevator car had left. It was after eight, almost twelve hours since he'd arrived for what he thought would be a calm and quiet day. He looked across to Joe's area. It was unusual to see it all in darkness, for typically Joe left much later than everyone else on staff. Without thinking, Doug walked through Margot's outer office and unlocked the door to Joe's. The smell of the Chinese food was now worse than ever; Doug still insisting that Margot not tidy it up, when she'd asked again late in the afternoon. Yet despite his need to keep the office as they'd found it, for the second time that day he sat at Joe's desk, this time in darkness broken only by outside lights, and put his head in his hands.

Startled by the chime of his smart phone, Doug answered and was taken aback to again hear the voice of his old and loyal associate, Stuart Flannery. Flannery had been the lead investigator on several of Doug's cases over the years. Now retired, he dabbled in the odd case as a private investigator while focusing on his more pressing priorities of fishing in the summer and ice fishing in the winter. Flannery told Doug he'd be over soon but meanwhile, he'd started poking around on a few things.

"The cops are keeping an eye out, unofficially. They are the best," Flannery said, "and good buddies of mine."

"I figured," Doug said, picturing Flannery, pencil thin with the pointiest head he'd ever seen. "Anything yet?"

"Nothing. Not sure what to think about all this. I can tell you, with the trial and all, it's looking suspicious."

CHAPTER 13

ANDREA SAT WITH HER BACK TO THE DOOR, her attention fixated on the TV screen, as Meg entered the room.

"Hey. Hey, any news? Sorry for being gone so long. Lots of catching up with the Blacks." Noticing her sister's red face and tears, Meg attempted to divert her attention by curving in front of the television and sitting beside her. "Any news on Joe?"

"It's *all* about Joe. But they aren't saying anything I want to hear." Andrea pulled a wad of tissues towards her nose and dabbed. She clicked the remote control's volume button to increase the sound as the screen filled with an image of Joe. He faced the camera, smiling in a black suit, pale green shirt and dark green tie. A rust-coloured wall, decorated with framed certificates too small to read, provided the background for his portrait. A blue banner of typed news scrolled beneath his picture. It read "Missing: Joe Sinclair, lawyer defending Chase McGill."

"That's an old photo," Andrea said without emotion and leaned towards the screen. "From before I knew him. I think it's from when he passed the bar."

Meg nodded. Although she had yet to meet her future brother-in-law, the photo made him appear younger than she'd imagined. He looked to be in his mid twenties. Meg took a moment to really look at his features, imagining him and her older sister as a couple. There was something striking about his eyes, even in a photo on a TV screen; they seemed to be looking right at her.

The female reporter's clear and determined voice continued as the photo faded into another one. This one showed a teenaged Joe, thin and hunched, walking amid a crowd of onlookers in front of a large stone building. With eyes concealed from the invading cameras, he stared downward. "Sinclair was the key suspect and was charged in the murder of fifteen-year-old Lauren Avery, Millerton's former mayor Gary Avery's only daughter, who was bludgeoned to death in 1997." A small picture of a pretty teenaged girl appeared in the corner of the screen, slightly overlapping Joe's. "But charges were later dropped due to lack of evidence. The Avery murder remains unsolved."

A male anchorman's voice interjected, "Thanks Donna. So many years ago but many Millerton residents remember that case like it was yesterday." The camera returned to the greying anchorman who turned towards it. "So where is Joe Sinclair? And why would he vanish on the day of this most important trial? So many unanswered questions. Stay tuned to Six O'clock Update. We'll be right back."

"Does Joe ever talk about that?" Meg leaned back in the oversized loveseat, hugging a pillow and slowly stroking her sister's back.

"What?"

"Joe, does he ever talk about the Avery murder?"

Andrea shook her head.

"I was nine," Meg continued. "I think I was protected from all the details. But it was the first time I ever remember there being a serious crime here, and one of the last. I remember kids talking about it at school and scaring me. Probably would have been better off to hear the truth than some of the stories they came up with." Her voice trailed off slightly. "You were her age, right? It must have affected you more."

"I don't remember it much. She went to Winston. Joe did too," Andrea whispered, dabbing a tear, and pausing her gaze on an arthritis cream commercial. "I don't know why they are rehashing all that. They should just be looking for Joe."

"They are. But it's news," Meg stated. "Unfortunately, Joe's well known for it, even though he didn't do anything wrong. It must have been hard for him though. Can you imagine? Being what? Fifteen or sixteen and accused of murder? It's amazing how successful he became afterwards."

"He's very smart. Very motivated," Andrea stated, her eyes still fixed on the television.

Andrea's cell phone rang and Meg felt her whole body jump, as did her sister's. They stared down at the phone on the table, the name Forester Sinclair followed by a phone number were displayed on the screen.

"You get it," Andrea said, and Meg did so.

"Andrea?" asked a firm male voice.

"No, this is her sister, Meg. May I take a message?"

"Meg, this is Doug Forester of Forester Sinclair. Andrea was here earlier today looking for Joe Sinclair. I'm not sure how much you know?"

"I know everything," Meg responded. "Please, do you have news?"

Meg listened to Doug's kind voice and words while simultaneously watching her sister's expression change as the TV screen lit up with a red Breaking News banner followed by the words "Joe Sinclair—Car and wife found—Sinclair still missing."

CHAPTER 14

MARGOT JOLTED from shattered sleep, momentarily unaware of her surroundings. She realized she'd dozed off on the sofa with her knitting twisted in her lap just moments after finally sitting down following a long and upsetting bath session with her mother. Her phone rang a second time. Doug's voice was sullen.

"Ryan Evans just called. They've found Taryn."

Margot gasped. "What? Where?"

"They found the car below Old Country's Edge, you know that part past Warrington where it gets really high?" His words were slow and methodical, as though his courtroom training had kicked in when his real thoughts failed from emotion.

Margot interrupted. "Doug, is she okay?"

"She's at Highlands. She's unconscious. Some kind of head injury they think. She's in ICU. They think the car went over the edge. It was practically buried in snow and really smashed up."

"Over the edge? At the part past Warrington? That's a terrible cliff! Why would she be up there?"

Doug shrugged his shoulders, "Well, it's one route to get to the farmhouse."

Margot frowned "A long route. What about Joe? Why was Taryn driving his car?"

"She wasn't."

"What?"

"She was found in the passenger seat."

"Oh my, how's Joe, then? Oh Doug, no. Is Joe?" She stood up and began pacing across her living room.

"No. I mean, I don't know. They don't know. He's not there."

"What? What do you mean?"

"Ryan says they only found Taryn. He's getting the police to call me. They can't find Joe. He said the snow's been blown around but they can see a trail, and there's some blood." He cleared his throat.

"Oh Doug," she cried.

"Ryan is as confused as we are. He told me that Taryn's been staying at his place for the last few months, but she was leaving yesterday—flying out in the morning to Israel like you thought. He has no idea why she was in Joe's car. He says the police will be calling me."

"Yeah, you said." She paced back. "Where are you?"

"Office still. Actually I'm sitting at Joe's desk. I tried you a few minutes ago but it just rang and rang, Flannery too."

"I was bathing Mom."

"I went ahead and called Andrea so you wouldn't have to. Hey, I need to go, Flannery's calling back."

Margot sat back down as Charlie, wakened by her voice, nuzzled into her hip. Assured that there was nothing she could do, she reluctantly agreed to await Doug's next update. She turned on the lamp next to her, the evening now upon them, and attempted to start her next knitting row three times before setting it down in frustration, the jittery energy of waiting thwarting her efforts to concentrate.

"They've got the helicopter and dogs. That car's pretty wrecked, it's amazing anyone survived." Flannery spoke quickly, out of breath, and Doug listened intently, imaging his friend making himself at home at the police station.

"And?"

"Well, the car was pretty much empty, usual stuff—some tools. Joe's cell phone was in the front and totally smashed up. I guess that's why he couldn't call anyone. Taryn's purse didn't contain a cell phone—which is kind of weird nowadays. I don't know."

Doug listened, then responded, "She was leaving the country yesterday."

"Oh?"

"Supposed to have been. She may have gotten rid of it."

"Oh, yeah, maybe." Flannery paused. "They've tested the blood they found in the snow. There wasn't a lot of it but enough to do a quick blood type and since Joe's blood is in the database, well, they've made a match on blood type. It doesn't mean it's Joe's—just someone with the same type as him. Could be anyone, but, I mean, it's Joe's car and Joe's wife so."

"So they think he wandered off to find help?"

"Looks like it. It's odd though, with all the snow drifting about, there's no way to tell where the footprints go. And they aren't really prints either, more like just a few little places where the snow seems more disturbed than others. That's where they found the blood."

"Okay."

"But there's something else." Flannery coughed lightly, then Doug heard him catch his breath and cough heavy and wet. Doug cringed slightly, unsure if it was the words or the familiar smoker's cough he'd come to hate.

"Go on," Doug said.

"In the trunk, well what's left of the trunk, they had to pry it open. Anyways, there was this gym bag, black?"

Doug wondered why Flannery's voice had ended in a question tone.

"Yeah, he goes to Smitty's gym," Doug answered the unasked.

"Yeah, but it's not that. No gym clothes. Uh, we found money. Sixty-thousand dollars. Cash."

Doug didn't know how to respond, so said nothing. He thanked Flannery for the updates then disconnected. The progression of information from the day churned in his head and he felt the familiar rise of indigestion stabbing at his chest. Thinking of his wife, who'd been nagging him to see a doctor about it, he muttered "okay" out loud and reminded himself to grab some TUMS from Margot's drawer. Absentmindedly, he reached for Joe's desk phone. The console was the same as the one in his office, so he knew how to look at last callers. He hit the button, scrolling through several calls from today with known caller ID's, then landed on the last call from yesterday. "4:30 PM. Unknown Caller 230-2808."

CHAPTER 15

HER SKIN STUNG in a diagonal line across her chest, as if being pricked by a thousand needles. She wanted to touch it, but her hand lay inanimate, pale and pink against the wrinkled white bed sheet. She could feel blood gushing with a pounding pressure inside her head. With each rotation left or right it felt as though her skull was about to explode. She listened, confused, to the faint patchy pulses and beeps from machines to her right.

"Taryn? Taryn? Hey, it's Ryan."

Her brother's hand reached for her lifeless one, and Taryn felt a flutter of clarity. She attempted to move her lips but their dryness scorched the syllables into a parched whisper and she choked unexpectedly, a roughness in her throat like she'd never felt before.

"It's okay, Taryn, don't speak. Everything is okay. You had a tube in your throat but they took it out."

She moved her eyes to where the voice came from and saw the shadow of her older brother's head and shoulders, a black formation against a white wall in the dim light.

"J ..." her words sifted through sand. "Joe?"

"Just rest, sis." Ryan placed his hand on her shoulder and Taryn heard him mutter something to someone at the end of the bed, then felt herself drifting further and further away. So tempting to fall back, so safe there. She struggled through the anesthetized haze to understand visions that flittered by as though clicking through a View-Master. Then, one solid memory pushed forward again and again and the frame finally stuck. She saw his face. Joe. Last night as he'd sat on the old leather chair in his office and looked at her as she'd stood in the doorway. His expression so guarded at first, then melting into a flood of tears. His face. As quickly as it came to her, it faded away and she felt herself falling backwards again into the muddled cloud.

Twenty-four minutes passed, but to Taryn it was only a second later. Her head hurt so much on the right side. She tried to reach up to touch it, this time her arm listened to her request and lifted, only to be brought up short by a thick wad of bandages. Her fingers recoiled and she turned her gaze back towards Ryan.

"The staircase," she whispered.

"No sweetie. You were in a car accident. In Joe's car. Do you remember?"

"Where's Joe? Did he fly down here?"

"No, you're here, Taryn. In Canada. In Millerton. You were in a car accident."

"Where's Joe?" she repeated.

Ryan didn't answer.

"I'm going to go and get the police." A female voice startled her from somewhere in the unshaped room. Taryn felt herself tense with irritation and lay silent for a few minutes looking only at her brother. She wanted to fade away but another, loud male voice startled her. "Taryn? Can you hear me?" The shrillness of his voice was grating. She shook her head in refusal, contradicting herself with the action.

"Sweetie," Ryan said, "this is a police officer. Can you talk to him?"

She reached again for Ryan's hand and felt him rubbing her arm with his thumb. No one was answering her about Joe. Where was Joe? She flashed again to the snapshot of him at the desk last night. The corners of his lips turning up, such pleasure at just seeing her. She wanted that moment again, not this pain and confusion. Whatever had happened before and after that moment didn't matter. *Stay here.* She willed her mind to focus on the picture of Joe at the desk in front of her, motionless, smiling. She closed her eyes. *Stay here.*

An intense blood curdling squawk and something resembling a dive bomber. Joe shook his head and felt his heart thumping. Staring up at the sky, he saw a large group of ravens that appeared to be having a family squabble. *An unkindness of ravens,* he recalled hearing the term once. Had he fallen asleep for a moment? No, that was impossible, and yet it seemed like the sun had completely retreated now. He waffled a moment, regretting his decision to leave her. He should have stayed by the car. What if she'd woken up scared and alone? And now, having heard what sounded like the whirr of a helicopter a while ago, Joe cursed that he'd done the wrong thing and prayed that they'd found her. Unable to see the source of the sound through the thick trees, he closed his eyes and listened, imagining they were above her, seeing the car and helping her.

But if it wasn't a helicopter, what if they hadn't found the car? Then Taryn was still up there, stranded, cold and injured. And he'd abandoned her.

When the car had finally come to a stop, Joe had felt his body thrust forward into the airbag and felt his hand let go of hers. That was the worst part of all, losing her hand. First when he'd consciously done so to try to gain control of the steering wheel before becoming airborne, then, in those moments when time stood still and all he heard was her screaming. If only he'd taken her hand again instead of his instincts taking over and forcing him to grasp the useless wheel. But as the car had moved on its own again down the cliff, he'd felt her pull away from him, then back, then away again, her body thrusting and crashing with the force.

As they'd finally landed, the noises of crashing and her cries had come to a dead, silencing stop, and he'd attempted to reach for her hand once again. But the final rocking motion of the car had pulled her away and her hand slipped from his for the last time.

He'd immediately turned to her, shouting her name over and over and getting no response. Her airbag had inflated as well, but unlike Joe who'd found himself slouched against it, Taryn was arched back against her seat, her neck awkwardly crooked towards the window, eyes closed, but her mouth slightly open, as though she had one last thing to say. Joe had tried to twist his body to kiss her but found it impossible. So reluctantly, he'd kissed his own fingers instead and brought them to her cheek. He could tell her head had hit the door frame or window, or both, given that they'd crash-landed twice. The window was smashed into dull, rounded crystals, creating a choker of jewels across her neck.

The most raucous raven dive bombed towards the others again, squawking at Joe with frantic intensity, as if saying, "Do something!"

He stood up from the spot he'd been resting in for five minutes— or had it been hours? His leg had grown stiffer and he noticed that his pant leg, although ripped, appeared stretched now by the swelling underneath. He tried to put his weight on the splinted leg with the help of a cane made from a branch he'd found earlier.

"Please." He looked at the raven, who oddly stared back. "Please tell me they found her." He cried and the bird stared blankly back, and then took off upwards, up to the rocky cliffs above the accident scene.

There was no longer any type of path to follow; the snow was deep and fluffy here, and the temperature getting warmer. It was the type of weather that often followed a big storm, the stuff that Christmas cards are made of. Joe stepped, one foot in front of the other, cane in hand, as he'd been doing for what seemed like days. He shivered, wondering at how the shivers seemed to come in waves now, lasting about twenty minutes and then retreating.

He stepped ahead, past the trees and broken branches. Step. Step. Step. *Just keep going,* he told himself over and over. As long as they found her, he didn't care. *Keep going. You are making progress. You aren't going in circles or you'd see your tracks in the snow. And you know from following the sun before it set that you were heading back towards town. You will find someone soon. It is crazy that you haven't already!*

Joe stopped for a moment, noticing the evening was brightening, the sky periodically clearing a path for a bright waxing half moon. The falling snow was now so small and soft that it seemed like the flakes defied gravity. They swirled in a motion like dust in a sunbeam in front of him, and he imagined Taryn as she'd been last night, standing in the doorway so unexpectedly. It was like watching a wish come true. He lifted his hand, allowing the snow to land on his black glove, then blew it off, willing a new wish with all his might.

Ten more steps, then ten more, then ten more. Every time he tried to count, he'd lose track. Utter silence but for the step, step, plunk of his two feet and makeshift cane.

CHAPTER 16

August 1997

THE ROOM SMELLED like unwashed armpits and the wall was an ugly shade of a colour that had no name. Joe pulled his sweatshirt around his slim body, keeping his arms tightly wound and his body hunched. The two policemen said nothing. The pudgy one sat in a metal chair directly opposite Joe, fidgeting with his collar and running his chubby hands through his greasy hair every few minutes. The thin one had a craggy face with etched lines, one especially deep running down the left side of his face from just below his eye to where it met his mouth. This one had scrunched his eyes a few times and observed Joe, a slight warmth to the hint of a smile on his thin lips.

The minister had eventually opened the church doors, dressed in jeans and a thick black sweater, with some sort of journal in hand. He'd opened his arms, literally, to Joe, who'd fallen through the doors in tears. When Joe couldn't get the words out, the minister had stepped outside, seen Lauren and almost collapsed himself. He'd then taken charge, leading Joe back inside the church to sit on a rickety armchair in a small office while he called the police and Joe's parents. The latter did not answer. In minutes they heard the wail of a siren and the kind minister took Joe under his arm and led him back outside.

The quiet churchyard was quickly transformed into a carnival of noise and chaos. Whining police cars—at least four, maybe more—had arrived almost at once, causing passersby to gasp and gather while Joe sat at the minister's protective side on the church steps. Frenzy played out in slow motion as police and other people buzzed about in confusion. Then with fine choreography, some measured and touched Lauren and the dumpster with blue-gloved hands and put evidence in thick Ziploc bags with large pink writing. Eventually, other cars pulled up, including the news van out of which several people flowed, including a woman in a purple suit, microphone in hand. Finally, the pudgy detective and his scrawny partner had arrived. Joe watched as they assessed Lauren, as though she was a spectacle to be discussed and examined. Then some uniformed officers nodded towards Joe and the two detectives came towards him.

It was the minister who'd pointed out that it would be better to talk to them with Joe's parents present and the two detectives had agreed, asking Joe if he'd consent to come to the police station and chat with them there. He agreed, but not before he'd told them his name, overheard by a purple-suited newswoman.

As he walked towards the police car, the minister promised to keep trying Joe's parents and ask them to meet him there. Joe smiled as the minister put his hand on his shoulder one last time. He preferred this. His mother shouldn't see Lauren like that.

Now they waited. And with each passing minute, the imprint of Lauren's face on Joe's mind grew darker and more menacing. He tried to close and reopen his eyes, attempting to recall her face the night before, with her flowing blonde hair and huge smile. But his efforts failed. All he could see was the blood, the hair on the wooden beam, and the memory that the last time he'd looked at her face, only one of her bright blue eyes had returned the stare.

Suddenly the heavy door thrust open and Joe was startled by the high-pitched squeal of his mother.

"Oh my darling!" She bee-lined for the chair beside Joe, pulling him close to her bosom. A whiff of Elizabeth Arden filled his nose and for a moment, he closed his eyes and imagined that she was in her long silk nightie, shaking him awake from a childhood nightmare at his bedside. "This is so terrible. Oh so terrible." She turned to the skinny detective. "We need to get him home."

"Yes, ma'am," he replied, stretching out his hand. "Sir." He turned to Joe's father, offering an overly-strong handshake to both of them. "I'm Detective Flannery, Stuart Flannery, and this is my partner Merv Small."

Joe listened to the light banter between them, finding a brief moment of irony amid the depth of sorrow, that the large, pudgy man was named Small. They'd introduced themselves at the church but those words had evaporated. He felt himself wanting to sob again as his father stood back across the room, surveying, as he often did, as though life was something to observe but not feel.

Then the rapid-fire questions began. What was Joe doing there? Where were he and Lauren going? When was the last time he'd seen her, spoken with her? Joe answered slowly and quietly, hearing his mother's loud inhalations each time Small punctuated a question. After what seemed like hours, but was probably only fifteen minutes, Joe's mother lifted her hands to her face and gasped.

"Why is this necessary?" Her voice trembled. "We need to get him home. Look at him, he's covered in blood!"

"Let them do their job, Dorothy," Joe's father spoke for the first time. He'd remained standing in the corner despite being offered a chair. He cleared his throat. "Stop coddling him."

"I'm not coddling him." She strained for clarity. "My God, think of what's happened." She waited until her husband nodded, and then turned to Flannery. "Why so many questions? My Joe just went to go meet his girlfriend and then found her like, like that! Someone beat that beautiful girl with a piece of wood? Hit her over the head with it? The way you explained it, I can't even imagine how awful this was for him to find." Her voice caught on the word imagine, the rest of the sentence trailing off. She cleared her throat. "And Lauren! It's not like he just found some stranger—this is Lauren. Such a beautiful girl! They were just in the basement last weekend listening to records." She began to cry.

Joe began to speak up and correct her that they were CDs, then caught himself, wondering why any detail in the world would ever matter again.

"Ma'am," Flannery leaned forward and looked in her eyes. "We just need Joe's statement clear and certain is all. We aren't trying to be hard on him." Joe raised his eyes from his bloody pant legs at Flannery who gave Joe a reassuring nod. "It won't be much longer. Let's take a break, get the boy a Coke, then we'll need to do some fingerprints."

"Fingerprints?" Dorothy squealed. "What on earth?"

"Just routine ma'am. We have to know which ones are Joe's so we can rule them out."

Dorothy buried her head in her hands. "Oh Arthur!" she murmured, glancing up towards her husband, who stood like a statue.

"Everything by the book." Joe's father finally spoke. "Dorothy, this is Avery's daughter we are talking 'bout. It's going to be high profile."

Dorothy shook her head and put her arm around Joe. "Who cares?" she whispered. "It's our Joe! We need to be worried about our Joe!"

Flannery led Joe out of the room and past a rusty Coke machine, which Joe declined. Following fingerprinting, they returned to the dingy room from which Small was now absent. Flannery insisted that Joe have a drink of water and they all sat a while in silence. Finally, Small reappeared and called Flannery over to whisper something inaudible.

The two detectives then sat back down across from Joe and Small proceeded: "Joe, can you explain why your fingerprints match those on the two-by-four that killed her?"

Joe looked up from where he'd been running his finger along the water glass. "I already told you." He sounded like a whining child, exasperated. "I picked it up before I saw her. I was wondering what was on it."

"You're right. You're right," Flannery tried to calm him. "It's just that the problem is, they are the *only* fingerprints on it. Can you explain that?"

CHAPTER 17

IT WAS THE SIZE OF A LARGE SHED, or small garage, made of vertical log panels and a pointy, black-shingled roof. Joe walked towards the door, which stood in the middle, between two windows so dirty that he could not see through them, nor could anyone have seen out. He reached for the cold door handle with his bare hand and felt it turn, but snow piled in front of it made opening it impossible. Using both hands he pushed the snow away until he'd cleared enough space to allow the door to swing outward. Overwhelmed by the scent of musty cedar, he stepped inside and closed the door.

The shed was about twelve feet long and eight feet wide, with floor-to-ceiling shelves along both side walls. Most of the shelves were filled with dusty glass jars and large ceramic jugs. In the middle of the shed was a solid wooden table with benches on either side. Joe pulled himself to sit on one of the benches. Despite there being no heat source, being shielded from the wind and inside a structure was a welcome change. Joe noted that the opposite end of the shed also had a door and two windows and he marvelled for a moment at the symmetry. Next to that door were two rusty hooks and on one of them was a puffy, red and black checkered jacket that resembled those of stereotypical lumberjacks. He hobbled towards it and wrapped it around himself like a blanket, with the opening towards the back.

Following a short rest, Joe stood again, perusing the jars and noting that many were full or partially-full of what appeared to be maple syrup. Cautiously, he unscrewed the lid of one of the jars, sniffed it, then dipped his finger into the thick brownish-gold liquid and put it to his lips. It was maple syrup for sure. Purposefully now, he scooped up another finger full, then another, gratefully thanking whoever owned the shed and feeling hopeful for the first time in hours.

After ingesting half a jar or so of the golden sugar, Joe returned to the table, this time considering its height and thickness. In one swoop, he lifted his injured leg as though it weren't his own and threw his body flat on to the table. Covering himself with the jacket, he took a few deep breaths. He'd just lie here for a few minutes to warm up then continue on his journey to find help. He'd just rest a moment.

CHAPTER 18

HOSPITAL NOISES OVERWHELMED every hope of sleep, despite the nurse's assurance that the latest shot of medicine added to her IV bag would help. Taryn's mind was clearer now, the accident still a complete blank while some of the events leading up to it presented in perfect order. The police had asked her so many questions. Why they were together? Where were they going? But they were so vague when she asked them where Joe was. Finally, Ryan asked them to stop talking and he calmly explained to her that Joe was missing. He'd left her and the car, to go get help it seemed, but had vanished. She strained to remember, and the memories surfaced—Joe tensed to grab the wheel with both hands, then the car was steering in the wrong direction, then the strange clang from hitting the guardrail. Then she remembered screaming. She could hear her own scream in her mind, a *no no no, God no,* then falling. Then nothing.

Ryan explained that Joe had left to get help and now they couldn't find him. The thought of how panicked he must have been pained her. She could picture him wandering off in the stark cold and her heart broke, remember how his used to beat against hers, remembering everything about him.

December 2009

Taryn straightened her pencil skirt and pushed her knees together, aware that the table left a wide open view to the shoppers bustling by. She checked her watch, one minute later than the last time she'd looked, and peered into the crowd comparing each male face against the fading newspaper clipping paper tucked inside her notebook.

"Taryn?" He surprised her by arriving from the opposite side and pointed to the photo then laughed. "I hope!"

She looked up "Yes, hello. Joe? Oh, yes, well I hope I'm the only one holding your old picture." She let out an unexpected giggle as a waft of fresh soap smell overcame her.

"Yes, let's hope so." He smiled, swinging his leg over the bench and joining her at the small table as he shook her hand. He looked older than she had expected. Despite knowing his age and that his sad and well-publicized story had occurred twelve years earlier, she still envisioned the rebellious, long-haired teen staring back at her from the famous photo. This Joe was clean shaven with short wispy hair that stood up ever so slightly, as though a stylist had left him moments earlier.

"Joe Sinclair." He said, surprising her with his formality and taking her hand in his. She felt a light squeeze and smiled.

"Taryn Evans. Thanks so much for agreeing to speak with me."

He nodded. His deep green eyes never leaving hers as he settled in with his paper coffee cup, motioning to ensure hers didn't need a refill. "I'm taking off my jacket" he said, folding the dark brown suit jacket onto the table and loosening his brown and grey tie. "It's warm in here."

"I think they put the heat up since it is so cold outside. They forget that people have coats on."

"Yeah, hey sorry for asking you to meet at the mall ... at Christmas!" he laughed. "I had to meet a client in the office complex next door at three."

Taryn smiled at his reference to the mall. The short row of stores joined together with a common hallway and the small, musty, upper level housing Millerton's only Chinese food restaurant and a small coffee shop didn't really qualify in her mind.

"No problem. A client, well that leads right in to some of my questions if you don't mind jumping right in? I have a class to prepare for this evening and I'm driving back to Toronto." He agreed and she continued. "So, as I told you on the phone, I'm doing my masters in journalism at U of T and I'm writing this story on the after-effects of being falsely accused as part of my internship with *The Star*. Of course, your story is so inspiring, with you going on to become a lawyer. I mean, I have to wonder if it was all that exposure to the legal system so young, or maybe hoping to help others going through it. Anyway, I've prepared ..." She felt herself stumbling over her words.

"Am I?"

"Are you what?"

"Inspiring?"

Looking down, she fumbled with more papers emerging from her knapsack. "Uh, well, yes. Yes, you are. I mean a lot of people would just be so, I don't know ... I'm jumping ahead of myself."

"Vengeful?" he said, bringing his coffee to his smiling lips. "My mother's word. 'Don't be vengeful,' she'd say." He paused. "I'm sorry, we're really diving right in here aren't we?"

She returned to her notebook, searching for focus. "I suppose I just can't imagine how it feels to know you've done nothing wrong and have everyone accusing you. I think I'd be angry. I mean, from what I've read all you did was fall for a girl. You were what, sixteen?"

"Fifteen."

"Yes. So young." Taryn thought of herself at fifteen, just ten years earlier. She couldn't imagine going through a murder trial. "I don't really know where to start. Tell me about the girl." She looked down at her prepared questions, none of which this was, and realizing she wasn't asking any of them.. "Lauren Avery."

"Not much to tell. I mean, like you said, I just fell for a girl. Nothing unusual. Teenage stuff. We were in high school, in grade ten. I guess she was my first real girlfriend with real dates. She was cute and smart. She wanted to be a cancer doctor." He paused and looked down. "The press never really focused on how smart she was, you know, when they covered it. That made me sad." He paused a moment while Taryn waited. "Anyway, we went out for a few months, movies, cheap dinners, one big school dance. It's all in the articles."

"Right. Yeah, it is. Just thought you might want to add something that's not in the articles."

"From what I remember, they covered it all pretty thoroughly. Too much, except for how smart she was." He took a swig of coffee. "I wish they'd written more about her as a person, not as a murder victim. I wish they hadn't written much at all. They broke a lot of laws covering me. Am I the only one?"

Taryn looked up, confused.

"The only falsely accused in your article?" he explained.

"I'm hoping to have three or four, probably three. You are just the first one who has agreed to meet with me. I'm wondering if I can find anything in common. You know, how people react to that, how they move on."

He shook his head. "I'm sure everybody's stories are pretty different."

She turned to her notes, willing herself to concentrate. "You found her."

"Is that a question?"

"No." She felt her face flush again. "Why do you think everyone immediately accused you? I mean just because you found her body. I read the transcripts and all the articles. It doesn't make sense to me."

"Well, there was this thing about fingerprints. When I came across the two-by-four in the dumpster, I picked it up. I didn't know what it was; I mean what was on it. I was curious so I picked it up. After I had it in my hands, I realized it was blood and," he cleared his throat, "well, blood." He turned his eyes downward. "But it turned out only my fingerprints were on it, so they didn't have anyone else to accuse, I guess. And I was turning into a bad kid, or so they thought. I mean, look at me." He turned the newspaper clipping back towards her and she felt her heart sink. He didn't look like a bad kid to her. He looked like a sad kid. Joe continued, "I smoked, I was starting to dress like some kind of grunge rebel, I was hanging out with the wrong people. Starting to stay out and party and not come home."

"Drugs?"

He nodded, "Yeah, drugs. It's no secret. But honestly, I'd just started trying them that year. The press and the cops accusing me made that to be way bigger than it was. Because of who she was."

"The mayor's daughter."

"Yeah. He didn't like her dating me in the first place, so when mine were the only fingerprints on the two-by-four, and I was high and hanging with the wrong people, it just fueled him. He had a lot of power and influenced everyone against me. And of course, Lauren and I were meeting because," he smiled and Taryn felt herself smile back. Joe Sinclair was an intoxicating blend of a cute little boy and a sharp, intriguing man.

"I read," she said.

He smiled wider. "Yep, two young kids going off to lose their virginity. Completely normal and innocent but, you know, when it all happened people said some awful things. Her girlfriends, they all spoke up telling everyone that she'd told them I was only after sex. That wasn't true, but I guess they all knew beforehand what we were going to do."

"Sure." Taryn thought of her first time and sharing it with her friends.

"So I was this young mixed-up kid, getting in with the wrong crowd, who apparently was off to go deflower the mayor's daughter while high on pot." He turned up his lips with a shy smile at the word deflower. "For lack of a better word. Then she's killed and I'm the only one who touched the murder weapon. It didn't take long for folks to turn on me."

"And they've still never solved the case."

Joe shook his head.

"So, what does it feel like to have everyone turn against you?"

"Everyone didn't."

She waited for him to continue.

"My mom always said I was innocent. So did my brothers."

"Your Dad?"

"I don't think he was ever sure."

"And now? What happened when you were proven innocent?"

"It's, it's never the same, you know. Once someone stops believing in you ... something's always broken from that point on."

She watched as pain cast a shadowy crease across his forehead.

"I want to hear about how it was then, later, when they figured out you hadn't done it and they dropped the charges."

"Tell me about you." He leaned back and stretched out his arm. "I mean, I'm sorry, I know we are short on time. But you mentioned this might take a few meetings and this first one was just to confirm we'd go forward? Sure, there's lots to tell I guess about me and my lawyer, who is now my partner, but there's time."

She nodded, captivated by his smiling eyes, amazed at how unexpectedly comfortable she felt, yet nervous at the same time. It didn't make sense that he wanted to know more about her, but she suddenly wanted to tell him, anything.

"Thank you. Well, yes, I am a bit short on time but, if you are agreeing to be in the article, we can do the rest by phone over the next couple of weeks. I can certainly give you the speedy version of me! I mean I told you, I go to U of T."

"Are you from here?"

She shook her head. "No, I'm from, well, all over. Born in Santiago, but I only lived there for one year. I've lived in all kinds of places. My dad is an archeologist. My mom was Canadian though, from down east. Anyway, they got divorced when I was four and then she died when I was seven and Ryan, that's my brother, was ten. We ended up travelling everywhere with Dad. It meant I lived everywhere, Thailand, Switzerland, Greece, a short stint in Iceland.

"But my brother, he lives here in Millerton. He married a girl from here. She's the one who mentioned you as a good story. They're pretty settled here with two kids. I stayed with them last night. Wow, I'm babbling. Is that what you wanted to know?"

Joe watched her animated face as she spoke and couldn't help but smile. He'd begrudgingly accepted her invitation as a favour to Doug. "An article mentioning the firm in *The Star* can't hurt and people love your story," Doug had said convincingly. Now he was sitting across from the most beautiful woman he'd ever set eyes on. Everything about her, the childlike giggling lilt in her voice, the way her eyelashes fanned down when she got serious, the way she twirled her pen in her slim manicured fingers. He couldn't keep his eyes off her.

Was this what he wanted to know? She'd asked. No, he wanted to know everything.

CHAPTER 19

"Well, there's a sight for sore eyes." Stuart Flannery made his way into Doug's office, leaning forward as he walked with a birdlike bob.

Doug looked up from a pile of dog-eared papers and old notebooks scattered across his desk, and rose to his feet. "Stuart!" He reached out to shake his old friend's hand, then changed his mind, wrapping his arm around Flannery's back in a warm hug. "So good to see you, old man. Thanks for coming over, especially so late."

"You too, Walleye!" Flannery laughed, referencing the famous fishing trip from years past where Doug had emerged triumphant. The fish, 24 inches and 5 pounds had grown in both length and weight through each telling of the story. The two men parted, nodding as years of affection swirled their mouths into wide grins. "It seemed odd talking about these things by phone."

They sat down, exchanging pleasantries; did Marlena still make that incredible butterscotch pie? Had Flannery found a woman yet? No, he was waiting for Marlena to realize Doug was no good. The two snickered at their longstanding jokes, twenty years and multiple cases in the making; a mutual admiration that withstood all passage of time manifested in this moment of levity and comfort in the late evening darkness. Although it had been months since their brief reunion at a mutual associate's funeral, the two dove into conversation without a gap.

"So, our lad." Flannery finally left the joviality behind. "No news yet. He can't have gotten too far. The wife awake yet?"

"Just got a call from her brother. She's awake but groggy."

"I heard she was pretty banged up. Her head hit against the side window and frame. That's got to be nasty. I suppose that's why he left to get help. But he'd have been better off stayin'. It's a shame. They've got the helicopter from Channel 4 that spotted the car still out looking, but it's awfully dark out there now. Good crew, those folks from Channel 4. And I talked to my old guys over at the station. They've gone out to the spot where the car went over the guardrail. I'm surprised no one noticed it from the highway, but they say it's just bent and twisted, not really smashed through. The car must have pretty much skimmed over top of it. Obviously no one was driving behind or in front of him or they'd have called it in. Mind you, Old Country's Edge isn't used as much as 21." He looked at his friend who stared down and sensed his speculations were going nowhere. "How are you doing?"

Doug looked up into Flannery's dark blue eyes encircled by his round wire glasses. The man never aged, but it was more from having the same craggy lines chiselling his face for the past twenty years than from a look of youthfulness.

"I'm just," he paused, "confused I suppose. Things just aren't adding up. Joe's been really off the last little while. He and Taryn broke up, you know."

Flanner shook his head. "No way."

"They did. They went through some stuff and he really retreated. Even from me. I found out this morning that he was supposed to have dinner last night with this woman that used to work here, Andrea. She came by here and acted like they were a couple. It's weird."

"But he was with Taryn in the car?"

Doug lifted his hands in the air indicating he had no idea what was going on. "Yeah, it's all a mystery. I guess we'll figure it out once we talk to him. Or talk to her more." Doug opened his eyes wide. "Stu, I know it was an accident and not some great mystery, but there's so much not making sense. Like this woman."

"Andrea?"

He grimaced. "She worked here for, I don't know, maybe six months. Started in the spring. She claimed she knew Joe from before so he brought her in. Then one night a few weeks into it, Joe confesses to me that he can't remember her at all. Anyway, it was bad, Stu, really bad."

Stuart Flannery sat back, listening, his left index finger affixed to his white trimmed mustache, knowing there was no need to prompt.

"She was dishonest. Not just dishonest, downright conniving. Margot noticed it first, that things weren't right. A few files went missing and Margot swore she'd known right where they were. Then Andrea came to see me to tell me she thought maybe Margot was a problem, getting forgetful. Margot forgetful? Come on!"

Stuart listened quietly, wanting to interrupt to ask how Margot was, but knowing Doug needed to continue.

"It was around that time that Margot started watching her more closely. One morning, Margot came in early, like always, and found her computer was on. She swore she'd never leave it on, and I know she wouldn't. You know Margot, she closes this place up like Fort Knox. No one is more careful than her. Anyway, Margot said she was the only one here and her computer was up and running. And it was wide open to the notes on an affidavit from a witness on a case I was trying. One that Margot was helping me with. And Margot would never leave a client's information wide open in the office like that. Well, being Margot, she looked it over with a fine-toothed comb and guess what? The file had been altered. Someone had changed the client's words in the document from what was on the recording. Changed it up so that the person's story was full of inconsistencies. I mean I can't give you details, but it was like the person said something was black and the document said it was white. It was hard at first, you know. No way to prove it was Andrea since it was on Margot's computer and Margot was the one signed in. Margot was a mess over it, but of course I believed her."

"So why would this girl, Andrea, do that? Why did you think it was her? Did she know the client or something?"

"No. That was the strange part. The changes she made, if anything, would have made it harder for me to get the client off. The only motivation I could come up with was to make me look bad, or more likely to make Margot look bad, look incompetent. I don't know. It was just a gut feeling that it was her. She was the newest one at the office and something about her just felt off. It was like she went out of her way to make Margot look bad. We finally confronted her. She denied it of course, and there wasn't much we could do. But then it happened again. Drink?"

Flannery nodded then declined ice as Doug reached into his bottom desk drawer, pulling out a small bottle of Glenlivet whisky and two tumblers and pouring them each an inch and a splash before continuing his story.

"It happened a second time. Margot was reviewing something she'd worked on in preparation for a trial, a different trial but also mine. That part was odd too. I mean, she works full time for Joe now, but on these two cases that got messed up, she was helping me. And she noticed it wasn't anything like she'd prepared it. Things were completely opposite in context. Again, of course, the last person recorded as altering the file was Margot. And this time, after the first incident, Margot had been even more careful about keeping her computer locked down. We asked Andrea and she got really mean and stormed out. I thought she was going to quit, but she showed up the next day; acted like nothing had happened."

"But you fired her eventually? Or did she quit?"

"Fired, yeah, soon after. About two weeks later, Margot came in to me one day just horrified, in tears. She said she'd gotten so suspicious that she'd gone through Andrea's resume and called the school where she supposedly did her legal assistant course. Apparently she'd never attended. Everything about her was fake. I kicked myself for not checking it out at first, but I had checked on a reference. I'd spoken to some guy who was supposedly her professor. I tried that number again the day Margot came in and, of course, some other person answered. I just hung up. It was all falsified. Live and learn. But then, Joe had said he'd known her.

"That was a challenge too. That was around the time that Joe started acting weird. As partners we discussed letting Andrea go that day and he was firmly against it. He didn't see any grounds since we had no way to prove the file thing. And he said her work for him was so impeccable that even if she had lied about going to school, he thought we should still keep her. It was really the first time he and I'd ever disagreed about a business thing, about anything. So that, plus him and Taryn breaking up, he just completely changed.

"Anyway, one day she said some things to Margot that got Margot all upset again. Personal things. Mean things. Brought up Margot's husband being killed overseas and telling her that this job was her only life and how sad that was. I lost it, I admit it buddy, I shouldn't have said what I did. I let my temper get in the way and I literally walked her out the door by the arm, told her to never come back."

Flannery squinted and smirked.

"What?" Doug asked.

"Walleye has a temper?"

"It takes a lot."

"Never seen it. She must have really been something!" Flannery thought a moment. "But you said you talked to her today and she said they were to have dinner?"

"Yes. She showed up here this morning, actually. That's how I found out Joe was missing."

Flannery took a long sip of scotch, letting it flow to the back of his throat before speaking. Always a straight speaker, he leaned forward, balancing the glass on his knee. "Sounds like they were together. Maybe you didn't want to see it, my friend."

Doug shrugged his shoulders. "No idea." He pushed some of the papers aside. "No idea what's going on with him. He comes in here and goes into his office, barely says hello. Some nights I think he sleeps here too. He talks to Margot a bit more than to me, but not much. Of course, he's totally caught up in this McGill trial. And you know how intense he gets. It's a stressful one—the biggest case of his career. That's another thing too. I met with McGill today." He paused, "But I'll get into that later. This Andrea, I don't know. He did really stick up for her that day I fired her. And today she acted as though I should have known they were due to have dinner. She seemed genuinely concerned actually."

Flannery nodded, deep in thought, his eyes wandered to the papers scattered on Doug's desk and landed on a newspaper clipping at the top of a box on the floor. It showed Lauren Avery's father. "What'd you dig up all this for?"

"I don't know. It wasn't intentional, really. I just pulled the boxes out of the file room looking for more recent case notes for McGill and saw this box too and some other ones from the early days. Just wondering where I lost him I guess, and felt like reminiscing. It's not all Avery trial stuff, some of it is just sentimental, from when he first came on board. I need to put a lot of it in storage but haven't yet. I guess I just felt like looking through it. The Avery stuff—it just happened to be in the first box." He sighed and Flannery saw the weight of the day pushing his friend deeper into the past. Flannery stayed quiet letting Doug's thoughts flow.

"Margot and I drove out to his house today. It's all packed up. I didn't even know he was moving. And this accident, I mean, if he was well enough to leave Taryn and the car, presumably to go get help, then where is he? Sure, it's rural down there, but someone must have seen him. Wouldn't he go find a cottage or a house and knock on the door? Or break in and use the phone? There's been a helicopter flying overhead for God's sake!" He swigged back his scotch, lowering the empty glass to his desk. "I mean, does he *want* to be missing? He had court today, and," he made a gruff sigh, "and this money in the trunk?"

"Sixty K."

Another long exhalation as Doug scratched his head. "Sixty K."

"Hundred dollar bills. Six hundred of them in packs of fifty, tied with rubber bands. The folks down in evidence counted it a few times. Non-sequential. Some old bills, some new ones. They were inside a pillowcase rolled up inside the gym bag. It's funny too, the trunk was so smashed up they weren't even going to look in it right away but something made them pry it open."

Flannery watched as Doug stared off at the wall across from him, waiting for his friend to absorb his words. Doug sat, perplexed, as though the painting of Fiji across from him held all the answers. For the first time all evening he refused to make eye contact, even when Flannery prompted him.

"You think he was depressed, or maybe with the stress of things he'd gotten into some habit?"

"Joe? Nah."

"You said he'd changed, withdrawn from you. The strain of that McGill case and breaking up with his wife. That can do a guy in."

"I've never known Joe to be depressed, not even at his worst. You remember? He had a lot of moods but he never got depressed."

Flannery nodded. "Sure, but I mean, divorce or separation and you said they'd been going through something else?"

Doug nodded, not mentioning the nursery but wondering how it had played into the separation.

Flannery continued, "I've seen cases you know, and heard of some others. Sometimes a guy can't take it and he offs himself. Sometimes they get messed in the head and take the ones they love with them."

Doug returned his gaze to Flannery, his face stern. "You think Joe deliberately drove off a cliff?" he shouted. "No way. Stu, I know you saw all kinds of things as a cop, even now as a private eye, but no, not Joe. Besides, he left the car! If he was depressed, which he wasn't, and even if he," Doug's voice cracked, "even if he wanted to kill himself, he'd never do anything to hurt Taryn. I don't know everything they went through these past few months, but I know he still loved her. Plus, she wasn't even supposed to be in the country."

Flannery frowned. "That might actually point to his frame of mind. Maybe he had her against her will?"

"Jesus, Stu! No way!" Doug yelled, then apologized, taking a deep breath and pausing for a long minute. "It doesn't explain the money!"

Flannery nodded, eating his words as Doug's face reddened even in the dim light of the desk lamp. "Yeah, yeah you're right, Walleye. I'm just rulin' everything out."

"Have I hired you yet?" Doug softened and Flannery smiled holding his glass out for a top up. Doug didn't seem to notice, his gaze returning to the painting, beginning another long stare of total silence.

"Okay, what about a habit then?" Flannery interrupted. "Any chance he was drinkin', druggin', gamblin'? Something that needed money? I mean it's not hard to end up there."

"Stuart." Doug interrupted.

"Ya?"

"Am I hiring you?"

"No. Jesus, Walleye, I'm all in. There's no hiring. He's my lad too. Why are you worrying about hiring me? I'm here to help you, my friend. This is me, not Stu Flannery, Private Detective, just me. This one's all on the house, buddy. Why would you even ask?"

Finally noticing Flannery's empty glass, Doug opened the bottle and topped him up. "Because I need something to stay between us."

"That's a given." Flannery watched his friend's shoulders slouch again.

"I don't want your old friends on the force to know, necessarily. I want your help without them for now."

"It's between us. Always," he said again.

"We're missing money," Doug began. "Here, at the firm. Twenty-three thousand that I know of. I just had to write a personal cheque to cover payroll."

"Damn."

The two men swigged their whisky at the same time, Doug finally returning his glass to the desk. He looked up. "This isn't just about an accident." Doug paused and lifted a document from his desk, focusing on the Forester & Sinclair letterhead. "Joe's in trouble."

CHAPTER 20

MEG TIPTOED INTO ANDREA'S ROOM, listening for the sounds of sleep but instead saw Andrea's outline, sitting up against her headboard.

"Can I get you anything?" Meg whispered. "Do you think you can sleep at all?"

Andrea sniffled as Meg came towards her. "No. I can't sleep. I was just thinking I'd turn the TV back on, you know for the eleven o'clock headlines. I had to turn it off before. I just couldn't listen to it anymore. They said they found blood in the snow."

"Yeah, I heard that too. But there could be lots of reasons for that. I mean, he might have cut himself or something. It doesn't mean he's hurt bad."

"Thanks, Meggie. Thanks for being here." Andrea reached forward to hug her and Meg noticed she hadn't changed out of her sweater. "Did you try his parents again?"

"Earlier, twice. Just voicemail. I don't think they've fully accepted me either," Andrea whispered. "Maybe we did jump into things quickly. It's hard for some people to understand. He fell in love with me so fast," she said, then went silent for a moment. "He loves me so much, Meggie."

"I know." Meg placed a reassuring hand on her arm. "Try to sleep, sis. I'm sure in the morning they'll find him and this will all make sense."

"I wish you could see how he looks at me."

"I will, tomorrow." Meg rose and began straightening the blankets over her sister.

"I know I come across kind of rough sometimes." Her voice was barely audible over the rustling of the blankets. Meg didn't reply. "To you too, Meggie. I'm sorry."

"It's fine, sis." Meg squeezed her hand. "I'm going to bed, come get me if you need me."

CHAPTER 21

ODDLY UNAFRAID despite the darkness and chilling silence of this second night, Joe felt comforted by the warm scent of cedar inside the shack. Sheltered from the heartless wind, he drifted in and out of sleep on the hard table. From deep within the dream where falling endlessly leads to a crash, he jolted awake. The faint call of an owl broke through the night and he swore he heard his name. Willing himself to stay alert, he fought his body's instincts to sleep and tried to lift his head up.

Every time he tried to focus his mind strayed down a careening path. Taking charge, he forced himself to think only of Taryn. Soon he was reminiscing of the night they met at the mall, and the all too short walk to her car, both knowing they were not willing for this to be their last encounter. He pictured her as she was that night, nervous and young but trying to act older. They'd stood in a gap of time, and she'd leaned against her car door, keys in hand, as they waited for one or the other to make the next move. Joe had hesitated a long time, for every kiss since Lauren had been nothing but a cold means to an end. But now, Taryn Evans was stirring emotions he thought he'd forgotten. He'd slid his hand between the small of her back and the car door, feeling the coarseness of her soft camel hair coat tickling his fingers and pulling her close to him, nudging hesitantly on her cheek with his lips, until certain she'd respond. Then they'd kissed over and over, standing under a cascade of snowflakes dancing in the glow of a streetlamp.

A winter of lingering phone calls led to a spring of eagerly anticipated, long awaited visits until finally Taryn completed her exams and arrived with a decision. She'd move to Millerton, at least for a while. She'd spend the next while working freelance towards her ultimate career goal of writing articles to help children around the world and while in Millerton they'd see if their being together was forever.

Joe fought his brain's discourteous attempts to change the subject as he started drifting again to thoughts of more recent events. The crisis of the past few months, like a poison, fighting its way to the front of his consciousness.

April

"Working late again?" Andrea stood at his office door, her short crimson dress making her legs look even longer than they really were, and flipped her flowing black cape across her shoulders. Joe looked up slowly, not wanting to let go of the idea in his mind as he input his notes from an earlier meeting with Chase McGill.

"Oh, hi Andrea. I didn't know anyone was still here." She stood in the doorway, moth-like, cape hitting both sides as it continued to swing. He lowered his eyes to the clock on his screen, surprised that it was after ten. Earlier, he'd texted Taryn to let her know he'd be late again but he'd anticipated closer to eight o'clock, hoping for a late Friday night dinner together. "It's awfully late."

"Oh, yes I think it's just us here." She smiled. "I wanted to finish up on the Bauer details, for Doug, you know. He needs things perfect for next week and I, well, I found things were just done so poorly. A lot of the files were downright incomplete."

Joe smiled. Andrea Vaillancourt had been with them for only three weeks but seemed to be working out so well. She was extremely keen; jumping in to help wherever was needed. And so exceptionally friendly, always stopping in to say hello in the morning and goodbye on her way out. He wished more of the clerks and assistants felt that level of comfort with the partners. He was pleased he'd run into her and agreed to bring her in. "Well, that's just great. We really appreciate your help. One thing though, Doug usually clears overtime before work is done, you know just to keep the client's billable hours on track. Did you talk to him?"

"Oh, I won't put in for it." She threw her head back. "I just like to do a good job. The clients shouldn't suffer and pay more because others missed things."

He nodded, amused. She was such a refreshing change.

She walked towards him, touching the lamp on his desk with her finger like a gloved butler and examining it for dust. "Don't you agree?"

"I do. I'm just surprised you'd give up your Friday night." He pushed back in his chair examining her more closely than he had in the past. She leaned in causing her cape to gape open and the square neckline of her dress to lower ever so slightly, revealing hidden white lace. Drawn to the deep curves of her breasts, he allowed his stare to linger a split second, then halted, suddenly fixated on the silver pendant that landed perfectly between them.

"Well, I don't have anything going on, nothing at all!" She said.

He looked up again, feeling suddenly caught.

"Hey, are you hungry?" She continued "I could go out and grab us a bite? Bring it back here."

"Thanks, no. I need to get home. My wife said she was heating up some of her homemade sauce for some pasta. Hopefully she's waited up for me. She's been tired lately." He wondered why he was sharing so much.

Her smile faded and she pursed her lips. "Oh, okay. I just thought maybe we could catch up. You know, *you* hired me and here I am seeing you every day and we've never really had a good conversation yet."

"Sure." He began shutting down his laptop. "Some other time?"

"I mean, we have this special connection, you know, with Lauren." She sat down across from him staring, blinking her eyes slowly.

"Oh. Yes, yes of course." He tensed, not wanting to have the conversation he had been dreading. He'd spent the past month since their initial random meeting on the street, wracking his brain to figure out how he knew her. She'd said she was one of Lauren's friends from high school, but Joe couldn't remember her from school and the truth was all he remembered of any of Lauren's friends was the blur of a few ponytailed gigglers who blended together in his piecemeal recollections from that summer. In his mind they'd all been named Jenny or Ginny. It didn't matter what they were called. Not one of them had approached him again. The moment the police had taken him away they'd all turned on him. "He wanted her to have sex with him that night!" they'd said. "He probably was going to force her. I heard he forced her," they'd said. "They found her that way, raped and beaten." Rumours weeded their way through Millerton those first months. It didn't matter that it wasn't true. High school gossip ran through the town in a torrent. Joe Sinclair was after Lauren and now she was dead. There was no room for truth with the Jennies and Ginnies.

And later, when Joe was free and had to return to school, those girls, those friends of Lauren's, were mysteriously at a loss for words. The rumours were no longer worth their weight in scandal. But Andrea? He didn't remember an Andrea at all.

"I've just wanted to say that I'm sorry." She tucked her hands together. "I mean all those years it's been and all those accusations." He felt heat from somewhere buried twenty years deep flood into his face. She continued, "I always knew you were innocent. I should have spoken up."

"Thank you, Andrea." He stood up. "I appreciate it, but it was a long time ago. We were all just kids. We'll talk more another day." He reached for his suit jacket on the coat rack in the corner.

She rose. "Sure, Joe. Anytime." A wide smile crossed her face.

Together they locked up the office, rode the elevator and headed to their cars discussing light topics such as how he and Doug had acquired the top floor of the Frosst Building. Joe pulled out of the parking lot, waving back at her and wondering why she sat in her car without starting it. He felt an odd sense of connection to his past for the first time in years. It felt good. Maybe she could share things with him about Lauren that would make recalling that summer less painful. Perhaps reconnecting with this woman was good for him.

Andrea sat in the driver's seat pretending to check her makeup in the rear view mirror until Joe was long gone. Joe Sinclair. She'd seen him look down the front of her dress. And she could almost taste his lips when his face softened at her apology. He must have needed to hear that for so long that he actually believed her. And the way he smiled at her and promised they'd talk another day. Another day and every day after that. *Soon my love.* She took a long, deep breath and then reached into her cape pocket and pulled out the spare set of keys she'd swiped from Margot's drawer earlier that evening.

CHAPTER 22

August 1997

THE REDHEAD WAS NICE. Margot was her name. She was younger than his mom but acted mother-like, asking if he was okay, did he want a muffin, could she get him some water? She led Joe past the faded sofa, through the arched doorframe and into the back office where Doug Forester rose from his chair.

They'd met last night when Doug had come to the police station. He'd walked in and introduced himself and somehow—amid the confusion of the big cop named Small, Joe's mother's tireless whimpers, and Joe's father's grating silence—the air had seemed to clear. There was calmness in Doug Forester's firm handshake and hope in his ability to look Joe square in the eyes and talk to *him* instead of the adults. This man commanded attention, taking Joe's muddled, bloodstained thoughts and slicing them to clarity. And Joe had watched as Doug turned to the skinny cop, Flannery, wishing him a warm hello. Joe liked this, since so far Flannery was the kinder cop. If they were friends, then maybe that meant something.

Last night had gone on forever: from fingerprints to handcuffs to a painful wait for a tired judge who'd finally rapped his worn-out gavel, announcing that Joe could go home. The drive was torture, staring at the back of their two heads. His father's shoulders stern and unforgiving, the print shop having been signed over to raise bail. His mother's shoulders slouched and shifting back and forth as Kleenex dabbed at her nose and words uttered repeatedly as though on an audio loop "That beautiful girl, that poor girl. Oh my boy, oh Joe. How could they?"

Joe had stared out the window as they'd driven through town, noting his father's avoidance of the park and wondering who he was really protecting. But in the distance up Drake Street, the glowing, devilish eyes of police lights still taunted. He wanted to go to bed and cry, partly for fear of his own life, but mostly for Lauren. Her family would know by now. Joe pictured her pretty mother collapsing in horror, and he became nauseated imagining her blonde hair, so much like Lauren's, and then pictured Lauren's, now matted in blood. He pictured Mr. Avery finding out too, and felt his own body heave in fear.

"I appreciate this second meeting. You must be exhausted." Doug pointed an open palm towards one of two brown-striped chairs then walked around to sit in the second one. "I know it was hard last night, with all the commotion. I really can't be a good lawyer to you unless we have some time to talk alone. Your parents have agreed."

Joe nodded and looked around the small office, painted beige on three walls, the exterior fourth wall exposing the original brick of the old building. His stomach curled in a permanent twist, now natural, as he listened and tried his best to care as Doug went through all the steps of the legal process. Doug Forester really knew his stuff. It would have been impressive at any other time. Eventually the lawyer took a breath.

"Does that make sense?" Doug asked.

Did it? What'd he say? "I guess so," Joe lied. He'd heard something about a pre-trial and setting dates. Something about the Crown Attorney doing something.

"It's a lot, I know. Don't worry. I'll be sure your parents know all the dates. And they will probably be at the rest of our meetings since you are a minor. But, I did just want to get to know you a bit better and understand what happened. Your mom's awfully upset, of course. And your dad, he seems angry."

"Yes."

"Just scared, I suppose."

The kindness in his voice pierced Joe's defenses and he felt a knot rising from deep in his throat. He wanted to cry and crumble into the couch. "I think he's mad about putting up the print shop money for bail," Joe said.

"You get bail money back."

"I know. But he also wanted to expand the shop. He wanted the city to approve it. Guess he figures that won't happen now."

Margot appeared with a pitcher of ice water, a blue plastic glass and a coffee mug bearing the raised three-dimensional head of the cartoon Tasmanian Devil. She silently handed the coffee to Doug, then poured a glass of water and handed it to Joe with a warm smile. He caught her catching him welling up with tears and she quickly turned away, leaving them alone.

"Joe?" Doug leaned towards him. "We're going to go over everything, but tell me what's on your mind right now."

"I, uh." Joe sipped the cold water, feeling it chill him all the way down. He was choking on his words and could imagine his father's stern disdain. "I just mean I didn't do anything." He felt his strength caving in. "I didn't do anything. I want ..."

"It's okay." Doug leaned in further, patting Joe's shoulder. "You want what?"

Joe buried his head in his hands, wiping his eyes as more tears, this time of embarrassment, poured down his face. A moment later he recomposed himself. "I want to see her."

Doug didn't ask who. "What do you mean?"

"I want to see Lauren." Joe turned his gaze to the brick wall, "I mean, I know she's dead and everything. It's not like I want to see dead people. I've never seen, except on TV, well except last night, but I've never seen—you know like at a funeral."

"What do you want, Joe?"

"I just want to see her. I want to be there. Do you think I can be there? I just want to say goodbye or whatever and tell her mom I didn't do this. Can I? Can I?"

Doug shook his head. "No, Joe. That's not a good idea. You know that."

"But I didn't do anything." Joe's voice rose. "Why is this happening?"

Doug shifted closer and pulled Joe towards him. "I don't know, Joe. But we're going to figure this out, okay? We're going to go over every detail and figure this out."

"Why don't people believe me?" Joe sobbed.

"I do."

CHAPTER 23

DOUG REVIEWED HIS CALENDAR, still hand written into a thick leather folder despite or in defiance of advances in technology. Using the Cross pen Marlena had given him for his birthday, he drew pointed stars next to the appointments he could possibly postpone. He jumped when his cell phone chimed from his coat pocket.

"Flannery," he answered without a hello, "any word?"

"No, Walleye. Sorry. Where are you?"

"Office."

"Okay, I'll be over soon. I'm going to cruise by the hospital to see if Taryn's up and willing to talk to me. Last I heard she is pretty with it now. They moved her up to a normal ward overnight."

"That's great." Doug meant it but found the good news heavy and incomplete.

"I ran that phone number." Flannery continued as Doug heard him hack a wet morning cough. Doug cringed but waited patiently for his friend to catch his breath. "I tried a reverse look-up on the internet last night but it didn't find anything, so first thing today I had Ruthie down at the station run it. It's a pay phone."

"Where?"

"Tracked it to a phone booth down by the marina. In fact, I'm there now. Thought I'd come by and check it out. It's one of the few left, you know. Who uses a pay phone anymore? I was surprised. It's right here on the corner of 4th and Dresden. You know where the docks are? Near the old Whistles?"

Doug said yes, thinking of the worst area of town, the neighbourhood that had somehow missed Millerton's most recent revival. The Dresden Road neighbourhood was where boats came to load and unload shipments. Unlike the rest of Millerton, which had lately boomed with prosperity and hope, Dresden Road reeked with falling down buildings and long-abandoned houses. The isolation of storage warehouses with broken windows and peeling paint contributed to its "don't walk there at night" reputation. Whistle's Bar, formerly a hot spot for young people at the turn of the millennium, was now a shell of its former self, reputed to be a shelter for junkies and their suppliers.

"There's no one around," Flannery continued. "Jesus, the city needs to do something down here." Doug could tell he was moving, likely walking about, as wind created unplanned cracks in the conversation. Doug heard Flannery say something else but only caught the word "more".

"Yes?"

"Ruthie got the call history off the payphone. Nine calls in the past week. Three to our lad."

"Hmm."

Flannery continued. "One to Reddy's taxi, that's probably not related. The other five to the same number."

"Whose?"

"Guess."

"Just tell me, Stu."

"Jack McGill." Flannery stated.

"Chase's uncle?"

"Yep. Well the uncle's house anyway."

Amber appeared at the door apologetically, holding a pile of papers. "Good morning, Doug?" Irritated, Doug held his phone away from his ear, showing her he was on it. "Sorry," she continued.

"It's just that Chase McGill and his uncle are here unexpectedly." She grimaced, awaiting his response.

"You hear that Stu?" Doug returned to the phone call. "They're here. Chase and his uncle."

"Okay. Cruising over to the hospital, then I'll be right over. Maybe they can explain who's been calling them from this shithole."

In the end, Doug didn't need Flannery or any of the information on the phone calls. For as soon as Chase and his uncle settled themselves on the sofa at the corner of Doug's office, the floodgate of confession opened.

"Chase's been awake all night, pacing the floor. Finally, after some prodding, he broke down." Uncle Jack leaned forward awkwardly, staring at his nephew. "Tell him."

"I wasn't totally honest with you," Chase said. "I uh, I was in the parking garage that night."

Doug nodded, all three of them knowing that Doug already knew. "Go on."

"I was there. But I didn't kill her, Mr. Forester." There was a long pause, with only the sound of Jack tapping his fingers on the arm of the couch, Doug hoping Chase would continue on his own.

"But you saw who did." It was a statement. Doug reached over to his side table to grab a legal pad. Chase nodded. "Did Joe know any of this? It's not in any of the case files."

Chase nodded again. "I told him the truth," he said. "But I'm not sure what he wrote down. These people, the ones that killed her, I uh, wuull, I think it was easier with the story the way we had it."

"They've been threatening you?"

Chase looked at his uncle, who nodded for him to continue. Chase nodded, "The thing is, I was okay with them threatening me. But they threatened my mom too. I don't care what they do to me, but she's already a mess and they said they'd, well you know they're capable of anything. But the thing is, since yesterday you know, Mr. Sinclair not showing up. First I thought it was the storm and stuff but then last night on the news them saying they found his car. I guess it was an accident but, wuull, the thing is, I just can't stop thinkin', maybe they've been threatening him too. Maybe they did this. And maybe if I don't say something." He stopped dead and Doug watched fear flicker in his eyes.

"They called your house. Who are we talking about here?" Doug turned towards Chase's uncle who nodded. He saw Chase's eyes squint, wondering how the lawyer knew. Doug explained, "They've called Joe too. And I think you are right, Chase. I think Joe was being threatened. My contact has established the same number that's been calling you was calling Joe. Can you tell me who they are?" A conflicted pause and Doug continued, "The police can protect you. I can call them."

A longer pause was broken by Amber's soft knock on the door. Annoyed, Doug excused himself and slipped into the outer office, silently closing the door behind him.

"I'm sorry," she said, "but he says it's urgent and might be related..."

Flannery stepped forward. "I made her interrupt you. You got McGill in there?"

"Yep."

"What'd he say?"

Doug scanned his office. Amber had returned to her desk, tuning them out.

"Someone's been threatening him. He witnessed the stabbing. He didn't do it. He wonders if someone's was threatening Joe too. Whoever made those calls."

"Yeah, okay. Well, I decided to come straight here after stopping by the hospital. I visited Taryn for a couple of minutes. She's awake, and lucid. She told me she'd been asking for me and was trying to get my number. I guess her brother told her I'd wanted to talk to her and she knew of me."

"Okay."

"She says the car's steering was tampered with. Says Joe mentioned it as they drove out and then when they were up on the highway before they went over, he couldn't control it at all."

"Jesus," Doug exclaimed. "Amber, call the cops."

Flannery shook his head and waving no towards her. "They're already on their way."

CHAPTER 24

Summer 2011

A PROPOSAL. She just sensed it. Taryn pulled her hair up into a loose bun, then let it fall again. Staring back at her from the mirror, she saw rigidness in her neck and reached up to rub her shoulders. Marriage. It hadn't entered her mind for a long, long time. Not since childhood when her friends would play bride and tie lavish pieces of lace to their hair, parading forward and marrying whatever stuffed animal, broom or unwitting younger brother was willing to patiently wait at the altar. In adult life it was a topic to be dismissed, guffawed at. Tied down? White picket fence? Not yet. Not me.

But then Joe Sinclair arrived. How cliché to say he'd swept her off her feet, but he had. From that first kiss by the car; no, before then, that first glance at the mall. Everything about him, from the way his left eye squinted ever so slightly smaller than his right when he looked at her so intensely, to the whole idea of the innocent ex-defendant straightening his life out from an apathetic, rebellious teenager to turning it all around and being top of his class at law school, then partnering with the very lawyer who'd believed in him from the start. Overcoming the sorrow of losing his first love so violently and being accused of her murder, he was never bitter, never a word of regret or anger towards those who'd doubted him, or his unapproachable father who'd lost faith in him altogether. Joe Sinclair was a hero, a role model. But his past wasn't the draw at all. It was just Joe. The way he woke up every day with a new song, usually an eighties anthem, stuck in his head and belted it out, every lyric intact, as he made his way around the kitchen. The way he softened when the topic of his mother came up, as though his sharp muscular body was suddenly wrapped in a soft blanket at the mention of her name.

If Taryn wanted to get married, dreamed of getting married, it was to a man just like Joe. In fact, before meeting him, she couldn't have even dreamed of all the things he represented coming together in one person. If Taryn wanted to get married.

She pulled her hair up again, in a ponytail this time, and brushed some lightly coloured gloss over her lips, then headed for the living room to wait for Joe. They were going to Gardenia Terrace, a lunch reservation, then a stroll along the river walk on this, the one-year anniversary of their beginning to date seriously after her move to Millerton. Usually disorganized about such things, he'd announced the reservation was set weeks ago and the lovely sentiment had been tingling her heart ever since. He was going to propose.

She reached up to the top of the couch back and gently stroked Gertrude, causing the tortoiseshell cat to stretch her front white-socked paw forward while opening one eye with a glare. "What do you think, Gertie?" She continued stroking her head while she eased into the motion, now amenable to the idea of a massage. "Do you think I'm the marrying type?"

There was no doubt, Joe was the one. But would marriage to a man who'd spent his entire life in the same city work for her? He was so settled here, working his way up to be partner in Doug's law firm. Would he ever really understand that she needed to help people in the roughest parts of the world and that the only way to do that was to go there? Taryn looked around her sparse living room, still undecorated after her arrival in Millerton twelve months ago, never really unpacked from her trip to university before that. Twelve months was the longest she'd ever lived in any city, or country for that matter, except for school. If Joe proposed, would he be willing to let her go, for months at a time, maybe more? Or was he picturing his parents' life: same city, same house, three boys climbing the same tree year after year? Millerton? Sure it was a great place, and Ryan lived here, not to mention it was only a two-hour drive from Mom's grave and the tombstone—bereft of a grave—that represented her father. If she was to settle somewhere, this was probably as good as anywhere else. She'd moved here to be with him, to test it out, but she hadn't unpacked.

She had to keep travelling and writing her articles. Organizations knew of her now, and her latest contribution to the *National Script* had raised so much awareness for child poverty that editors and mentors had glowed that her career was set. Maybe she and Joe could work it out somehow. She'd continue travelling the world and pushing her career forward while Joe and Doug made Forester and Sinclair into the finest law firm in town. He'd probably appreciate the free time to focus on his cases and the time apart would keep the magic going. Her upcoming trip to Peru would be a good test: three months apart with only one trip home in the middle. The tinge returned. Every time she brought up Peru she saw him change right before her eyes. His words and expression mismatched. He'd say he was proud of her but end the conversation with downturned eyes and an utterance of "be careful", leaving her excitement hanging like thick smoke in the air.

Two hours later, Taryn sat at Gardenia and took in the moment. Swans and ducks took methodical dips and walks along the shore of the calm Argent River. A warm spring breeze blew in through the screened porch. The steak and goat cheese over arugula were long gone as was most of the bottle of Sauvignon Blanc. Mango cheesecake crumbs framed by two silver forks lay on a white china plate. Joe's spirits were high and, as always, Taryn felt herself lost in his jade eyes as he regaled her with another story about his brothers, then took on a serious tone as he spoke of his parents.

"I know it's not ideal now, I mean with me and my father, but my mother doesn't see that. They are still as in love today as they were when they met, maybe more so."

Taryn nodded, thinking of her own parents' constant movement so her father could find the latest archeological dig, her mother silently accommodating and towing Taryn and Ryan along. Then, after her mother's death, Taryn and Ryan following their father's latest adventures from place to place, school to school, and language to language until they were old enough to find their own way.

Joe continued, swirling the water in his glass, "Well, anyway, again, Happy Anniversary!" He clinked his water glass to her near empty wine glass. "We should get more wine." He looked over his shoulder for the waiter.

"I'm okay," Taryn whispered. *This is it,* she thought to herself and, as if on cue, he fumbled in his pocket.

"I love you, Taryn Evans." His voice and face softened.

"I love you too, Joe."

"Taryn. I've loved you since that first moment, but now even more. If you'd asked me ten years ago if I'd ever feel like I could love a woman, or ever feel secure enough to think of loving someone forever, or ever feel comfortable enough with someone. I'm rambling." He smiled. She leaned forward, wondering if the thumping in her chest was noticeable.

"I'm not saying it's all going to be easy." He went on, "I still have my demons, you know that. And I know you want more than this, more than Millerton, and that's tough for me because, well because it scares me. I mean you don't just want to travel like most people, but the places you want to go." He paused. "It's amazing you know. It's part of why I love you but it scares me to death. You want to make the world a better place by going to these places everyone else avoids and writing about them. I mean, that's just so incredible. But ..."

She nodded. This was the segue she needed. "Yes, Joe. I know it's hard. My brother hates it; my friends hate it. Everyone worries so much. But it's who I am. I can't live in a world where people are suffering and I'm not helping them. If you love me, and want to be with me, then that's the package." There, she'd said it. She'd countered on an offer that hadn't even been presented yet.

Joe fumbled the ring box under the table, rubbing its fuzzy top with his thumb. What if she said no? What if she said yes and then went off to some war torn country and got attacked, murdered, sick? He closed his eyes tightly as the tricks and methods from years of therapy had taught him. *I can't control what happens. I love her too much to risk not having her.* He opened his eyes again and looked at the woman he loved. She looked concerned, uncomfortable, still holding the stem of her empty wineglass. *Just say the words. Just say the words.*

"Joe?"

"I know. I know that's the package. I know we won't be anything like any other couple. Not like my parents, not like Doug and Marlena—we'll be our own thing. Joe and Taryn Sinclair: the accused defendant who became the lawyer and the news journalist with a death wish."

She winced. "I don't have a death wish."

"I'm rambling again. I know it's not a death wish. It's just scary for me." She nodded.

He continued, "But, speaking of Doug, I need to say this 'cause it was him who made me realize what I want. He and Marlena have been married a long time. I told him a while back that I thought I'd found the perfect person in you because I could picture living every day for the rest of my life with you. You know what he said?" She shook her head.

"He said, 'That's only half of it. It's not just picturing living every day with them, it's picturing any day without them and realizing it's just not possible.'" He wiped his forehead then pushed back his chair to stand momentarily beside the table. Onlookers at the surrounding tables smiled knowingly as he dropped to one knee on the floor at Taryn's side and looked up at her, opening the ring box with one hand. "Taryn, I can't imagine living any day without you. Will you marry me?"

CHAPTER 25

"I can't believe it." Margot tugged at the plastic covering the roast beef wrap, pulling it halfway down and handing it to Doug.

"I know. The press is having a field day. Everything happened so fast this morning." Doug took a bite of the sandwich. "I went with Chase and his uncle to the police station and he told them everything."

"I heard so many sirens. I didn't even know we had that many police cars. And it's those same ones who did the shootings last year?" She asked but knew the answer. "I hate that those types are in Millerton now."

Doug nodded. "Me too. Pretty major drug bust though. Hopefully they were the only ones. Can't imagine a city our size would have another organized ring like that. You not eating?" He looked at the dark circles under her eyes as she shook her head and picked at a loose thread on her skirt. "We'll find him."

"It's been almost two days, Doug." She yanked at the thread, finally breaking it. "Two days ago we were all here watching that snowstorm. And Joe was getting ready for Chase's trial and we were sitting here stupidly not knowing he was being threatened, not knowing Taryn had decided to stay in Canada, not knowing that Chase, that poor boy, was really innocent but being threatened too.

And where could Joe be now? They must have got to him, Doug." Her voice quavered.

"We don't know that. He and Taryn went over the guardrail together. There's no way they could have gotten to him down there. He went off to find help. If we can't find him, they can't either, right?"

"Then why hasn't anyone spotted him with their helicopter? It's daylight again! Noon—they've had a whole other morning." He shook his head. "I think he found help and came back to the city and those criminals got to him, Doug. Who knows what those people are capable of. Oh my!"

"Margot, eat something." He tore his sandwich, handing her half. "We need to stick to what we know. And you need to take care of yourself. Why don't you head home?"

She shook her head, refusing the food. "I don't have to. My aunt came in today to help me. She's going to stay over tonight and take care of Mom, so I'm free to do whatever needs doing." She bit her thumbnail and continued, "What do you need?"

Doug smiled. She never changed. "Nothing. Besides the obvious."

"Then I'm going to go visit Taryn," she said. "I want to hear from her what she told Flannery about the steering. I can't believe those people are trying to kill Joe!"

"Not sure we'll ever prove that. Flannery says the car's too damaged to know for sure if the steering was tampered with."

"But Taryn said it was busted." She frowned, "And I want to understand her story about the night of the accident better. I hate getting these half messages from Flannery and her brother. I need to hear it all from the horse's mouth. Plus, I just want to see her and know she's okay."

"Sounds good." Doug took her hand. "Margot, everything is going to be okay."

"Come with me?"

"I'll come up later," he assured her. "I'm going to hang around here a while longer. Flannery said he'd be back with an update. Once those dealers are charged, they'll let Chase go. One of them already admitted to killing Gloria," he said. "Just some details to iron out. I want to be available for the kid."

"Sure." She looked at the lines on his face, creased deeper than she'd ever noticed before. "He saw the whole thing?"

Doug nodded. "He did go to the hospital that night for help. And he did go inside and found her. Apparently they talked about him going into a program there at Highlands. He said she wanted him to get admitted that night but he had to go back and check on his mom first. Gloria was just finishing her shift so they walked out together. She even offered him a ride home." Doug paused a moment and Margot watched his mind working. "It's weird, given how everyone thought he'd killed her. I mean, if that part of the story had ever come out everyone would have really thought he'd killed her, her being so trusting and all.

"They got to her car and those thugs were there. They weren't looking for her. They were looking for him. I don't know the details on how they knew he was there; they must have been following him. I don't know. Chase's mother owed them a ton of money. They didn't mean to stab Gloria; she just got in the way. They took off, and then Chase took off. I guess someone saw him running away."

"And he couldn't just tell the truth about the whole thing?"

"He said the threats started right away. And he knew these guys; knew what they were capable of. That kid was so messed up and so desperate to save his mother. He really thought that going to jail was the best solution. Didn't give a damn about himself. Figured he'd just rot in jail and die."

"So why hire Joe? Why lie to Joe?"

"He didn't. Remember, it was his uncle that hired Joe. Plus, when we were too pricey for the uncle, *we* started paying for the whole thing 'cause Joe was so passionate about it. Not to mention it was good publicity for us."

"I know, but why didn't Chase just refuse. Why didn't he just confess?"

Doug stroked his chin and frowned. "It's all so confusing today, a lot of information to process, but the best I can figure is that he and Joe started to connect. I think somehow over the past year he changed his mind and really wanted Joe to get him off. He told Flannery this morning that the threats had lessened lately. They weren't threatening his mom anymore. I think maybe he started believing they were going to leave him alone. With the shootings last year and stuff, they had more troubles than Chase McGill.

"And I think that, after hanging with Joe, the kid started believing there was hope. He started wanting the truth. You saw him today, he's straightening out. The uncle's been good for him, and Joe too, I think. Smart kid though, the minute he realized yesterday that they might have come after Joe, he changed his whole story again. He even had me convinced that we'd been greatly mistaken. He was ready to go down again, this time to protect Joe."

CHAPTER 26

THE TEA MUGS RATTLED on the metal tray as she ascended the winding stairs.

"Andrea?" Meg's voice was soft against a sombre silence broken by the gentle creaks of her footfalls. "Andrea?" Her tone rose slightly in volume, so as not to startle her sister if she were finally asleep. She pushed the bedroom door inward and peered into the dim late afternoon light. Bed blankets were tossed in a heap, leaving the bare, wrinkled sheet wide open and empty. Meg turned her attention to the door of the ensuite bathroom. Empty.

"Andrea?" Meg stepped towards the rosewood nightstand and brushed the bridal magazines out of the way to make room for the tea tray.

"I'm in here." Andrea's voice came from the depths of the narrow walk-in closet.

"Oh? Well, I've brought you some tea, and some toast. You should try to eat something." Flicking on the light, Meg's eyes adjusted to the scene before her. Her sister sat at the back of the closet in the same shabby yoga pants she'd had on for two days now. Her knees were pulled in to her chest and her green cable knit sweater was pulled over them, stretching it into a formless cocoon. Andrea looked up with eyes rubbed pink, raw cheeks and cracked lips. Her hair fell dishevelled over her shoulders.

"Oh, honey." Meg rushed to her sister's side and placed her hand on her knee. "What are you doing in here?" Andrea batted her lashes, long fans against vacant eyes, at her younger sister. "Andrea?" Meg tried again, this time reaching for her shoulder. "Honey, let's get you back to bed."

"I just wanted to see it." Andrea said to the carpet, and then lifted her eyes towards the back of the closet where the puffy white garment bag hung on a hook. The zipper had been pulled down all the way to the bottom and billows of white tulle escaped through the crack. "I wanted *you* to see it. Why haven't you asked to see it? Don't you *want* to see it?" Andrea moved her head slowly towards Meg and as their eyes met, Meg felt herself recoil as something familiar from long ago flashed and then dimmed in her sister's expression.

"Why haven't I, uh, well there's just been a lot, I mean."

"It's my wedding dress, Meggie. Remember how we used to dream about what our wedding dresses would be like? Remember when I came back home that Christmas? You were what, twelve? I gave you that bride Barbie doll and we'd laugh and tease each other about these very moments. The day we'd have real wedding dresses. I can't believe you haven't asked to see it, Nugget!" Andrea stood up, Meg following her lead. "I mean, when we talked on the phone last month you wanted every detail, and now you've been here what? Two days? You've hurt my feelings Meg. Surely the web link I sent didn't do it justice."

"Of course not. But Andrea, I really think you should be resting."

"Help me into it? I really need your opinion on a couple of things." Andrea stepped forward and pulled the gown from the bag, placing it on the carpet in a circle as rumples of lace and satin flowed outwards. She scooped herself a circle in the middle, pushed down her pants then stepped inside, facing the large oval mirror on the inside of the door. Meg picked up the yoga pants and began folding them neatly then unfolding and folding them again as her sister whipped her sweater off over her head and tossed it to the floor.

Meg could feel Andrea's eyes drilling into her as she busied herself tidying the closet. Finally, Meg responded to the unspoken direction. She helped pull up the bodice then began fastening the endless line of satin covered buttons. Andrea let out an audible sigh, her eyes fixated on her reflection in the mirror. She pursed her lips and winked her left eye ever so slightly. "Well?"

Meg slowed down her fingers as though keeping the dress undone could stop time. Flashes of memory, of something from years ago, nudged at her mind. She fastened each button up her sister's spine as a frigid nerve crept up her own.

"Well, er, it's beautiful, of course." Meg whispered, watching Andrea watch herself.

"I need a better mirror, one that goes all the way to the floor. I can't see my feet in this one and that's my biggest fear, you know. When they altered it last week, I thought they took too much off the length and I only want the tips of my pumps to show." Andrea heaved the train up over her arm and swivelled to leave the closet. "Help me down the stairs, Nugget, and we can look in the mirror on the front hall closet doors. My shoes are right there; can you grab them?"

Meg picked up the open shoe box of satin pumps and sat down on the edge of the bed. "I really think this can wait, Andrea. I'm not sure you should be doing this now. Please have some tea. You haven't eaten all day."

Andrea swivelled in a whoosh of ruffles. "DAMN IT MEGGIE, ARE YOU STUPID? GET THAT AWAY FROM ME!" she screamed. "YOU'LL SPILL TEA ON MY DRESS!" She spun back towards the bedroom, then turned back again softly. "Gosh, Nugget, I'm sorry. I guess I'm all nerves. But seriously, tea near my dress? Are you crazy?"

Meg gulped back tears. "Andrea, I just don't think this is appropriate. You're not well from all this worry. I'm going to call Mom or maybe the doctor."

"What's not appropriate, Meggie? I need your help for God's sake. The wedding is in less than three weeks! I need to get this sorted out! And don't you DARE mention Mom again."

"Wedding? But Andrea, Joe's ..." She stopped in mid-sentence by instinct, watching her sister's wild eyes darting back and forth. That look. The memories flowed back. That year when Meg was nine and Andrea was fifteen. The year she never understood and no one had ever explained. The year Andrea went away. Meg listened to the shouts from the staircase that Andrea needed help with her train, needed help with her dress for her wedding to her missing fiancé. Terrified, Meg let her body slip off the bed on to the floor and reached for her sister's cell phone.

CHAPTER 27

May

TARYN LIKED THE SOUND the sharp knife made as it cut through the waxy layer of the red and yellow peppers. Sliding the seeded centres onto a paper towel, she collected the pepper sticks and arranged them around the dip bowl. Her usually roomy kitchen island of dark grey marble was a scattered assortment of glasses and plates in various states of cleanliness, while off to one end sat the huge cake box, untouched. Taryn stood and stared through the wide open doors, pleased that the weather had cooperated for Joe and Doug's annual firm barbeque. She could hear the low mumble of adults in the adjacent great room, those few seeking relief from the warm day. Louder was the larger crowd beyond the triple French doors to the deck, watching children beyond on the grass assembled in makeshift games of ball hockey and badminton. Unconsciously, she brushed her flat stomach and held her hand there for a moment. Her eyes followed Joe who scooped up a young ball player in a fit of giggles as that tall blonde, Andrea, headed towards him, touching him lightly on the shoulder and throwing her head back.

"She's something." Margot rose from the ottoman, having witnessed the same.

Taryn feigned that she hadn't noticed.

"She just rubs me the wrong way," Margot said. "I liked her at first. She was all perky and eager to help out. She fooled us all."

"Andrea? What do you mean? Joe speaks highly of her." Taryn returned to restocking her vegetable tray while Margot stacked dirty plates and collected disposable dishes and napkins.

"They all do, even I did. I don't know, just a gut thing. I don't trust her. I've caught her snooping around Joe's computer and then this one day, I had a file out and it went missing. Later Joe and Doug were frantic looking for it and she sat there and said nothing. Then, the next day it turned up and suddenly she was proposing a change to how they were handling the case. The two of them were all excited over her idea." Margot looked up to see Taryn had stopped moving and was squinting back, concerned. "Oh, I'm rambling, hon; it's just a feeling I get. I mean look at her." The two women looked back out to see Andrea seated next to Joe on one of the deck benches. The tall blonde leaned in and hung on every word he spoke, tucking her blonde hair behind her ear, only to find it falling forward again when she laughed.

Taryn looked at her dear older friend and took a deep breath to squelch the acid in her stomach, then spoke with a slight laugh: "What? You think she's after Joe?"

"Ah, hon, I need filters on my mouth. I just find she's like that with all of them, all the men. But I'm also concerned for her work. Like I said, she had an idea for that case and they all acted like it was the greatest thing they'd ever heard. And in the end, the whole thing was a mess. I just don't get why she'd hide having the file. I mean, we are all a team, she could have just said she was reviewing it because she had a new idea."

"Well, all Joe's said is that he has this new legal assistant and that she's really smart and helping him a lot." She continued to watch out the window as Andrea pulled out her phone and asked another guest to snap a photo of her and Joe, arm in arm. "I guess she knew him from high school, knew Lauren. They ran into each other one day and caught up and she needed a job. Today's the first time I've met her." Taryn paused. "She is pretty."

"Look who's talking." Margot smiled. "Well, enough about her. It's still early and I shouldn't be so judgy. I'm sorry, I need to stop monitoring everyone else's moves and focus on myself."

Taryn nodded letting her reply of, "I've been saying that for years," remain unspoken.

Margot continued, "I'm like an old mother hen worrying about Doug and Joe all the time. They're big boys, smart boys. And Joe's so happy with you, hon." She reached for Taryn's hand.

Taryn looked at the selfless woman, thankful for her always being there. She noticed the lack of lustre in Margot's face, the sadness that remained permanently in her eyes. "You do worry about all of us, and your mom. I don't see a lot of Margot care going on."

Margot smiled. "I don't mind. I had my great life with Sam. Only eight years but it was still worth a lifetime. And he died doing what he wanted to do, defending our country. But right now I do have to focus on Mom. Alzheimer's is a horrid thing, and the comings and goings of Forester & Sinclair sure do keep me going."

Taryn turned her gaze back to the French doors. "Joe's certainly caught up in this McGill trial. How are things with you two?" Margot's question unintentionally opened a window of vulnerability in Taryn's eyes.

Taryn faked a smile and turned to the pantry to grab a box of crackers. "Good." Turning back, Margot's question lingered in the air. "Well, yeah, as good as ever. I mean, you know, he works too much, cares for the clients too much, but that's nothing new." She paused, "And there's just always that lingering ... I don't know how to describe it." She giggled quietly, "I don't have to tell you."

Margot nodded. "Joe's like a hurt little boy sometimes. It's always there."

"To some degree, yes. He really does live in, I don't know, fear? He's bright and confident and then sometimes the oddest things will come out in the weirdest ways." She stopped herself realizing she wasn't making sense.

Margot nodded again. "I've known him longer than you, dear." She laughed and Taryn smiled. In some ways Margot was like a second mother to Joe, and Doug like a real father. "It was hard those early days after the murder, all that acting out and carrying on. He had a lot to sort out. It made sense in some ways, jumping from woman to woman meant no one could leave him, and if someone hurt them he wouldn't care. But once he met you, that all stopped. I think the real Joe came back."

Taryn nodded. "I know. We've talked about it at length, especially before we committed to getting married. I understood. That horrible night messed him up in so many ways. Just the thought of it all and the therapy he needed afterwards."

Margot nodded, thinking back to those early days and the young, terrified boy sitting in the old office.

"It makes things hard, even today." Taryn heard the words opening a door into a deeper conversation she so needed but hadn't anticipated having today.

Margot sat herself down on a kitchen stool, pouring from an open bottle of wine into two glasses.

"I should really go be a hostess," Taryn diverted as Margot slid a glass towards her.

"We've got time for one glass."

"We've just had our fifth anniversary, you know that," Taryn said, sitting down beside Margot at the kitchen counter. "We've talked about children in the future and I made it clear, well we both understood, that I had some things I wanted to do first, career wise."

"I recall. You are still young."

"Yes, we are. There's time."

"Are you?" Margot lifted herself from the chair slightly and leaned forward as Taryn stared at her wine glass without taking a sip. "You *are*?"

Taryn smiled. "No, well, I don't know. Joe has been suddenly very keen to get started. Pushing me actually, which surprised me. He'd always held back before. His old insecurities, I suppose."

"And?"

Taryn's eyes misted. "I am late. I haven't even told Joe yet. I mean, it's very unlikely. We aren't even trying but this one night, well, it is possible." She laughed and continued, "But it has me very confused. Just the thought of it because," she hesitated, uncertain about continuing, "I've been offered the most amazing opportunity, Margot. It's huge. Bigger than we'd ever imagined."

Margot noted the way her face beamed and eyes sparkled at even the thought of it.

"It's a contract to go to Israel for a year. I'd be journaling about the Gaza Strip war and following families who have literally lived their entire lives in the conflict. The magazine offered me the cover and one of their affiliates is close to offering me a book deal. It's so much more than I ever thought possible." A tear glistened against her cheek.

"Taryn, that's incredible! Congratulations!"

"Yeah, thanks. No one knows. Not even my brother."

"Joe?"

"I told him. He tried. He tried, Margot, to be happy for me."

"Oh, he is happy for you."

"He is. But he can't be, not one hundred percent. He's so afraid."

"It's a scary place. Anyone would be worried."

"But Joe especially. I know he doesn't want me to go. He wants to switch our focus and get pregnant. I don't know what to do. I really can't pass this up. I really can't. I love him so much and I know marriage is compromise. But this opportunity is a game changer. And the fact that he doesn't want me to go, it makes me the scared one. And now, with me being late. Is fate making me turn it down?"

CHAPTER 28

MEG FOUND ANDREA on the bottom step of the staircase, her puffy skirt encircling her as though she had no legs. Tears streamed down Andrea's face and Meg was surprised to see what looked like black streaks from old mascara despite her sister's makeup-free face. Stopping a couple of steps above her, Meg sat down, both sisters facing the mirrored closet door. Nervous to speak, Meg watched as their eyes met in the reflection.

"It could have been fun," Andrea mumbled, continuing her stare.

"What could have been fun? Andrea?"

"This. This week. Us. Together for the first time in, how long?"

Meg mentally calculated the answer at six years without saying it out loud.

"We've had our phone chats and you seemed like you really wanted to be part of this wedding. I really felt like I had some piece of family again, for the first time. Asking you to be my maid of honour, it could have been so fun."

Meg cleared her throat, gripping the edge of the stair carpet with her fingers. "Andrea, I, it is fun." She spoke carefully. "I'm honoured to be part of your wedding. It's just that I'm worried like you are, about Joe."

"Stop ruining it. Why do you ruin things? I thought when we'd started calling each other this past year things would be good." Andrea turned her head now to look at Meg directly.

"I'm not. I don't ruin ..."

"I wanted to show you my wedding dress and you act all weird and threaten to call Mom!"

"It's not a threat. I was worried. Andrea, listen to me. I'm just concerned about you being so caught up in a dress when we don't know where Joe is yet. And with his wife, uh, ex-wife, being found in the car and her being in the hospital." She choked on her own words. "On the news they said she was his wife. Why would they get that wrong? Things just aren't adding up for me." Meg watched her sister's expression turn stone cold, her eyes darting to the right and upward. "Andrea? Andrea?"

Andrea turned again, her back to her sister and grasped her full skirt in her hands, tugging it upward then tossing it down in fury. "My own sister. My little sister." She murmured as she threw the dress skirt up and down almost tearing a piece of lace from the front.

"Andrea, I think you are just too upset about Joe. Let's get you upstairs and out of your dress. You don't want to rip it or get it dirty."

Andrea spun her head back to Meg and made a *hrmph* sound, then stood and ascended the staircase, almost running. Meg followed her back to the bedroom and watched as Andrea contorted her arms violently behind her to undo the back. Two pearl buttons dropped to the floor and rolled under the bed.

"Andrea? Let me help you."

Standing now in her bra and panties, Andrea hurled the gown onto the bed. "Obviously I don't want your help. You, you're just like everyone else. Talking about Taryn. Taryn. Taryn. Taryn. That bitch! What was she doing in his car? Was she stealing him away?"

"I don't know, honey. No one will know until we find Joe. Or when Taryn tells everyone what was going on. But Andrea, listen to me," Meg reached for a throw and covered her sister's shoulders. "Things don't make sense. It's not just her being in Joe's car. Why hasn't Joe's family returned your calls? And what about those people at the office? I called Joe's partner, Doug just now, and he acted like you'd have no reason to be asking about Joe. Is there something you aren't telling me?"

"You fucking bitch." Andrea let out a loud groan of frustration, lifting her arms so the throw appeared like a canopy, then letting it fall to the ground. She took off back downstairs through the hallway and into the living room.

Meg stood, dumbfounded, feeling heat rising in her throat and familiar knots in her stomach from deep buried places. Those feelings she'd never quite understood that rarely surfaced, but when they did she was overcome with anxiety. This time, she remembered.

She was nine and terrified. Her mother sat at the metal kitchen chair in her striped shorts and halter top, her bleached blonde hair streaked with black. "It's going to be okay, Meg", her mother had whispered through the draw of a cigarette. Meg had risen from the table and walked through the long, dark hallway of the apartment complex, finding Andrea on the concrete front steps, solemn in a black T-shirt and jeans, a small duffle bag beside her. Her older sister stared straight in front of her.

"She's sending me away, Nugget." Her voice was flat.

"Where?" Meg whispered, reaching for a hand that snapped away.

"A hospital. Can you believe that?"

Meg wrinkled her face, suddenly worried. "Are you sick?"

"No Nugget, I'm not sick. She's the sick one."

Confused, Meg sat on the step and curled her knees into herself. She turned to her big sister, thinking of times they'd played and cuddled, the Andrea she loved. "Andrea? Is this because of me?"

"Some other things." Andrea folded her arms.

The front door creaked open and their mother appeared, taller in platform sandals, carrying her purse strapped across her chest. "Andrea needs some help," their mother said. "We don't want her hurting anyone or herself." She tossed her cigarette down, stomping it with her toe and twisting her leg back and forth. A taxi appeared from the corner and pulled into the driveway. "Meggie, I'm trusting you to stay home alone and be a big girl. I'll be a few hours or so dropping off Andrea, okay?" Meg had nodded, uncertain but afraid to ask more.

Now Meg descended another staircase, slowly letting a framed view of her sister unfold within each pair of railings. Andrea sat in her underwear with one of the large grey blue sofa cushions across her chest and lifted her eyes towards her.

Meg meandered across the carpet and sat a safe distance across from her, summoning the courage to speak. "Andrea. Please listen to me. I came here because I love you. You are my sister. Even though it's been six years since I last came home and more before that, it doesn't mean I don't think of you. I am so happy to be in your wedding."

"You left."

"What?"

"You left, as soon as you could. Eighteen was it? Or seventeen? Plus all the summer vacations. Outta here she flew. Off to her daddy and all his money, to the other side of the country."

Meg swallowed. "Andrea, it just made sense for me to be with my dad. And I wanted to go to UBC."

"University. With daddy's money."

Meg felt herself curdling inside and anger rising despite her need to keep her sister calm. "I can't help it if my dad had money. I can't help it if my dad stuck around." She heard her own words and knew she'd ignited a powder keg.

Surprisingly, Andrea didn't blow, just sat there with the tip of her fingernail in between her two top teeth. She smiled then and let out a soft giggle. "Yeah, the only one who stuck around. Of the parade of men Mom had. How'd you luck out like that, Meggie?"

Meg shrugged her shoulders.

"I don't think mom knew who my dad was." Andrea giggled again. "Isn't that crazy?"

Meg nodded, fearful of the calm.

"How many men do you suppose there were, Nugget?"

"I can't. I don't know. What difference does it make?"

"All kinds of them, eh? Rich, poor, tall, short. What an amazing way to get by. Good old Ellen Vaillancourt, the slut of Millerton."

Meg gulped. "What's done is done, Andrea." She looked at her sister's half naked body. "Aren't you cold?" She stood to grab the throw from the ottoman, then both women jumped at the sound of the doorbell chime. Meg went to answer it.

"Oh hey, again we meet." Dominic stood with an arm up on the doorframe, staring down at Meg and winking ever so slightly.

"It's not a good time," Meg stated, then suddenly, surprisingly, Andrea appeared behind her wrapped in her overcoat.

"Dominic, I need you to leave," she said. "My sister and I are knee deep in something. Can you come by tomorrow?" Meg watched as her sister flicked her hair and gazed at the man with a warm smile.

"Tomorrow's way too late." He winked and spun on his heel to leave.

Amazed, Meg turned back to her after they closed the door behind him. "Andrea, you're not behaving right. Something's wrong. You are all over the place with your moods. One minute you are all kind and sweet, like to that guy. What's up with that guy anyway?" Meg passed her sister to flee to the kitchen and grab her purse and coat. "I know you are worried sick, but I'm going out. I need some air."

Andrea looked confused. "Where are you going?"

"I'm going to Mom's for the night. Look, I love you and I really don't want to leave you here with Joe missing. But I can't take it." Meg pulled on her boots, hopping a moment on one foot and losing her balance in frustration.

"Meggie!"

"Goodbye, Andrea. I'll call you later. You need some rest. And that guy is just weird. Don't let him in here."

"I'm sorry. I just get to remembering how things were. You know, with you and your dad. He'd always come and take you places and send Christmas presents."

"I don't feel like dredging up the past, Andrea."

"Remember that one year, you went away with him for Christmas, skiing?"

"Sure."

"You know what I got that Christmas, Meggie?"

"Andrea, I'm not doing this!" She tied her scarf around her neck. "I'll call you to check on you later."

"DO YOU KNOW WHAT I GOT FOR CHRISTMAS THAT YEAR, MEG? MEG!"

Meg opened the front door and kept walking to the car without looking back. From the open door she heard her sister yelling and felt the one syllable of her own name clawing at her back.

CHAPTER 29

August

THE ANTICIPATION WITH WHICH SHE HAD AWOKEN
had transformed into disappointment. Taryn stared ahead at Joe
from her seated position on the front foyer bench as he stood balancing his travel mug in one hand, scrolling his emails on his phone
with the other; eyes downward as though she was not even there.

"Joe?"

"I don't want to talk about it anymore," he finally said, popping
his phone into his pocket and reaching for the door. "I guess I will
see you in six days." His voice lacked inflection. She hadn't meant
for this to happen. She watched the door close behind him, even the
sound of the latch shutting softly was lifeless and defeated.

Tears stung her eyes and she took a large gulp of breath before
rising and heading upstairs. Despite the balmy weather, she felt
chilled and headed towards the master bedroom seeking the warm
wrap of a sweater. She stopped at the door to the baby's room and
stepped inside. The synthetic freshness of paint smell swirled against
the long lasting blast of the fresh wooden beams beneath the drywall.
The newness made her happy. The walls had been finished just a
month ago but left unpainted until a week ago Friday when the

sonogram news was confirmed. A girl it was. And no sooner was that confirmed than the baby had a name: Madison Jane, the Jane part after Taryn's mother. By Saturday morning, Joe had started applying the first coat of "Ballerina Gown" to three of the walls, while the back wall with the two windows awaited the darker toned "Palace Rose".

"That back wall will have the white shelves between the windows for all her toys and dolls." Joe had laughed as Taryn shook her head imagining just how many toys Joe would buy for his long-awaited child.

Taryn lifted the plastic throw cover off of a chair and sat down. He was so good to her. He would be so good to them. Was she doing the wrong thing? She closed her eyes imagining Maddie Jane. They'd already begun calling her this since the first time it flowed off Taryn's tongue. She pictured her snuggled in a pink onesie; a curvy little baby bum, dimpled elbows and tiny toes. She pictured her older, in pigtails and sundresses. She would show her photos of faraway places and teach her to bake apple pies. And Joe would teach her to ride a bike and make her feel protected. She imagined their other future children too; one more, perhaps two, maybe even three.

It wasn't that Taryn didn't want them all. From the moment she realized that Maddie Jane was coming, she'd been overjoyed with unprecedented love and so much emotion that she never looked back to ask why fate had made her a mother-to-be so suddenly. They were planning to start trying for a baby this year or next anyway. So coming off the pill due to side effects and transition-ing to other methods hadn't exactly failed. It had just brought the inevitable forward.

Everything about Maddie Jane made Taryn's insides flood with love and hope. She longed to see her tiny face, hold her tiny finger, sing her to sleep with the songs her own mother had sung. She longed for those quiet, tender times with Joe and Maddie Jane. And, like she'd seen with Ryan's kids, she longed for those wide-eyed times of wonder when the things adults take for granted are seen by children for the first time. This baby, their baby, and the others that followed would complete their family and, now that Maddie Jane was halfway here, Taryn couldn't imagine her life without her.

Her thoughts returned to the present morning and she felt the bleakness come back. Why was she doing this? Why, when Joe was so adamant that she stop her travels, was she insisting on this trip to Chile?

Because it was safe, that's why, she argued to herself. Yes, her life the past five years had truly been risky. She admitted this. Her freelance career as a journalist covering children of war took her to places most people would avoid at all costs. But by doing so she'd established herself in the profession. She had relationships with NGOs and government agencies; contacts at World Vision, Save the Children, Doctors without Borders and Child Save. National and international publications now sought her to cover stories. "Tell the world what is really going on," they'd say. And she did. "Your stories bring the truth forward and help us in so many ways," they'd say. Stories of orphans and refugees, poverty and sickness, slavery and abuse. Taryn took on each story as though her own life depended on it, often becoming so engrossed that it affected her well-being. And while the professional accolades were many and her reputation had provided her with enough work to allow some time off, she was driven by the children themselves. Each child she met, each smile erupting in response to a small, kind gesture, each tear wiped to calm the desperation, drove her further. Joe tried to understand. And most of the time he loved her for it despite himself.

Despite passing up the Israel opportunity after confirming she was pregnant, she'd focused her efforts on her writings from her previous trip to northern Kenya, visiting a Somalian refugee camp with Doctors Without Borders. Taryn had settled into the idea of being home, preparing to finish a series of articles for publication and some related short articles for a few other magazines that had expressed interest. Joe and Taryn had planned and discussed that there would be no more trips until long after the baby came, and

Taryn was fine with that. It would give her time to review her past articles and tie them together. In the back of her mind, she had the spark of an idea for a book.

But two weeks ago, Evelyn Sanders from Child Save had called. Would Taryn be interested in one quick trip to Chile? Six days, in and out, to a place that was completely safe. There was no conflict there, just a quick story about the after effects of the earthquake and the rebuilding. It was a nice change of pace for Taryn, the chance to write a story and try to promote public awareness that they still needed funding. Just a quick trip to a safe city in the country where she'd been born, not to mention a nice chunk of change. There would even be a doctor and two nurses travelling with her. Taryn accepted, without even consulting Joe. That wasn't the norm, but the words had just come out.

CHAPTER 30

DOUG COULDN'T STAND IT anymore. Most of the clients had agreed to cancel but, somewhat understandably, this over-anxious woman had insisted on coming in. It was her last meeting with him before her larceny trial next week and she had questions needing answers. Sure, she'd seen the news and understood that Doug's partner was missing, but really, men take off sometimes, she'd said. Her own experiences of the past nudging their way into today's reality.

He'd listened. He'd answered. He'd jotted down notes on his yellow legal pad with pointy stars next to the questions that did need following up. He'd follow up, of course, just not today. Not until the world made sense again. He did everything he could to not rush her, to reassure his guilty client that things would be okay as he walked her to the elevator and shook her hand with confident eye contact.

Now, a half hour later, he drove aimlessly out of the Frosst Building's parking lot and debated heading home for an hour's reprieve, then remembered that Marlena had gone ahead with her charity auction meeting. A roomful of zealous and curious women wasn't what he needed right now. So instead, he turned in the opposite direction of home, past the shops and businesses of Millerton's downtown core that buzzed with daytime traffic and parking challenges and on through the newly-revived residential area full of modern glass and oddly-angled townhouses.

Soon he found himself in the older, well-manicured neighbourhood where Joe had grown up and where his parents still lived. Taking an unplanned turn, he slowly drove the car towards the Sinclairs' welcoming yellow-bricked bungalow. The house inviting him in with its large wooden front porch, perfect rose garden, and huge, aged trees. Two cars were parked in the driveway and Doug imagined that Dorothy and Art Sinclair were inside. He knew Dorothy was worried sick. He'd called her earlier that morning to offer support. As for Art, he was likely silent and detached, just as he was every time Doug met him. Doug pulled the car up to the curb across the street and sat a moment, looking through the wide-shuttered windows of the house for a shadow. Torn about showing up unexpectedly, he sat. It was rare that he saw Joe's parents, mostly during the preparation of Joe's defence, then later at big occasions like Joe and Taryn's wedding. Was showing up unexpectedly, despite Joe's disappearance, the right thing to do? He lied to himself that his hesitation was due to protocol, knowing it wasn't that at all. Of course Dorothy would love to see him. It was Joe's father that kept him in the idling car.

From the first day they'd met, Art Sinclair had been harsh and, as years passed and Doug got to know Joe better, it was clear that Art had always been this way. He wasn't a bad person, never laid a hand on Dorothy, Joe or his brothers. It wasn't even the harm of violent words that necessarily caused anguish to those around him. Instead it was the air that hung in the spaces between sparse words, an atmosphere of disapproval. Despite Joe's innocence and despite his achievements, Art's contempt lived on, like a living, breathing soul, forever encircling Joe's successes. And by extension, Art's undefined scorn managed to poke at even Doug's otherwise undeniable confidence.

He'd call Dorothy again later, he thought, pulling the car away from the house and turning onto the next cross street, then turning slowly into the wide driveway that led to the church parking lot and marked the edge of Bryan Park. He put the car in park in the first spot closest to the church's back door and stepped outside. In the years that had passed since driving Joe here to try to recall the details of finding Lauren, the shrubs that lined the churchyard had been removed and replaced with a pale cream vinyl fence, the apartment building behind the church had not only been erected but now bore signs of aging, it's structure no longer the latest and greatest in Millerton architecture.

Doug walked past a few other parked cars towards the back of the parking lot and stood in the empty spot where, to the best of his recollection, the dumpster had been. In his mind's eye, he remembered Joe on that December morning with the weather so similar to today's. Teary-eyed and red faced, Joe had stared at a newly replaced dumpster, then raced back towards the church steps, vomiting uncontrollably.

In Doug's experience, it had been smart to bring witnesses and defendants back to crime scenes. Things came back in physical places that hid in memories' virtual ones. And, four months after finding Lauren, the crime scene sterility long gone, he'd convinced Joe to come. To try to remember the lady with the poodle, the older man who had nodded when Joe extinguished his joint, to try to remember the girl running across the edge of the park, the woman in the long skirt with the little boy.

But Joe's reaction that day was unlike any other clients'. If Doug hadn't already been convinced the kid was innocent, his reaction there would have sealed his belief. Joe's story remained crystal clear, not even the slightest hesitation or missed word as he'd leaned against the railing of the church step, hunched over holding his stomach, sobbing. Doug forced him to talk, one more time, about finding the beam of wood. For although Doug had convinced himself, and could convince a jury, that the construction worker's fingerprints could have been washed away in the rain the day before, what about the murderer's? Lauren had died within minutes of Joe finding her. How could Joe's be the only prints on the beam?

"I don't know. I told you. I told the police. I don't know," Joe had pleaded, causing Doug to put his arm around him.

"It's okay. Maybe the killer wore gloves. We've talked about that." Doug gave a reassuring squeeze to Joe's shoulder. "Maybe this wasn't a good idea after all. Let's go back to the office."

Joe stood up straight and wiped his eyes, then turned them towards the new dumpster and stared through reality back into an absent August night.

"What if the killer only touched the duct tape?" he mumbled.

"What? What duct tape?"

"There was some duct tape on the ground. Just a small piece, it was all curled up right beside Lauren. What if that tape had been on the wood before and the killer only touched that, and then somehow it came off?"

Doug walked back towards his car and leaned against the door, facing the park and imagining the sweltering August night of Lauren's murder, the subsequent things he and Joe had discussed in the months that followed. Maybe he was right about the duct tape. The police lab had catalogued it and it did have prints on it but no one they could identify. The lab also checked later whether the tape had left residue on the wood. It was chemically indeterminate. Maybe Doug could make it sound possible, maybe even plausible enough to convince a jury.

Now nineteen years later, the duct tape and beam remained catalogued and waiting with the other evidence from Lauren Avery's unsolved murder.

It was a source of deep and lasting regret to Doug that he'd put the already traumatized young client, now his friend and protégé, through the trauma of re-enacting such a painful episode when, in the end, none of it had had any bearing on the case.

February 1998

Another scream that made her heart pound. *Not again.* This was the second night in a row and the second night that he'd screamed out just as she had started to fall asleep. Melodie leapt from her bed and raced to Jarret's bedroom.

"Mommy!" he yelled repeatedly until she buried his little curly-haired head against her breast and felt the warm tears wet her nightshirt.

"Jarret, sweetheart. Again? It was just a bad dream darling." She leaned forward and clicked on the bedside lamp allowing the smiling faces of T-Rexes and other dinosaurs to glow. "Can you tell Mommy what you saw?"

Jarret lifted his face and rolled his fists into his eyes, frowning as his lip trembled and he shook his head.

"Nothing? You can't remember anything?" Melodie rubbed his back and felt her own tears welling from worry.

It had started in the past month and a half, since Christmas. Nightmares, almost every night, they came. She'd taken him to see the doctor and school councillors and was awaiting a psychiatrist's appointment. No one could figure out what was troubling poor little Jarret although the recent split between her and Glen was everyone's best guess despite Jarret denying it. She'd changed his diet, ensured he exercised, even tried adjusting his schedule. She'd asked him over and over if anyone had hurt him, bullied him, touched him?

Night after night she sat, rocking her boy back and forth. Glen had tried to figure it out too. He'd been so supportive despite them not being together. Glen said sometimes Jarret had nightmares at his place too, when he visited on weekends.

Melodie desperately tried to figure out what the triggers were. Today had been like any other Saturday. They'd gotten up early, watched cartoons, had some pancakes, then he'd come with her to do some grocery shopping. After that, they'd gone to the park and she'd watched him build a snow fort with a neighbourhood buddy.

Then they'd had an early supper, watched a Disney movie and she'd put him to bed, silently praying that tonight nothing would haunt him. Tired herself, she'd gone to bed early, only to be awakened to yet another blood curdling scream.

"No Mommy, nothing."

"And you'd tell Mommy if it was something? You know you can tell Mommy anything, right?"

Jarret sniffled and nodded.

"Let's try to think if there was something about today and about yesterday that we did the same, because last night you had bad dreams too."

He nodded.

"Yesterday you had school and today you didn't. Yesterday you visited Daddy after school and today you did not see Daddy." Melodie wracked her brain for a common thread, knowing that it was unlikely there was one after so many weeks of trying to figure it out. "Today we had pancakes, yesterday we had cereal," she continued, looking up as their faithful golden retriever, Abby, sauntered into the bedroom and lay protectively by the bed.

"What about Abby? Is Abby ever in your dreams?"

"I don't remember, Mommy!" Jarret cried, frustrated by her constant questions.

"Okay, sweetheart. I know, I just want to figure this out, you know." She reached down and patted the dog's head, thinking how Abby had faithfully sat on the snow today at the park while Jarret played.

"The park!" Melodie sat up straighter. "We took Abby for a walk to the park last night after dinner and we went again today!"

Jarret nodded.

"I wonder, hmm. Have we ever tried to see if we went to the park on the days you have the bad dreams?" She knew it sounded ridiculous, but Melodie was out of ideas. "Let's look at your journal." She reached for the ring-spined notebook she kept in his bedside table drawer. The one she'd started on her quest to understand her son's nightmares. "Okay, you had a bad dream today, last night, that's Friday, and before that was Wednesday. Did we go to the park on Wednesday?"

Jarret shrugged his shoulders while Melodie held the pen to her lips. "We did! We did, remember we took Abby for a walk and I thought she might be sore from her shots at the vets. So that was Wednesday. Then you had a bad dream last Saturday and we went last Saturday because you played with Liam. Wow. Okay, four for four." She scrolled back through the other journal entries. "Hmm, hard to say but, wow, there may be a pattern here!" Startled, she looked at her son, still plunking tears from his lids. "Sorry buddy, Mommy got distracted looking at this." She pulled him close. "It's okay, buddy. It's always okay, remember. Someday these will go away and remember dreams aren't real, they can't hurt you." She held and rocked him until she felt him fall back to sleep, then sat alone at the bottom of his bed, delving into the recesses of her brain, horrified.

It had taken her a few weeks to muster the courage to return to the park last fall, after the horrible news of mayor Avery's daughter being murdered. But Jarret loved it there and he'd been protected from the news. Besides, despite them being there that exact night, they'd been way over by the swing set. They hadn't seen or heard anything. The police had interviewed Melodie, then let her go, agreeing after a quick conversation with Jarret that they'd seen nothing. And that was months ago. Jarret's nightmares only started when Glen left.

The next day she and Glen brought Jarret to the park.

"I just thought we should both be here."

"Yeah, that's cool, Mel. But why do you think it is the park? Just based on the timing of the dreams?" Glen brushed snow off the rickety picnic table and sat down while his son climbed up the sledding hill. "He's so happy here, and we both bring him, all the time."

"Yeah, just the timing. I've been trying to remember and it seems like almost every time he has the nightmares, it's after we've been here. I know it sounds weird, but I've tried tracking everything else and nothing else has a pattern."

"So he'll have a bad dream tonight." Glen stated, his condescending tone irking Melodie.

"Well, I don't know, do I? But I think so, maybe, yes. I just thought maybe coming here and having both of us nearby in case."

"In case?"

"Well maybe if we push him a bit he might remember something. Maybe something happened here?" She turned her eyes downward, trying hard to recall if she'd ever left him out of her sight. "Could someone have approached him?"

"Mel?"

"Well, he's always supervised! I don't know Glen. I don't have the answers, I'm just wondering."

Glen looked at his ex-wife and smiled. She did think she always had all the answers. That was part of the problem. But he wasn't here to argue. Jarret was their number one priority and he agreed, if there was any chance of getting to the bottom of the nightmares, it was well worth it. They'd let him play a bit then sit him down for a chat.

About ten minutes later, Jarret returned to sit next to them.

"So buddy," Melodie began, "when you play here at the park, how do you feel?"

The boy smiled and slurped on his straw. "Good."

"That's good. Does anything about the park ever make you feel sad, or scared?"

He scratched his head. "I dunno. No. It's fun."

"It is fun, buddy." Glen chimed in. "Everyone likes the park. It's just that Mommy and I wondered if ever you were here when it wasn't fun. Maybe some time that we don't even remember—like maybe you fell down or someone said something mean?"

He shook his head. "I dunno."

Glen shook his head at Melodie as if they were wasting their time. She peered across the snow-covered park, imagining how it was in the summer.

"What about Abby, Jarret? When we are walking Abby, do you ever feel sad or scared?"

He shrugged his shoulders. Melodie looked at his face and felt an overwhelming sixth sense, something her ex would never understand.

"There's something, Glen," she whispered. Glen rolled his eyes and shook his head. "Mother's intuition. I really think there's something about this park and Abby."

She turned to Jarret. "Sweetie, did anyone ever say anything to you while you were walking Abby? Like maybe those times when I let you hold the leash?"

He shrugged his shoulders and Melodie reached for Abby's collar, stroking the soft fur. "I wish Abby could talk." She smiled.

Suddenly, Melodie watched her son's eyes widen and his face flush. Glen leaned forward, "Hey buddy, what's wrong?"

"The lady!" he shouted and Melodie ran around the table to embrace him.

"What lady, Jarret? What are you talking about?"

The boy sobbed. "Mommy! Mommy no! The lady, the girl from the dreams! I remember now. Oh Mommy!" he whispered while his parents embraced him from both sides. "In my dreams we are here with Abby and I'm holding her leash and Abby runs away. Like when I saw the lady."

Melodie struggled to remember, barely. "Uh, well I remember one night last summer when I let you hold Abby and then you dropped the leash and Abby took off and you chased her into those bushes. That night?" She turned to Glen and mouthed, "That night."

Jarret shook and sobbed. "Mommy! That girl. In my nightmares, she is going to kill us. NO Daddy, no Daddy, help me!"

Glen held his trembling son's body in horror.

"What lady? Wait, a lady or a girl, Jarret a lady like Mommy or Grandma?"

"No, like Kimmy's kind of age," Jarret replied, referencing his babysitter.

Melodie shrugged her shoulders. "Honey, I don't remember anyone. I just remember you were walking Abby and you chased off after her. You were upset and when I caught up to you, you were crying and wanted to swing and I said it was too late and you started screaming. I thought you were mad that we couldn't swing. Oh!"

Glen stared at her

"Glen that was that night!"

Jarret rocked against his father's chest, and spoke through a quivering lip. "That girl was all blooded."

"Okay, sweetie." Glen pushed Jarret's head into his chest and let him sob and rock. "Good boy. You are such a good boy. Daddy'll take you home now and then we'll talk some more, okay?"

"I think we should go see a doctor," Melodie whispered.

"And call the police," Glen mouthed back to her so his son couldn't hear.

The little boy with the lady in the long skirt and the golden retriever remembered, months later, seeing the running girl covered in blood. On the actual night he had blocked it out. Blocked it out for months in fact, until his father moved out and he no longer felt as safe.

A week later, Doug got to make the call he'd been hoping for. All the charges against Joe were dropped.

CHAPTER 31

August

THEY ALL SPOKE OF MATIAS. Those who'd been in the region for weeks, even months, spoke of the five-year-old boy so often that Taryn knew instinctively that her upcoming article, or at least part of it, would revolve around him.

First there was his story. The earthquake had devastated his home, his neighbourhood, his school. More tragically, his father had died right in front of him as they'd walked that morning through the square to buy bread. Returning home, he'd found his older brothers dead on the tile floor, one trapped beneath a cabinet, the other bleeding from his head after being hit by a flying beam. Months later, Matias' mother, dying of a broken heart, remained distant and detached from the young boy and most of his care came from an ailing and fragile grandmother.

Despite earthquake relief, his mother and grandmother remained in the family home, living exclusively on what remained of the main floor. The upper story of the house had been reduced to a flat heap when the failing structure had folded. They spent their nights in the large open room, in a row of three sleeping bags provided to them by the Red Cross. They cooked soup on a rickety stove fueled by gas, since electricity had not yet been restored, and they went to the bathroom outside, usually in the field behind the rubble of their neighbourhood.

Moreover, there was talk of his resilient nature. His wide, inquisitive eyes and blooming smile had captivated the aid workers who struggled and fought to find Matias and his remaining family an adequate home. They assured her that the little man's personality would leap from her pages causing those in faraway lands to feel connected in sorrow and send much needed charitable funding.

Taryn looked forward to meeting him as they drove along the broken, winding roads through the square and up the dilapidated street to his damaged home. The formerly rectangular structure of blue and grey looked like an accordion stretched in mid-song and Taryn gasped for the people living inside, fearful that some godly musician would push the ends of the row of houses together, allowing it to collapse into itself.

Her colleagues had not been wrong. Within a few minutes, Matias had captivated her. He sat on her knee, describing with hand gestures and quickly spoken Spanish an array of stories that were so full of life, it didn't matter that she didn't understand. Their team translator did her best and Taryn's own childhood Spanish was a dusty memory, but Taryn really didn't care what he was saying. It was the spirit and happiness that rose from this place of despair that she needed to portray in her story. At one point he pulled his hands towards his chest and pushed his tongue out panting, then let out a woof. The translator explaining from Matias' grandmother that prior to the earthquake they'd had a little dog, Gitano. But on the day of the earthquake, the dog had run out the front door in search of Matias' father, never to be seen again. Sometimes, his grandmother explained further, Matias insisted the dog was still upstairs in his now flattened bedroom. He'd told her, she said, that sometimes as he lay awake in his sleeping bag, he'd hear him barking.

Over tasteless tea, Taryn sat with Matias's mother and grandmother, learning of their story and hardships while her colleagues from Child Save did some final sweeps of the house. They had received news that morning that a funded apartment had been found for Matias' family and were packing their few belongings in boxes. The plan was for Taryn to finish her interview while they prepared, then the whole team would drive the family to their new home forty kilometres away.

Ninety minutes later, her teammates had put the grandmother in the jeep and were escorting Matias' fragile mother slowly down the road to their other vehicle. Taryn and Matias stood on what was left of the porch with the team doctor, staring up at puffy clouds and pointing out shapes, distracting the boy from the idea that he was leaving the only home he'd even known.

With the mother settled, the doctor hopped off the porch to the safe ground below and reached up to pull Matias down, then assist Taryn navigating the steep step. It was then that Matias spun around to avoid the doctor's strong embrace and screamed a loud, "No!"

Diving back into the house, Matias tore towards the broken-down staircase.

"Gitano!" he called. "*Gitano, nos vamos.*" Matias put his small foot on the first step, taking hold of the rickety railing.

"No, NO Matias!" Taryn called after him. "Gitano's not here!" But the boy's will forced him onward, ascending the steps in an instant, to the higher section where there was no longer a railing. "Come down!"

"Taryn?" She heard the doctor's voice call from outside. "Taryn, what's going on?"

"Matias!" she pleaded, then put her right foot on the first blue and white cracked tile step, shifting her weight back and forth to test it. Feeling it solid beneath her, she lifted her left foot on to the second step, then gingerly skipped the next one and climbed upward. Using the length of her body she reached up, barely grasping the little boy's grimy sock at the ankle. "Matias! Matias, Gitano's not upstairs!"

With that she felt his sock slip between her thumb and finger, while his tiny foot kicked forward, pushing him higher and higher to the top of the landing.

"Taryn! NO!" The doctor flew through the front door as she climbed up higher, reaching but failing to secure the little boy's legs in her embrace. She paused a moment to catch her breath and heard the doctor's footsteps on the bottom steps. Then, as she felt his arms taking hold of her hips, they heard the cracking noise.

In a split second it was over. An angry snap of crumbling wood then the rumble of breaking tiles. The doctor yelled and fell backwards, releasing Taryn as the staircase collapsed beneath them. She fell hard onto the tile floor facing up and screamed as little Matias fell the entire height of the staircase, landing on top of her.

Taryn realized later, berated herself when reliving it in the days that followed, that calling the dog's name along with English words only confused the boy and validated his belief that the dog was upstairs. Little Matias had landed without a scratch, only the jolt of fear causing him to cry out. The doctor suffered only a broken wrist and ran to check on her, forcing her to move her arms and legs without pain, to turn her neck without injury. There, for a split second, it seemed that the three of them had beaten the odds. But she didn't care about that. She didn't care about anything except her baby.

And then she felt it, the warm flow of blood between her legs. And with it a pain so intense in her belly and so mournful in her heart that she wanted to lie there staring at the grey dusty ceiling forever.

CHAPTER 32

MEG WIPED HER TEARS while guiding the rental car up the street. She had no intention of visiting Mom; she'd just needed an excuse to get out of there and away from Andrea. She'd spent most of the afternoon driving around and visiting places from her past. Now, hours later, after grabbing a sandwich at a downtown cafe, she drove through the crisp early-evening air, thinking again of her sister's vile tone.

On a whim she turned the car right on Argent, a main thorough-fare that led towards the river, then left down a winding riverfront road where the houses increased in size and the owners increased in wealth before stopping the car in front of the Millerton Yacht Club. The lavish, white, three-story building was a fairy-tale vision. Christmas trees on the lawn cascaded with blue and white lights, and huge red bows decorated every post on the way up to the door. Meg could see lights were on in all the windows and the number of cars in the parking lot led her to believe that a late-afternoon event was in progress. This time of year, Christmas parties were likely held daily at the most beautiful and famous venue in all of Millerton.

She got out of the car and made her way up the long, winding walkway, pausing every few moments and pretending to take in the beauty and smell of the blue spruces while in reality pacing her way through an undefined dread. The information that might lie ahead, something she couldn't articulate, weighed on her heart.

A few minutes later she opened the wide wooden doors and stepped into the incredible three-storey lobby, decked out for Christmas with holly garlands and a tree that reached all the way to the rafters. A few partygoers mingled in dark suits and cocktail dresses as muffled conversations and laughter filled the air. Looking down at her jeans and black boots, Meg pulled her jacket around her, as though covering her UBC sweatshirt would mask her casual appearance.

Finding the administrative office, Meg peered inside and found a well-dressed woman of about forty who stared down at a stack of papers while gnawing a pen.

"Beatty party?" she asked without looking up, and then gradually moved her eyes to Meg. "Oh, can I help you?" she corrected herself, having noted Meg's casual appearance.

"No, ahem, I'm sorry to bother you." Meg noted the woman's "get on with it" expression, causing her to fluster even more. "I'm wondering, well," taking a gasp of air, Meg composed herself, "are you involved in the reservations for events here?"

"Yes. I'm one of the two event coordinators. But typically we need an appointment and I'm sorry but we are very busy tonight."

"Sorry, I kind of just came here without thinking."

"Would you like to make an appointment?" The woman reached for her computer mouse and looked at the screen to her left.

"Actually, no. I was just wondering," Meg stumbled again, "my sister is getting married here in a few weeks."

The woman's tight composure lifted and a smile formed on her face. "Lovely, how can I help?"

"Andrea. Andrea Vaillancourt and Joe Sinclair? The wedding is New Year's Eve."

"Oh? Oh, yes." The woman paused and appeared overcome. "Do sit down dear. Ah, you must be Meg! I'm Jill by the way. Have a seat."

Meg nodded and the woman continued. "I've been following the news today. Have they found him?"

Meg slid down into a chair opposite the desk and felt herself lighten. This woman knew Andrea and Joe. "No, not yet."

"It's horrible. I heard last night on the radio that they found his car? It's so strange. I wanted to call your sister, you know, but with everything…it's hard to know the right thing to do in these circumstances."

"Yes."

"And this business about his, wife?" Jill dropped her eyes then lifted them to Meg's gaze, seeking the inside edge on the news story.

"Wife? Oh, the woman in the car? Taryn?" Meg felt herself explaining more than she'd planned. "No, she was his ex-wife."

Jill nodded. "Oh. Yeah, well that's the press isn't it? I sure thought that was odd," she grumbled. "How can I help you then? I think until we know more we should just leave the wedding status quo. I mean, if they find, er, well, depending on what happens we'll figure it out from there."

"Yes. That's not really why I'm here."

Jill frowned.

"I guess, I was just, well this is going to sound funny I know, but I just wanted to come in tonight and make sure that there really was a wedding. I mean, I mean that things were in order." Meg watched Jill's confusion grow. "It's just some of the things Andrea said. I'm sorry, I'm not making sense. Thank you for your time." She stood.

"There's a wedding. Of course!" Jill reached for a huge padded book and flipped through the pages. "December 31st, 5 o'clock. Platinum package with string quartet—the whole nine yards. It's going to be incredible! Your sister's been in here at least ten times finalizing everything. And how she'd go on and on about you, Meg!"

"Okay, great. Sorry to have bothered you. I'm sure it seems weird me asking." Meg tugged at her purse strap and thanked Jill who repeated her concern at Joe's disappearance, urging Meg to call her if there was any word.

Meg turned away towards the door. With the full lobby in view again, she caught sight of a tall, handsome man standing alone, reading something on his smart phone. He looked up at her briefly and smiled then returned to the screen. Meg stopped in her tracks and turned back towards Jill.

"Jill, one more thing?"

"Certainly."

"Joe. Joe's been here planning the wedding too?"

Jill stopped what she was doing and placed her hands on the arms of her chair. "Actually, no. It's been a bit odd come to think of it. But some men are pretty hands off about these things. Andrea's assured me he's on board with all the plans. And you know with this McGill trial and all, Andrea explained how busy he is. He could just never make it in. One time he was supposed to come in and I have to tell you I was looking forward to meeting him, but he got held up in court or something."

Meg sighed and bit her lip.

Jill continued, "I feel like I know him though, with all that Andrea's told me. Honestly, I was expecting to meet him this week when they come to finalize the music. Hopefully he's okay and we can do so. Why, Meg? Is there something I should know?"

"I ... I don't know."

"Well, I haven't met him but he's certainly on board for the wedding despite his busy schedule. I mean, he's paid for the whole thing!"

CHAPTER 33

"I've been waiting." Dominic's voice came through the dusk.

"Oh for fuck's sake!" Andrea screamed and tried to slam the front door as he kicked his foot inside preventing it from shutting.

He laughed and stepped inside, observing her. "Jesus, you're a mess."

"I thought you were leaving." She stood firmly in the foyer, not allowing him to pass any further.

"I am," he said. "And so are you."

"This again?"

"I'm flying home tomorrow," he said. "Just been trying to catch you to say, you know, good riddance." He chuckled ever so slightly.

"Fine."

"Not fine." He grabbed her by the arm, hard.

"Let go of me!"

He thrust her arm downward, releasing it. "Look, girl. I'm done, you're done, your little fiancé," he laughed, "well, he's not only done but missing."

"Shut up." Andrea pulled her coat belt tight, winding it around her wrist. "How many times have you said we are done, Dominic, and then months later you appear at my door? Come on, this little situation of ours has worked for both of us, you'll be back."

"Not this time. Not worth it after yesterday. Look, girl, I'll look the other way for the sixty grand. Whatever, it's a drop in the bucket compared to all the money I've spent on you. I didn't mind as long as I could have you whenever I wanted. But now, what's in it for me now? Plus, you're *way* too fucked up for me, girl. I can afford anyone I want now. I don't need your sorry piece of tail."

"Fine! Go. Let me go. I told you it was over a long time ago. I'm getting married."

"Yeah, yeah, I know. I met him remember? But let's be clear here. I forked over that sixty grand for your little fiancé, love of your life, was it?" He chuckled and shook his head. "But as of tomorrow, I'm flying home to Havana. And I'm selling this place, all of it, all the units are going on the market. And I don't plan to set foot in this boring crappy city again."

Andrea flung her head back. "Dominic. I have to go. Let's talk about this some other ..."

"No, don't do that ignore me shit. I'm done with you, girl. What was it I used to say to my friends? The wildest lay of my life? How many years, Andrea, and how much of your stupid bullshit just for that? Stupid me, you are so not worth it." He stepped back and re-opened the front door then turned towards her and spat on the floor. "Tomorrow, girl. My flight out of this shithole and the For Sale sign's going up. You're homeless."

With that he slammed the front door hard.

"NO!" she screamed, banging her head against the window in her fur trimmed overcoat over top of her bra and underwear. She rested her cheek against the cold window, blinking her eyes wildly, trying to absorb everything. Dominic was lying. If Joe wasn't found, Dominic would come back. He'd miss the special things she did for him and let her keep the house. And if Joe was found, they'd get married and she wouldn't need Dominic at all. And Meg, Meg would come back too. That stupid little girl rushing off like that to visit Mom.

Their mother, Ellen, always such a scrawny thing, tying her blonde hair up in bright-coloured hair bands like a throwback from a 1960s beach movie. Andrea pictured her as she'd always been, standing at the bathroom counter applying thick blue eye shadow and dark lipstick, awaiting one of the endless stream of men.

Just that one moment of attention, it was all Andrea ever wanted from those men. But instead they'd come and go, walking past Andrea as Ellen led them through the shabby apartment. And little Meg with her dark brown pigtails, oblivious to the comings and goings, spoiled by her own father's gifts; the doll house, the party dress, the ski trip. Meg's father cared. He stuck around, if not with Ellen, at least to be involved in Meg's life.

But for Andrea, the years went on and more men, one by one, came and went, in and out of their lives without a moment's notice of her. Until, that one, when Andrea was fifteen. Not only did he stay and come back but he'd talk to Andrea, include her and Meg in some of their home-cooked dinner dates. He bought them presents and gave Ellen beautiful things and it seemed as though things were finally changing. The other men stopped coming around and Ellen started dressing just a little bit better, a little less make up. He talked to Andrea about the things she cared about, movies and music. Sometimes he'd stop in and they'd chat for a good half hour before Ellen appeared from the bedroom for their dates. Andrea already loved him. Sometimes when she looked at him she caught familiarity, like she recognized him from somewhere else, but she decided that was due to how much it was meant to be. This was her chance to have a dad like Meg.

But then, months after he and Ellen began, the girls were summoned to the sofa for a talk. Ellen sat down across from them and spoke in a quavering voice. He'd still be around, she said but they were never, ever to mention him to anyone.

Andrea pulled her face from the window and exhaled slowly. Why did everything good get ripped away? Everything in her life, rip, tear, rip, tear. She tied the overcoat belt around her and let the end wrap tightly around her wrist until it hurt, then headed to the kitchen, opening the fridge and slamming the wine bottle down on the counter with such force she was surprised it didn't shatter. She poured a glass and gulped it down, then poured a second.

Meg's green maid of honour dress, hung over the doorframe. Perfect. She pictured her pretty, naive little sister standing there yesterday in that dress, looking like an angel. Distaste rose in her mouth. *It could have been so fun.* Pulling the kitchen drawer open, she reached for the scissors and walked towards the dress, carefully unzipping the clear outer bag then running her fingers over the sparkled bodice and along the crevices of the pleats at the waist. Noting the large price tag hanging off the collar, she opened the scissors and clipped it off, letting it fall to the floor. Then she wrapped her hand around the cold, hard handles of the scissors and lifted them up to chest level, thrusting and listening to the tearing sound as the blade made its first puncture into the bodice. She then repeatedly stabbed, pulling the scissor blades in a downward motion after each jab to slice the top in two as sequins fell to the floor, and then fully shredded the skirt as a satisfying heat rose in her cheeks. Panting as she finished and smiling at the messy strips of green satin and chiffon, she sat a moment at the counter and slugged back the rest of her wine.

Meggie as maid of honour. What a joke. What was she thinking? That that little girl could possibly fathom a wedding as glamorous as this? That she could possibly understand a love like Andrea's for Joe? Meggie questioning *everything* Andrea did. BITCH!

She sat back, this time swigging another gulp of wine directly from the bottle. The questions repeating again and again. Where could Joe be? Why was he with *her?* Why? Why was *she* with him and why had he left the car?

"WHY?" she shouted, sweeping the countertop with her arm and knocking her empty wineglass and a couple of unlit votive candles to the ground. Damn Taryn. This is the last straw, the last obstacle to her and Joe being together. Her Joe. Her amazing Joe. She'd loved him for so long. Ever since that night so long ago.

She stepped over the larger portions of the smashed glass, allowing a few tiny shards to cut into her bare feet. Then, she slipped her cut feet into her boots and, with only the overcoat wound tightly over her half naked body, reached for her car keys and left.

CHAPTER 34

September

THEY SPOKE ON THE EDGE of conversation; the words they wanted to say too crushing to bring into routine, normal days. They did what needed to be done, paid bills, did laundry, spoke with unwavering voices to their worried families on the phone.

The moment Taryn had called five weeks ago, Joe had insisted on flying to Chile, only to be discouraged by her persuadingly stoic voice. No, she'd see him soon. She was well enough to fly and the doctor would be accompanying her for part of the journey home. So instead, Joe had stood at the airport baggage claim holding a senseless bouquet of flowers, each second dragging on forever until she'd appeared at the top of a crowded escalator. Her knapsack hung on slouched shoulders, her tousled hair fell in front of her face. She saw him and blinked without smiling, then stared dead ahead until she arrived at the bottom and the two fell into a wordless embrace. Joe felt her trembling against his shoulder and gulped hard to keep from sobbing out loud in the bustle of strangers.

The first week, a tightly wound torture of niceties. Joe pushed. She withdrew. He wanted to hold her. He wanted to shake her, to make her open up. But instead Taryn fell silent. She spent days in her office stacking pages of articles and stories she'd written into organized piles on the area rug. At night, following brief words about the household or robotic questions about Joe's trial preparations, she'd retreat up to their bedroom, curling her body into a C shape as far to the edge as she could, her back towards the middle.

Joe would lie awake, trying hard to keep his tears cloaked, as he listened to the quiet noises of her breaths and sniffs buried deep into their sheets. Twice he reached for her and felt her recoil, once soliciting words that cut. By the second week he couldn't take it any longer. He wanted to talk, or better yet yell, something, anything to smash a hole in the pain. He woke at 4 AM, dusted in the vision of a confusing half-dream and lay silent, willing her to admit she was awake. Finally, he spoke.

If only he could take it back.

"Tar?"

He heard her breathing pause.

"Tar, I know you're awake."

She swallowed loudly. "Yes."

"Tar, look at me." He debated flicking on the bedside lamp but realized the full moon outside the window was bathing the room in soft silver. She propped herself up on one elbow and finally faced him. She looked so frail, a partially bare shoulder draped in a soft T-shirt. "Tar, we need to talk about it. And I'm worried about you. I'm worried about us. We can get through this. Maybe you," he paused at her blank expression. "Maybe *we* need to see a doctor or something?"

She nodded. "No. I'm okay."

"Well, okay. But I don't think you are babe. I mean, not really. Tar, this is the most difficult thing we've ever gone through. But I know we can get through it. People get through this. I know they never fully get over it but they do move forward. I love you."

She sat up then and pulled her knees into her chest as she began to sob. Joe waited for her to speak, touching her back, thankful that for the first time since her return she was not turning away from him.

Relieved, he thought that she was going to open up about her pain. But when she did turn to him, the sorrow in her eyes was unfamiliar.

"We'll never get over you blaming me. I will never get over that," she said and he shook his head. "You think it's my fault." Her voice rose, clear now, angry.

"No."

She nodded, biting her lip. "I see it every day, Joe. Every look you give me. Every word you don't say. You say other people get through this? Sure, people lose babies and grieve together and yes, they get through it, Joe. But other people don't blame each other."

"Taryn, I don't blame you."

She exhaled, sitting straighter now. "Joe. Admit it. Come on, we were barely speaking when I left."

"Yeah, but ..."

"Why? Because you thought it was too dangerous for Maddie." Her voice broke and she took a moment to swallow. "For the baby. And you were right, weren't you? You were right! You were right!" With that she rolled sideways, away from him, sobbing into her pillow.

"Tar, no. Tar, come on. I was worried for sure, but I was wrong. You said it was safe and, well it was safe. Tar this was an accident."

She didn't respond.

"Tar this was an accident." He sat a moment trying to think of what to say. What was the right thing? Regrettably, he chose the wrong words. "Maybe you blame yourself." He saw her body tense. "Maybe you are angry with me for blaming you because *you* blame you."

He heard her gasp and she sat up again, chest heaving. "All I did was try to save a little boy!" she cried and jumped out of bed.

"Tar. Tar, I know," he pleaded.

"And that's what you can't forgive me for!" Screaming now, she reached for her housecoat strewn across the bottom of the bed and put it on, tying the belt furiously.

"No."

"Yes, Joe. I see you looking at me and I know what you are thinking. You think I put those children ahead of us. You think I put that little boy's life ahead of our little girl's."

Without thinking Joe answered. And as he said the words he knew the truth that lay in words unplanned could shatter steel.

"You did."

CHAPTER 35

"Thank you for seeing me." Meg sat down on the edge of the chair.

"Of course," Doug said, setting his smart phone to silent and placing it face down on the oversized desk. "I hope I can help. This is about Andrea?"

Clearing her throat, Meg lowered her eyes. "Well, I really don't know where to start. As I mentioned on the phone, she's not doing well at all and, well that's why I was hoping you could help me. Give me some insight into what's going on with Joe being missing. I mean, it's just been so confusing. She's really not coping."

Doug felt concern for the beautiful young woman in front of him but none for her sister. Not knowing what to say, he heard himself lie but heard in his own voice the questioning tone, "I'm sorry to hear that. Why not?"

"Mr. Forester, I really ..."

"Call me Doug."

"Doug." Meg cleared her throat. "I really don't know all the details of what went on when Andrea worked here. She's told me a few things and, well, I guess it all just doesn't make sense to me." She heard him inhale and looked up to see him stroking his fine grey evening shadow of whiskers. He nodded and she continued. "It seems, to me, like Andrea was let go for no good reason. Anyway, the thing is Joe's family isn't returning her calls. It's just so strange. I tried calling Joe's mother myself and only got voicemail. He's been missing for two days now and no news at all except what we see on the TV and, of course, when you called us yesterday. I'm so confused and now, and well, Andrea's not acting right. I figure, with you being Joe's partner, you might know more of what is going on? Or maybe you could call them? Joe's parents, I mean."

Doug continued nodding, squinting his eyes at the young woman before him. She was obviously distraught.

She continued, "I'm concerned for her. She has, well, she's had some problems in the past."

Doug watched a large tear escape her left eye. She whisked it away in shame then stared, wide-eyed and sorrowful, awaiting his response.

He strode around the desk to offer her the box of tissues. Pulling up a chair beside her, he waited while she dabbed her eyes and nose, then spoke, "Meg, I hadn't heard of Andrea having problems but it doesn't surprise me given her behavior here. I am sorry. I'm sure you love your sister very much. But the issues we had this past summer and fall she brought on herself. And I do not understand why she is so desperate to reach Joe's family."

Meg raised her hands and cocked her head like an alert puppy. "Well, why wouldn't she?"

He began calmly. "We wanted nothing to do with her. We told her so that last day when we had to let her go. Since then, I don't know. I didn't think she and Joe have been in touch but, well, I really don't know now."

"What?" Meg crinkled her face in total confusion.

"I can understand with him being missing she might be concerned, like we all are. But to call Joe's parents seems intrusive. Even I have only been calling Joe's brother and one call to his mother because I know she is just beside herself. And Andrea coming here yesterday was completely out of line. She told Margot they'd had supposed dinner plans and that shocked us both. I don't know what she's told you, but things here were bad. I'm sorry; I know she's your sister. But we had to fire her. And quite honestly, I think, given the circumstances with Taryn, that you should just go home and we'll keep you posted on Joe."

Meg plunked the tissues back on the desk and Doug watched as her face flushed. She looked a bit like Andrea now, the edges of her cheekbones more pronounced. "Doug, my sister is a mess. She's been wandering around the house in her wedding dress in a complete state; her moods are switching like crazy. First she's worried sick and then she starts talking as though nothing has happened."

Doug's brain processed the information in pieces. "I didn't know Andrea was getting married. I didn't even know she was with anyone."

"Wait, wait. Andrea and Joe are getting married on New Year's Eve. That's why I'm here, in Millerton. I flew home to pick out my dress and stay with Andrea to finalize all the plans. I've just come from the yacht club. The wedding is all set. But now, with him missing, it's all just so sad and confusing." She began to sob. "Why would that Taryn be in the car? She's horrible. Andrea told me what she did, trying to get Joe back after he left her." She looked up to see him shaking his head back and forth in frustration. He reached out and put his hand on top of hers.

"Meg, no. I don't know what Andrea told you or why, but you've got it all wrong. Taryn is Joe's wife. They've been married for," he paused and she saw him lift his eyes for the answer, "five years, up until a few months ago she left him, partly because, well partly because of your sister from what I've gathered."

She let out a heaving sob.

"I'm sorry Meg but your sister did some things here that were not only unethical but criminal. We agreed to look the other way if she promised to leave."

"There must be some mistake."

"I don't think so. Meg, I'm sorry. We have proof of some of the things she did here at the office, but we never went after her. Just asked her to go away quietly and get out of our lives, especially Joe's. After Taryn left, Joe withdrew from us too. We didn't know what was going on in his mind. When Margot told me Andrea came by yesterday saying they were to have dinner, it scared the crap out of me."

Meg dropped her wet face into her hands as flashes filled her mind. Andrea in the wedding gown with those dead eyes, those eyes that Meg had seen before. "Oh my God," she sobbed.

"I hate that I've been out of touch with Joe these past few weeks, but if he and your sister were in touch, or dating, I'd be surprised, after what she did. And they are most certainly not engaged. I don't know what your sister is thinking or why, but I'm certain Joe wanted nothing to do with her. Now that you're here some things are coming back to me. That day we let her go she said some things that didn't make sense. Stuff about her and Joe."

"Oh, God," Meg repeated as flickers of memory pulled at the nerves in her mind. She sobbed and Doug waited patiently for her noisy cries to soften to the point where words could form again.

He nodded encouragement.

"I don't know what to do. She's at home alone. I've tried my mother but my mother is, well she's not able to help. She and Andrea don't talk. Andrea's been sick before, you know, when she was younger. She went away when she was in her teens. I was too young, I didn't understand. Then I moved away. But lately, these last few months Andrea started calling me and telling me about Joe and the wedding. I thought Andrea marrying Joe would be so good for her. I mean he sounded so great. I had no idea. Doug?"

He nodded again, allowing her to finish.

"Has this all been a delusion?" She stared at the floor, sniffling, then as clear as the man in front of her she saw a vision from the past. "I think my sister is sick."

Doug listened intently.

"I think it is like before. When I was nine," she said. "When I was nine and Andrea was fifteen. That's the last time."

"Last time?"

"The last time I saw that look in her eyes like I saw today. I'd all but forgotten."

"Tell me," Doug said, leaning back in his chair, arms crossed.

CHAPTER 36

October

JOE HATED WHAT HE'D SAID. But no amount of saying "I didn't mean it" could ever make it true. As weeks passed, Joe came to realize that trying to convince her that he didn't blame her was a hollow lie. What he needed to say instead was that he did mean it but that loving her and her need to help those children of the world was worth more than anything to him. But in the weeks that lay ahead, he never got the chance.

Seven weeks after Taryn's return from Chile and five weeks after his fateful words, Joe found her seated on the bottom edge of their bed on a rainy Saturday afternoon. He'd gone in to the office to work on the McGill trial that morning. As he walked into the room he gasped; for the first time since coming home she'd done herself up in a crisp, sky blue sundress; her golden brown hair hung in soft curls over her shoulders and her face glowed from a touch of makeup. As beautiful as she always was, today she looked especially so. Her legs were crossed and she turned her head towards him.

"Hey. Wow, you look gorgeous. How are you feeling?" he said, sliding in to a spot next to her and inhaling a whiff of jasmine.

For a while she said nothing, then: "Joe. I've made a decision." And before he could understand why tears were rolling down her face, she finished, "I'm leaving." She stood up, brushing the skirt of her dress flat.

"No, Taryn. I know we have to work though losing the baby." He cringed. He had tried so hard to reconcile during those early weeks after her return.

"It's not only that, Joe. Come on."

"Taryn why are you avoiding everything? We need to talk about the baby."

She spun on her heel. "No, Joe. We don't. I thought I knew you."

"Taryn. This is ridiculous. Leaving me? Taryn I didn't do anything wrong. I love you and I love what we have."

"Seriously? Don't lie to me, Joe!" she spoke, defeated, heading towards her office. "I'm not stupid. How long have you been lying to me, Joe?"

He looked at her face, so thin and crushed, her eyes so permanently rimmed in red these past weeks. "Taryn, this isn't like us."

"I SAW THE EMAILS, JOE!"

"What? What emails?"

She spun around and grabbed a small stack of papers from her desk, then sat down in the chair facing him and began reading from the first page.

"September 3rd, 2:00 AM— from HER: 'Oh Joe I can't take it. It's been an hour and I'm going insane.'"

"September 3rd, 2:40 AM—from YOU: 'Andrea, let's try for tomorrow night. I'm going insane too.'"

"September 7th, 3:00 AM from YOU: 'Andrea, babe, I'm free now if you're ready. Open the wine and put on that black outfit.'"

"*Babe,* Joe. You called her *babe!*" With that Taryn broke down sobbing. "How could you do this to us? How could you do this after we lost Maddie?"

Dumbfounded, Joe grabbed the papers from her hands. "Taryn, I didn't write this! Where did you get this? What the hell?"

She stared at him in disgust. "I'd just lost Maddie. We'd just lost Maddie, and you went off to ... fuck some ... oh she's so awful." She threw the papers down on the desk with a swat.

"Calm down." Joe approached her. He hardly ever heard her swear, and when she did it always sounded so forced. "Taryn, I'm not interested in Andrea."

"Margot didn't even like her. And Margot likes everyone! You fired her, Joe. You and Doug fired her. Why would you?"

"I didn't write this!" Angry now, Joe got down and kneeled at her lap, grabbing her wrists in his and forcing her to make eye contact. "Taryn, where did this come from?"

She took several deep breaths in the minute or two that followed, gathering her thoughts. Then calmly she explained. "I went downstairs first thing this morning after you went to work. I went in your office. I wasn't snooping, Joe. I was reconsidering the Israel contract and I wanted to get the contact number for John, that associate of yours with the Israeli embassy. I had a few questions for him. You were out so I thought I'd just go onto your laptop."

Joe nodded. "That's fine."

"And your stupid password is always the same so I thought I'd just go in and get it."

"Okay." He wanted to smile at her pointing his bad habit out again, but couldn't.

"And your email was open and there was this one from today. From her. About you two moving ahead. Moving ahead? I don't know what that meant and I got curious and started reading it, the whole thing back and forth between the two of you." She pulled the first paper off the stack and began reading again.

"October 12th, 9:41 AM—from HER: 'Joe, this fall heat, I can't take it, I need you to lick some ice cream off my back.' October 12th, 11:21 AM: 'Babe, I've got to work on the trial today. But I'll tell her even later and pop over. Save me some of that ice cream. I can't wait to see you.'"

"I'll tell her even later," she repeated and began to cry harder. "Did you go? Did you leave work and go lick the ice cream, Joe?"

"STOP. This is insane. This is crazy. I didn't write these!"

"Joe, it's right there in your email. Today! Why are you lying? Please just admit it."

"And look at this other email, Joe, she's thanking you for a necklace? There was a photo with it. Some selfie of her boobs and a silver pendant."

"What? No. I'm going downstairs to look at this." He stood up, angry and determined, his heart raced as he headed for the staircase, then paused at the doorway to the baby's room, and slid down the wall, sobbing. He listened to her as she walked back to the bedroom. A few minutes later she emerged with her suitcase, her words now surprisingly calm.

"Joe, I called my contacts. The offer for the book on the Gaza strip is still open. I'm taking it." He stared at her, her voice clear and determined. "I'll be leaving for Tel Aviv as soon as things get organized. It will take some time to get all the paper work in order— work visas and things. That's why I was looking for your embassy contact. I am going to go stay at Ryan's until things are in order."

Without emotion she continued as he stared. It was like a switch had flipped. Robot-like, she said, "I don't think it's wise for us to keep the farmhouse."

"Tar?"

"Joe, listen. I'll be gone for at least a year. This place is too far out and rebuilding it has been such a money pit." She swallowed and he began to sob again. "I know that I could take you for way more than half of our assets, given what you've done, but I just couldn't be bothered. Sell it all and just transfer half."

"Taryn, I didn't."

"I think that realtor who sold it to us in the first place would be good because he knows the history and I've researched a packing company that is willing to come in and take care of everything."

"You can't just decide all this."

A large tear rolled down her cheek, finally breaking her robotic tone "I can Joe. I have. You don't sleep here anyway; you're always at the office." She frowned "Oh, stupid me. I suppose you're not and you've been lying about that. But either way, you aren't here, so with me gone too, why are we bothering?"

"I have been sleeping at the office. Because I have the trial coming up. And sleeping here is so hard, Taryn, you can barely look at me!"

"And I can't bear to go near the baby's room and I know you can't either. We can't stay here, Joe." She continued along the hallway to the staircase. He stood and tried to help her with her suitcase and she recoiled, yanking it loudly down each step.

Let her go to her brother's and get her head together, he thought. Maybe it was a good thing for her, to be with Ryan and his wife and children. And maybe she was right about this house too. He watched from the porch as she rolled her suitcase clumsily down the driveway, her small frame lifting it into the trunk of her car as the warm October sky painted a blue background against their massive red maple trees. A snapshot of his life he knew he'd never throw away.

Returning to the house, he immediately went to his office to reread the emails, this time on screen. "Damn it," he said aloud and buried his head in his hands.

CHAPTER 37

MADELAINE STRAPPED ON HER SNOWSHOES and sat on the bench for a moment to let the sun's rays warm her face. She stared at the brilliant winter sky, more vibrant than on any summer day, and silently thanked her blessings that she lived in such a beautiful climate. The storm on Tuesday contrasted today's gentle stillness, both providing her with enormous pleasure. The pleasure, in fact, from the contrast itself.

Standing, she did a few of the stretches her physiotherapist had prescribed and looked ahead from the gate at the untouched snow ahead. This time last year, after her second knee surgery, she couldn't have imagined that she'd be snowshoeing again, but her commitment and exercise routine had gotten her back in shape. In another few months, hopefully before winter's end, she'd be able to try a quick cross country ski. She mashed the first oversized footprint into the snow and then propelled herself forward to take her second step, then her third, getting used to the moisture in the snow, which was causing each step to sink down into the perfect, untouched trail. She raised her sleeve and glanced at her watch, there was about an hour of daylight left. "One hour only," she'd promised Frank. She'd have to be sure to be back five minutes early so he didn't worry. She'd check the time again when she reached the clearing they called Heaven's Triangle. It'd probably be after 4:30 by then, her turning point to head back. Once night fell she'd be close enough to the house to be safe.

Inhaling the cedar and observing the scattering of pine needles guiding the trail, she set off on one of her favourite activities, day-dreaming masked as snowshoeing. She let her mind wander past tall spruce trees, remembering Christmases past and imagining how this coming season would be, with her newest grandbabies on their parents' laps as they gathered around the tree. Madeleine couldn't wait to have them all home again. With each crunching step she began imagining how perfect it would be, what food she'd prepare ahead of time and what she'd cook on those special days, picturing the family sneaking into her kitchen, stealing bites and laughing just like old times.

Twenty minutes down the trail, she paused at the fork. Knowing Heaven's Triangle was about ten minutes ahead if she kept going straight, she looked to her left down the less open trail that led to the sugar shack. The sugar shack was an old wooden shed that Frank had built about thirty years earlier when he'd had a notion to start collecting sap. Always the dreamer, Frank saw opportunity in everything, especially their fifty-acre property. One year a Christmas tree farm, one year sleigh rides, and that year their future millions in maple syrup. Long abandoned, the shack had remained a hideout for the kids during extremely complex games of hide and go seek, then later, to Madeleine's purposefully blind eye, a place to which her teenagers escaped. In the last ten years, the shack had been left abandoned, save for her or Frank occasionally wandering out to check and see if it had fallen over or blown away in a bad storm. Then last year, as though his upcoming milestone birthday had lit a spark, he'd resumed the maple syrup production, declaring that while they likely wouldn't make millions, he sure enjoyed it on his pancakes. Suddenly curious, having not seen it in over a year, Madeleine turned her foot to the lesser trail and began crunching down the path.

The sugar shack stood before her, not looking anywhere near as worse for wear as she'd expected. She approached it with a crooked smile escaping her lips, thinking of Frank as a young man, holding his first batch of sap and explaining how this would change everything for them. Snow had drifted up against the wobbly door. Unable to kick it away with her snowshoes on, she removed them and began clearing it with a combination of her boots and her mitten-clad hands, pushing the snow back like a dog digging in the dirt, until the door had enough clearance to swing open. She pulled the large wooden latch, which stiffly resisted, causing her entire body to pull back. She laughed to herself and tried again, this time pulling the door back with her.

Squinting in the darkness, striped by a sunlit pattern from cracks in the wooden slat walls, she stepped inside and screamed.

CHAPTER 38

"It was just weird. I mean, I didn't know what was going on. We didn't exactly live a fairy-tale life." Meg had moved to the leather sofa in Doug's office and sipped on a cup of tea he'd prepared. "My mom, our mom, she didn't have any money and she kind of, well I guess moving from man to man kept her set financially. That year my mom had been dating this really wealthy man. We both liked him but the thing was, we weren't allowed to speak of it. I realize now that he was married to someone else. But at nine, I didn't get it. I just did what I was told."

Doug nodded.

"He was nice. I remember he used to bring us dinner on Friday nights, from Burger Town." She drifted into reverie a moment and Doug patiently awaited her return. "I liked him okay. Gary, that was his name. But Andrea, oh my God, at first she loved everything about him and then, once Mom said we couldn't speak of him, then she hated everything about him. I didn't understand why." Meg drifted again and Doug noted her grasping at her purse straps.

"Did he? I mean ..."

She looked up at him, unsure, then realization crossed her face. "Oh, no, nothing like that. I mean that I know of. No, it was more about him being married and not committing to Mom and us. I do remember one night Andrea coming in to my room in tears. She said I shouldn't be nice to him because all he really cared about was his real family. Then all of a sudden it was like everything changed. Andrea changed. One night she came home. It was late. I was already in bed but I heard a commotion. Our apartment was really small so I left my bedroom and went down the hall to the dining area and, oh, God."

"What is it?"

"I hid behind the buffet cabinet while Andrea screamed at the top of her lungs and ran by with the scissors from the kitchen drawer. My mother was running too, fleeing. She didn't notice me. Then, after what seemed like forever, Andrea put the scissors back in the drawer and walked slowly towards me." Her voice trailed off

"*You don't understand.*" Meg whispered.

"I'm trying." Doug said.

"No, that's what Andrea kept saying, that I didn't understand. She'd whispered to the cabinet as she went by and I realized then that she knew I'd been there the whole time. Then Mom came back. Yes, oh my gosh, I remember!"

"Tell me."

"Andrea was standing there laughing, but not fun laughing. She was laughing like a scary person. And my mom was screaming at her 'What did you do? What did you do?' I kept hidden behind the cabinet. I was so scared. How could I have forgotten all this?"

"Our minds protect us."

"Andrea saw me. I know she did."

Meg sat with a look of horror on her face. "Oh."

"What is it?"

"I just remembered. She had blood all over her."

CHAPTER 39

ANDREA SWERVED TO AVOID AN ELDERLY MAN in her way as she turned on to Argent Street. Gripping the steering wheel, seething, she pushed the gas pedal with the toe of her pointed boot, swearing and mumbling under her breath. "This city, this god-damned piece of shit city with its stupid Christmas lights, all in the same blue alternating with white like God forbid some rebellious store owner might dare to break this year's council decision and flash a red tree or a yellow star. Morons. Every last one of them." Why on earth had her mother stayed here? And why on earth did she ever come back after her years in Toronto after she'd left the hospital?

Those first years back here when Andrea, at eighteen, finally returned to live with Ellen back in that dump on Regent Street following increasingly long outpatient passes. Ellen was pushing forty by then and her main source of income, swooning men, was drying up. So she'd turned even meaner than before. Why hadn't Andrea just up and left and gone back to the nice big city and started over? So what if she had no cash? Ellen had taught her how to handle that and Dominic, that Cuban geek she'd met while waitressing in Toronto, he was loaded. He was dreadfully smart and renowned for his illicit computer skills, but he didn't have a single social skill in that disgusting, hairy body. Dominic would have funded her anywhere. But no, she'd returned to Millerton for Meg. For Meg, who'd increasingly turned around and abandoned her.

By the time Meg was twelve, she was spending every holiday and summer with her dad and had already settled on doing university out west. She was already getting perfect perky little boobs and had the tiniest waist, the perfect little body to go with her gorgeous skin, big doe eyes and shiny dark hair. Soon Meg would get all the boys, and nice boys too, not like the ones who feigned interest in Andrea and her mother. Meg was smart. Straight A's in subjects Andrea didn't even try, and she danced, she danced like some kind of natural angel, already at a grade level in contemporary and ballet that was years ahead of her age, paid for, of course, by her perfect dad. Meg would end up with some nice boy. Someone like Joe Sinclair.

The last forty-eight hours had turned the whole world upside down. No one understood how it had all gone down. That it was some sort of fate that afternoon this past March that she'd seen him on the street after moving into that townhouse. She'd parked on the street to pick up a few things at the hardware store and, head down, stepped out onto the sidewalk and literally plowed right into him. It wasn't planned or orchestrated. It just proved to her that this was how it was meant to be.

He'd been rushing, frazzled, and immediately apologized without even looking at her face, ensuring she was fine while balancing his paper coffee cup to keep it from spilling on her.

"Joe?" She'd smiled, feeling her entire body snap with current.

"Yeah. Oh, hi?" he'd said, his face completely blank.

"Andrea. Andrea Vaillancourt." She'd beamed a smile at him, tucking a lock of her looped curl behind her ear.

He remained blank at first but lied, she could tell. "Oh, yes, nice to see you." He'd fumbled as she'd chuckled inside watching him squirm. Of course he didn't remember her. He'd looked at her twice before but never seen her.

"Nice to see you as well," she'd said, pulling her wrap off her shoulders despite the cool March air as he'd checked again that she was okay and apologized a second time for walking into her. He was older now, of course, but that crooked smile, those flecked eyes. She remembered the way the light had hit them in the news broadcasts. She'd sat, glued to the TV those nights, after she was sent away. And she adored those newspaper clippings, especially that one of him smiling, standing next to his mother on the courthouse steps, when Doug Forester finally announced to the world that the charges were dropped. One of the nurses at the hospital had left that newspaper in her room at Andrea's request and Andrea had slid it into her drawer next to her panties. Joe would like that. She knew. And now, here he was right in front of her, smiling and making sure she was okay. He was looking right at her and caring for her. She'd awaited this moment her whole life and here it had happened randomly. Fate was finally on her side.

"I hear you are a lawyer now." She put on her most interested voice and expression, watching him still struggling but knowing that soon it wouldn't matter that he didn't remember her. She could convince him of anything and then he'd be hers.

"Yes, yes for quite some time now." He'd smiled and raised his eyebrow, *those flecks in his eyes.* "Hey, I'm so sorry. I seem to have forgotten where I know you from."

Liar.

Andrea batted her lashes, pretending she was hurt, then smiled confidently. "School. Well, high school. I went to Millerton but, you know, those combined dances and such."

He nodded, straining "Oh, ok. I think I only went to one of those." His voice trailed off.

"Yes. Yes, of course that would be true." She said, all knowing, watching his face strain, thinking about that dance. Andrea knew he'd been captivated only by perfect Lauren Avery in her turquoise dress. But Andrea had been there, watching them all night, laughing, dancing, giggling, then later making out in the alcove of the stairs by the music room. She'd heard them whispering and breathing and closed her eyes imagining it was her. He'd had no idea. But that didn't matter now. This was her chance. "I was a friend of Lauren's," she lied.

"Oh, right. Andrea? How are you?"

This was so easy. This was opportunity knocking when it had never even brushed the door before. Ideas came quicker than she could speak. "I've been meaning to look you up and get in touch."

"Oh?"

"Yes, I recently went back to school, you know. I took one of those online things. Well most was online but some was in class." The words gushed out with detail that wasn't even contrived, making her beam a wide smile. Detail made lies so much more believable. "I took a legal assistant course and recently finished. I got to thinking how you have one of the bigger law firms here. I don't know if you are looking?"

"Oh, well sure. Doug Forester and I have been growing really fast. We're always looking for help these days. I'm in the midst of a big case and Doug has a thousand things on the go. You should drop by." He reached into his inside suit pocket, flipping a business card like a magician and handing it to her. "Call us and we'll set something up. Hey, I've got to run. It was nice to see you again, Andrea." He smiled, his left eye slightly more squinted than his right.

Liar.

It took so little effort it was almost a joke. A quick trip to Talbots with some of Dominic's stash money to get a few nice outfits, a glossy, well-paginated resume listing details of the course she found on the website and a few reliable references. Dominic could easily drop his accent to speak to Forester and Sinclair as the keen professor of legal ethics who had a special fondness for Andrea's thorough and professional work. All that would take was one quick roll in his sheets. And what else would they check? One respected professor's reference and she was a shoe in. Besides, Joe Sinclair already knew her, or thought he did, and he'd never want to admit that he'd forgotten one of Lauren's friends so easily.

It wasn't that she wanted to be manipulative. But when something like this happened after all these years of thinking about him, she had to seize it and make it happen. And she could tell by his smile and how kindly he'd checked that she was okay, he was already falling for her.

She was in. Working at the office side by side with her prince as they fell even deeper in love.

CHAPTER 40

The night of the accident

JOE HEARD A SMALL NOISE and looked up from his laptop screen. Taryn stood before him, at the door. She reached for the doorframe, a momentary wobble, and smiled.

"Tar?" he whispered. *Pinch me.* She was wearing soft pale blue jeans and oversized fuzzy boots, a long lavender sweater hung shapelessly beneath her opened jacket, her hair dishevelled from melted snowflakes that tossed her bangs into her eyes.

"Hi Joe." She paused, as though words weren't enough and stepped a few feet towards him. Clearing her throat, she kept advancing. "Bad time?"

"Of course not."

She seated herself across the desk from him, sliding into the chair in a liquid motion and stared.

"I, I thought you'd be gone by now. Was your flight cancelled because of the weather?"

She shook her head and he saw her face blush ever so slightly. "No, I mean yes, cancelled, but by me." Her eyelids lowered in a slow motion blink. "Joe?"

He felt himself bracing but was unsure why. "What is it ba ... Tar?"

Her face was fully flushed now. "Joe, I don't want to go." She began to sob and he slid a box of tissues across the desk, then rose to close his office door. Returning to her shaking shoulders, he took the chair alongside her and held her hand, waiting until she looked back up into his eyes. "I don't want to go."

"Okay, Tar that's up to you."

"I don't just mean Israel."

"Okay." He nodded, so afraid to read into her words it was as though he felt a box forming around him. She looked so beautiful, even in this state, and somehow smaller than usual. His heart ached to hold her tight.

"I've made a terrible mistake."

He nodded and stroked her hand with his thumb. "Tar, what is it?"

"I don't want to go to Israel, Joe. I never told you but, do you remember Ardi, from Child Save?"

Confused, he nodded, vaguely remembering the many contacts Taryn had acquired over the years.

"Well, before I took the Israel assignment, Ardi called me and offered me a job. It'd be something I could do from here, coordinating their missions, and honestly, I'd have even more impact on saving the kids than I would on any writing assignment." She spoke clearly now, determined, the old Taryn. "And I didn't even mention it because of everything else. I just wanted to leave, you know?"

"Yeah." Their eyes met, tears matching tears now.

"You're crying now." She smiled and reached up to wipe a tear from his cheek with her thumb. That point of contact, the start of a shudder in his body.

"Tar, you should do what is best for you, what is in your heart. Don't make escaping us a reason to turn down something you want."

She looked away then pulled her hand away from him and buried her face in her hands.

"Tar?"

"Joe, how did everything get so bad?" she sobbed and he let the answerless question dissolve in the air around them while time lost measure. She continued, "I don't want to leave, Joe."

"Okay, Tar, it's okay, just call off the trip. And then call Ardi, or take time off, whatever you need babe." He chastised himself for the babe reference. It came so naturally.

"I don't want to leave *you,* Joe."

She'd said it. The truth had escaped into words for the first time. Suddenly calm, she sniffled and interlaced her fingers, hearing him gulp beside her. She turned back towards him, the defeated face, pale and detailed with lines from the past year.

A long pause forced her to say it again. "I don't want to leave *us,* Joe."

He couldn't speak. Instead he leaned forward, pulling her in so her soft hair fell against his face while he stroked her head. He closed his eyes tight. Was he dreaming this? How could this be happening? Everything he'd prayed for, but so much pain lurking to pull them apart. Overwhelmed, he began to sob until the two, rocking, finally pulled apart. He kissed her softly, then deeper, then finally pulled away resting his lips on her forehead.

"Is this for real?" he whispered.

"Joe, all morning, all the way over here after I called to say I was heading for the airport, I've been trying to find the words to explain it all. I guess, well underneath everything the truth is I just want us to be together so much. I want it like it was before, only better. I want a family. Dr. Hinton says I can try again. I want it all Joe. I have since the day I met you."

He kissed her again. She pulled away to continue. "All this year, all this bullshit with *her,* Andrea," she gasped. "I was so wrong. I see it now."

"No, I..."

"It all came to me this morning. Let me explain. It's so odd. I went to the farmhouse, to get those last few things we talked about.

Remember how I wanted that silly photo of Gertrude and, of course, my passport from the safe."

"Yes."

"I was at the house. *Our* house. Alone. And I just stood there in the kitchen by the coffee pot, staring at the walls and I just started to cry. I just wanted it back. Saturday mornings, scrambled eggs, you in those ugly striped pajamas, everything. When I finally stopped crying, I couldn't stop thinking about Ardi's job offer versus me flying off to Israel. I kept thinking about how if I took the offer I could stay here and maybe, maybe we could start over? But it hurt, you know. It just hurt so bad."

"I'm sorry."

"No, Joe. You don't have to be sorry. It all hit me right then, well, a few minutes later."

He waited, uncertain, mesmerized by her steady voice.

"I went upstairs to grab my passport from the office safe and went past the main bathroom and, for some weird reason, I stepped inside. It smelled like you. I think that's why I went in."

He smiled and laughed quietly. "I've been using that bathroom instead of ours when I go home. I don't know why. But I haven't been there lately."

"It still smelled like your cologne. I guess that drew me in. There I was standing, staring at myself in the mirror and I reached up to open the medicine cabinet. Joe, it was like something came down and hit me. But I remembered."

"Remembered?"

"That party, Joe. You remember the office summer barbeque at our place for your firm?"

"Of course."

"Andrea. Andrea had been up in the bathroom. I remember I came inside and upstairs to grab some sun block and found her coming out of there. And I was surprised, I mean we have a bathroom downstairs and there she was upstairs in our house."

Joe shrugged.

"Joe, I'd noticed the medicine cabinet was open. She'd been snooping through our stuff. I'd totally forgotten about that day."

"O-kay?"

"Why would she be up there?"

"I don't know. Maybe the downstairs bathroom was busy. People snoop in other people's houses. But about Andrea, there are things I need to tell you."

She turned so their knees met and took his hands in hers. "There's more. I remember. I remember the look on her face when I saw her and I remember that later the papers in my office weren't how I'd left them. Joe, I've figured it all out. You weren't lying. I am so, so sorry."

"Let me tell you what I know now." He said but she kept talking.

"I got to thinking about that day and how she was upstairs and then just all the things, the emails and the necklace. Joe, you were telling the truth. You didn't send those emails and you didn't buy that necklace. It all hit me today. Oh Joe, I should have listened to you! The emails! I went back to Ryan's house, to gather my luggage, and the whole way there as I sat in the taxi forever in this storm, it all made sense. And then I realized I subconsciously forgot the passport and Gertrude's photo. It was like a sign. When I got to Ryan's, I found the box where I'd put those printed emails. I'd kept them, you know?"

He shook his head. "I understand."

"I found them and read them again. This time I read them without being mad. I mean I really read them. And you know what?"

"What babe?"

"You didn't write them. If I don't know how you speak and write by now after all these years! You don't talk like that. And on one of them, one that I hadn't read to you, you spelled Margot's name wrong— no T. I've never known you to do that. Joe, *she* wrote those emails to herself. She must have gotten into your account."

He nodded. "She did. Well, sort of, I'll explain. She got into my email accounts and other things too."

"Why didn't you tell me?"

"How? Tar, I'd already lost you. And some of it I just found out today. There's so much more."

"I read those emails three times this morning, Joe. Cancelled my flight and just sat there on the floor reading them. Each read through it made more sense. She's crazy, Joe."

"I know."

"I mean really, really sick. Margot never liked her. She set you up, set me up to destroy us. And the necklace!"

"It was like Lauren's."

"What?"

"That necklace she said I gave her. It was the same as the one Lauren always wore, the pendant. Lauren's was an L with the small flower at the bend. Andrea's was identical, but an A, same flower. When I saw Andrea wearing it, back in the summer, it looked familiar but I didn't really remember until later."

"That's sick, why would she wear the same necklace as Lauren's? How would she even have known?"

He nodded. "It's not hard to know. Lauren's wearing it in the most famous photo that went around that year and since. I guess she was trying to get my attention."

"I'm so, so sorry, Joe. I didn't believe you, and I didn't know that was like Lauren's. I thought it was just some stupid necklace. It's just sick, Joe. She scares me."

"Me too."

"It was all lies, to get us to break up. She wanted you so bad she manipulated everyone, and hacked emails. Joe, I am so sorry I didn't believe you."

He closed his eyes to push the pain away, then opened them and looked at his wife, frail and fragile. He could have her back.

"She's not going to ruin us, Joe."

"Never," he said, pulling her close again. "I love you, Taryn." He cried, then stood and guided her towards the couch where they made love, then lay together in comfortable silence watching the snow swirling beyond the window.

In the empty office Joe and Taryn held each other as though the gap that had existed between them had dissolved into something more beautiful. Finally, he rose and left his office without a word, returning moments later with a bottle of cabernet from Doug's office and two plastic cups.

"I think we're here for a while. I can run next door to Golden Sun and get us some food if they're still open," he suggested.

"In a minute." Taryn put her wineglass down and pulled him back towards her and they made love again.

CHAPTER 41

"She stabbed your mother?" Doug sat back, his courtroom interrogation voice escaping unintentionally.

Meg paused and scrunched up her face. She stared at Doug for a long moment, as though memories were tapping at a glass shield they couldn't quite break. "No. I don't know. Not yet. It was weird though. I remember all the blood now, on her dress and she came towards Mom again with the scissors. Maybe she hadn't put them away. I don't know. They were screaming. Screaming. I was running my finger along one of the carved edges of the cabinet legs, back and forth, back and forth."

She sat still again, head tilted, staring at the carpet, then said, "I'm sorry. I'm sorry this is all coming back to me fast. I had forgotten. I guess I was so terrified."

"It's okay. I understand. And I'm used to it, sometimes clients have to remember horrible things too. Please take your time."

Meg looked around the office, trying to gather her words. Her eyes dropped to a banker's box, open on the floor next to Doug's desk. Rumpled papers flowed out the top, one paper, partially covering the top corner of a black and white newspaper photo of a man. She looked from the photo to Doug and back again.

"What is it?" Doug asked.

"That's Gary. My mom's boyfriend."

CHAPTER 42

GARY. THAT WAS HIS NAME. Andrea knew he was different before she even met him. Her mother was sitting in front of the vanity mirror on the old scratched dresser applying her makeup and the girls came in, as they often did, to watch. But today her mother's blonde hair appeared healthy and gleaming, without the usual dark roots and split ends. She applied a dash of mascara to clear eyes, without her usual blue smear of cheap shadow. Gary, she explained, had treated her earlier to a day at a spa; a real spa, with the best French products for esthetics. He wasn't like the other men she'd dated. They'd been seeing each other for over a month already after meeting at the Goodwill; he'd been there for philanthropy, her to find shoes for the girls. Tonight, he was bringing dinner for all of them and she so wanted the girls to accept him. "Be polite ladies," she went on, smirking her mouth as though she knew what that even meant. Gary liked polite. Gary liked everything orderly and beautiful, and Andrea soon learned and observed that.

He had money. He was kind. He treated their mother like a lady, and after a while, it was almost as though Ellen began to believe it. He'd come by with dinner or the latest movies from the video store. He bought them presents and really, really seemed to care. And he paid more attention to her than to Meg. Gary was going to be *her* father. Finally she'd understand what that felt like.

She didn't want to go. It was her mother, pushing her, convincing her to get out. The combined dance between two high schools would be a great opportunity. Andrea knew what her mother really meant was a new group of kids to explore who didn't already hate her. She debated going all day, pulling out the wrinkly dusty rose dress her mother had purchased from God knows where. But she had to admit, with Gary in the picture her mom did seem more engaged in her and Meg's lives, and buying the dress was a nice gesture, after all. So, by six-thirty she'd showered and done up her hair as best she could, stepping into the dress and finding a pair of shoes that were way too tight but matched okay.

The dance was being held at the other high school, Winston, then next fall it would be the opposite and they'd host it at her school, Millerton High. Andrea wasn't sure where the idea came from or why, but it had been a tradition in Millerton for her whole life and probably Ellen's whole life too.

The other school wasn't far, so Andrea pulled a warm sweater around her shoulders and headed out, arriving at the front of Winston High about twenty minutes later.

She stopped in her tracks. She knew this school well from the outside but had never stepped inside. Nerves knotted at her stomach and she wondered why she'd come, especially alone. But, last night, lying in bed listening to the sound of Meg breathing and some residual rain drops tapping against the metal siding of the house she'd had an image, a fantasy. A tall, slim and handsome Winstoner would see her from across the room and walk towards her, arm outstretched, while her fellow Millerton High classmates stood with their mouths gaping open that she, Andrea Vaillancourt, could attract such a prince. He would ask her to dance, then later escape the party to sit, perhaps on those big front steps, or perhaps to his gleaming car. Andrea imagined it all over and over again. The momentum of the dream pushing her forward now.

But here, looking at gathered clumps of chatty, squealing teenagers, she'd never felt so alone. Could she even get up the nerve to step inside? The prince of Winston probably wasn't inside. And if he was, wasn't he already dancing with one of those satin-clad, lipsticked girls who kept bustling past her?

Andrea turned her back to the school to leave before anyone noticed as a large black sedan pulled up, almost cutting off where she was about to step. The passenger door flung open and out stepped a beautiful blonde girl. Her hair was gathered in an updo, with tiny white ribbons and flowers interwoven through it. She lifted up her overblown turquoise dress so as not to step on it with her matching shoes.

"Pull over and park!" a high voice commanded from the back seat as the other door flung open as well. "I want some photos." The older woman, but not by much, stepped out of the back seat, fussing with the teenage girl's dress and purse. "Lauren, darling, come stand over by that beautiful oak tree," the woman instructed as the sedan pulled forward and parked off to the side. "Where's Joe?" the woman asked.

"He should be here soon," the girl answered, scanning the pockets of teens standing across the lawn. "Oh, there he is!" She shouted and began waving her arm back and forth. Mesmerized by the commotion, Andrea stood and watched as a slim, dark haired young man shuffled towards the girl.

"Oh, Joe!" the older woman exclaimed. Andrea couldn't help but notice her slim figure and short skirt. If this was the girl's mother, then she must have had her when she was a child.

The young man walked towards them, kissing Lauren on the cheek and handing her a flower corsage in a plastic container. But just then, as Lauren fumbled with the box and examined the elastic wristband, Andrea caught his eye. He looked past Lauren and directly at her, nodded and smiled.

He was perfect. He was the prince from her fantasy. His dark hair was cut close to his head but a bit longer in the front creating a shaggy, edgy look. He had a smile that flowed from ear to ear, and seemed to make his eyes pierce. He put his arm gently on Lauren's back, awaiting instruction from the slim, older woman, who grew increasingly frustrated at the slowness of her still absent husband.

"Dad's getting the camera!" the woman said, way more excited than the sentence warranted. "Over here!" she pointed her finger towards the young couple, now staring at each other with subtle, secret expressions.

"Coming, Dalia! Photos of my beauty!" Andrea heard the man's voice from behind, familiar. She turned and their eyes met, both frozen by the sight of each other, his eyes growing wide in fear. Suddenly he looked away, walking right past her as though she wasn't there. "Yes dear, let's get these photos."

"Gary?" Andrea thought she was speaking in a normal tone, but heard her voice catch such that the 'ary' trailed off.

He continued towards the young couple, snapping photos of them while Andrea watched. Finally, after the photos were done, he and the slim woman hugged their daughter, Gary kissing her on the cheek, and then the two turned back towards the car.

Andrea felt her face go scarlet. With each step he took to pass by her again, her heart jumped another beat. She wasn't going to move. As solid and steadfast as if her heels were permanently impaled in the grass, she stood, staring. Gary walked past, his arm around his wife, his head down. As they got closer she tried again. "Gary," she said, firmly this time. He kept walking. She clenched her teeth and began following him. "Gary? It's Andrea. GARY!" she shouted and the woman turned towards her.

"Can we help you dear?" the woman asked and both turned towards Andrea, Gary behind such that his wife could not see his expression as he shook his head slowly from side to side and glared at her with eyes that shot more warning than a rifle.

"Uh, oh, no never mind." Andrea shuffled away, turning back towards the tree, where the Winston prince stood, arms around the puffy-dressed Lauren, pulling her in tight for a lingering kiss.

CHAPTER 43

MARGOT PULLED THE KNITTED AFGHAN up to her neck, unable to get over the shivers that had plagued her for the past couple of days. Nothing seemed to work, neither tea nor wine. Charlie nuzzled next to her and rested his chin on her leg, then cocked one ear unexpectedly. Having had a quick visit with Taryn, she'd returned home, awaiting a second long night of insomnia.

"What is it boy?" she asked, stroking his ear, then hearing the footfalls on the porch followed by firm knocking.

Doug stood before her on the porch, his face beaming in the dim porch light, as she pulled open the door.

"They found him," he said, pushing his way inside and pulling her into a hug. "Flannery called me and I came right over here from the office. He's heading to Highlands by ambulance. Let's go meet him there!"

"Oh my!" Margot screamed and began to cry. "Is he okay?"

"I don't know. But he's alive!"

The hospital was eerily quiet as she approached the information desk. Andrea advanced slowly, surprised by how few staff were present. A few feet from it she stopped herself, before a nurse looked up, and turned back towards the door.

"Can I help you?" The round-faced nurse stood before her in a pink shirt.

"Oh, no. I'm fine. I think I just got turned around from when I visited yesterday," Andrea lied. "Taryn Sinclair."

"Are you family?"

Andrea tightened her overcoat and smiled. "Yes, I'm her sister. I just flew in from Vancouver."

"Oh, she was moved out of intensive care last night." The clerk said with a smile. "5 West, it's closest if you take those back elevators. The staff up there will help you."

"Thank you so much," Andrea said and scurried towards the elevator bank, pausing to smile widely at two nurses who stood awaiting its arrival.

CHAPTER 44

The Day of the Accident

He wanted to shake her. Violently shake her and whack some sense into those muddled eyes that stared back at him with so much desire; shake her until the words from her mouth actually made some sense. She stared at him, with wide round eyes, rambling on about gold tablecloths and red napkins.

"Andrea." Joe sat down on the sofa, trying to remain calm. "I don't know what you are talking about."

"Darling, why are you being like this? Our wedding is coming and you've been so busy with work you haven't even come to the yacht club to finalize anything with me. You work too hard. That's going to stop. But what I was saying was how I need you to come over later, for dinner. My sister, Meg, is flying in. She should be here by now actually, but with the weather, I think it will be quite a bit later this afternoon." She sat down next to him and her spicy perfume with an overlay of cigarette smoke overpowered the air. He wanted to gag. "You'll come by for dinner, right?"

"Andrea, something is wrong."

"Say yes." She snapped her head towards him.

"Andrea, are you listening to yourself?"

She leaned towards him further and put her face right against his, as a child might. "Say *yes*."

"Yes," he whispered. Anything to calm her down.

From the time Joe awakened that morning to the rough bristles of the office couch against his face he'd known today was the day. After weeks of investigating, weeks of sorrow over losing Taryn, and months of the constant pull on his shoulders of the biggest case of his life, he was down to two choices. He could do what a big part of him longed for, wither away beneath the soft throw and remain trapped in the darkest cave of his life or, he could stand up, put one foot in front of the other and make things right. He chose the latter. Today, he had a long meeting with Chase in preparation for the trial tomorrow. Despite Chase constantly changing his story, this time Joe knew they finally had the right version: the Truth. And tonight, once everything was settled, he would talk to Doug about the trial. Come clean on that. Come clean on everything.

But this morning, before Chase arrived, Joe would gather all his evidence and head over to Andrea's. He'd looked up her address from the office files. It was just a few blocks away, not a problem even with the storm that was starting. He needed her to admit everything so badly he could taste it. He dreamed of the moment he could prove to Doug that everything he'd thought Andrea had done was true. More importantly, despite Taryn leaving today for the other side of the world, he had to get those answers. Answers he knew wouldn't change anything, but at least could properly wrap the end of their marriage in a shroud of reality.

At nine in the morning, Joe gathered up the files and went to tell Margot that he was stepping out just as his cell phone rang showing Taryn's brother's number.

"It's me," she'd said, detached, and went on to explain that her flight out was today and she'd now realized her passport was back at the farmhouse. Would he mind her coming by to get it and also that old photo of Gertrude? He made small talk back to her about her trip and the storm and she responded, in equal small talk, inquiring how late he was working and ending with a suggestion that he should sleep at the office. Joe wasn't sure why she'd suggested that. He wanted to believe that through her emotionless voice he caught a hint of concern, an invitation back to civility, then questioned if instead it was a jab from her perception of the affair. Little did she know that he slept there almost every night now.

That October morning when Taryn left, after watching her car until it vanished, he'd returned to his home office to re-read the emails he'd supposedly sent. With his limited computer knowledge, he'd looked at all the ways they could have been created and come up empty. Everything he saw indicated that he had sent them, just as Taryn had believed. He had spent the rest of the day in a state of bewilderment, walking around the farmhouse knowing he couldn't stay there. The next few weeks consisted of endless tasks; doing what was necessary to shut the house down, calling the realtor and packing company as Taryn had suggested.

His last day at the farmhouse, Joe walked from room to room, inhaling the lingering scents of her beloved candles, the crisp whiff of her perfume from her now abandoned pillow. He sat for minutes or maybe hours at the kitchen table, remembering hot coffee poured into oversized mugs on lazy mornings and braided apple pies presented on late summer Sunday afternoons. He stood at the door to his office, thinking of his longstanding dream of eventually spending some work days here, when the caseload allowed it. He imagined having lunch with his children or stopping by Taryn's office upstairs just to stand at the doorway watching her write, her mind so caught up in her stories that she would not even notice him. Finally, before leaving, Joe had sat down in the middle of Maddie's room looking at the crib and rocking chair still covered in plastic. He'd reached for the screwdriver he'd planned to use to put up the toy shelves and considered taking the crib apart but couldn't. Instead he popped the screwdriver into his gym bag and made a decision. He'd instruct the packing company to leave this room as it was, at least for now.

While a hotel was an option, somehow the comfort of the office he knew so well and the familiar, itchy, lumpy couch would be his home for the next little while. In the morning, he'd go to the gym a few blocks away, get in a swim or some time on the treadmill, shower there and return to the office after Margot had arrived. He couldn't possibly trouble her or Doug with all of this, he convinced himself, knowing that really he just couldn't face them. Sharing the loss of Maddie with them would be too painful, and facing the fact that he'd brought Andrea into their world and caused risk to their office and sadness to Margot was more than he could take. Instead, he'd lay low, and divide his time and energy between Chase's case and figuring it all out, piece by piece. Taryn wasn't coming back. He knew that. But, if the chaos of the past few months could be extinguished under a layer of truth, he could at least find his way up for air. The first day at work following a tortured sleep on the couch, he'd started researching computer security companies for a consultant to help. And one week later, a young man in thick hipster glasses arrived at his door.

"No, you're absolutely right you were hacked. We've traced the IP to Ms. Vaillancourt's computer. Yes, absolutely, it was her, there is no doubt."

Joe listened, pleased to have solid proof as the man continued using the word absolutely at least once every sentence.

"Now, as you requested, we also did a full security check of your home and your office here and we found what you suspected. You are absolutely right that there is money missing. The transfers originally flowed from your and Mr. Forester's main business account, through your payroll account and then out to a numbered account. Lately, though, we see a breach from this other account too, the small one, 497 322 016, do you know that one?"

Joe nodded after double checking the number. "It's the slush account for cases we are helping to fund. Most recently I've been controlling it for a big case I'm on. And you have all the documentation on this?"

"Absolutely."

"And how do we find out who the numbered account belongs to?"

"Already done, sir!" the consultant beamed. "It had a few hops, the money I mean, but in the end, there were small payments electronically transferred to Ms. Vaillancourt as well. Sir, this is a criminal matter. I mean, I don't have to tell you that as a lawyer. I'm obliged to bring this forward, sir."

"Understood." Joe agreed. "But give me a week or two."

"Sir, that's not a good idea. We can certainly put extra security layers on your accounts, but the reporting of the crime, I'm not comfortable delaying."

Joe nodded. "Yes, add the security, right away. But please, let me deal with something before you bring this forward."

The keen consultant proceeded to pull out a stack of forms, reluctantly agreeing to hold off and making it clear he was uncomfortable doing anything without Doug's consent. However, the young man's ethics lifted when Joe agreed to purchase the premium package with his own money.

Over twenty thousand was missing from the payroll account and another forty thousand from the fund that was currently paying for Chase's trial preparations. She'd hurt their firm and Margot and Taryn. This was the day he would confront her.

Now, he sat next to her as she babbled away as though acting in a play, insisting he join her for dinner. "Andrea. Just stop." He took her arm with a harsh snap. "I've been here for fifteen minutes and you haven't answered a single question. Do you want me to call the police? I was giving you a chance to explain and all you've done is babble. Are you well?"

She pulled her arm from his grip, leaning back into the couch arm. He watched as she ran her fingers through her hair then stuck them into her mouth. "Andrea? Andrea do you need help?" He didn't know what to do. Was she having some sort of breakdown? "Do you need a doctor? Andrea?"

She sat silently staring at the carpet a moment then turned back to him. "No, Joe, I'm sorry. I'm fine, It's just a lot of things you've thrown at me. Could you ask me things one at a time instead?"

She was acting perfectly normal again, the actress had ended the play. He felt himself backing up, cautious, reconsidering his idea to come here. But he had nothing to lose and he needed answers.

"Fine. Let's start with these emails," he said pulling the pages he'd printed and handing them to her. "You wrote these?"

"Yes."

"I mean both sides of them. My responses too."

She frowned. "Of course not, darling. You wrote those."

Joe counted to three in his mind to stay calm. "No. I didn't. And someone who knows about computers says that you wrote them. They came from your computer. Do you remember writing them?" He found himself speaking as if he was about to scold a child.

"No."

"You didn't write these?"

"I wrote them to you. You answered. Darling, why are you asking me these things?"

"I wrote them." A strong voice came from the hallway and Joe turned to see a scruffy, dark-skinned man in a long beige sweater. He was flashing a large-faced, diamond-studded watch and had rings on almost all of his fingers.

"Dominic! What?" Andrea turned her head towards him. "What are you talking about?"

"I wrote them. Hey, you must be Joe, the fiancé."

Joe stood now. "I'm Joe Sinclair. And you are?"

"A friend." The man stepped forward. "I was, a friend, of hers," he snickered. "Look man, I'm sure you two will be happy ever after and all that. I'm done with this. I'm sorry, I was just fucking with her brain."

"What?" Joe said. "What are you talking about. Who are you?"

"It doesn't matter. Look, Andrea and I go way back and sometimes when I'm here, in town, I drop in is all. We have, whatdyacallit? History. From way back in Toronto. I drop in, right Andrea?"

Andrea's face was scarlet. She turned to Joe. "Joe, that was before. Before us."

"Enough!" Joe yelled. "Am I in God damned Crazy Town? There is no *us*." He watched her slide back again, rubbing her hair. Joe turned to Dominic. "Why would you write emails as me?"

"I was fucking with her mind," Dominic said. "Stupid, I know. I'd popped in to town for a quick one a few months ago and found her obsessing over you, her new boss, her prince, she called you. She'd finally found you after all these years. She said she'd sent you an email and when you didn't reply she'd got all bitchy. So one day I just replied as you and got a thread going."

"You replied, as me."

Dominic smirked. "Stupid, I know. It just seemed to make her hornier. Every time you, well I, replied to her she'd get all hot and bothered and we'd have a grand old time. So I just kept going."

"How did you reply as me?"

"Easy stuff. Replied to some texts too"

"He's a genius," Andrea said softly and Joe turned to Dominic for clarification.

"With computers, yeah. My whole life. Lots to be made in the hacking business."

"So why didn't I ever notice these emails? I never saw them until my wife found them. MY WIFE found them."

"Yeah, yeah they never actually got to you or came from you. At first I did it from a fake account that just looked like you sent them. She didn't notice," he scoffed towards Andrea. "Then later I got inside the ISP, that was more of a challenge. Makes life interesting."

Joe looked at the lumpy dishevelled man, wondering why he was confessing but not really caring. "Then how did my wife find them?"

"Buddy, Jesus, get over it. I was just fucking around. But when Andrea got all caught up in you, it wasn't just a game anymore. I started to realize you two were seriously happening so I stopped messing with her. That's when I decided I'm getting out of here. Funding Andrea has been good for a while but if she's really with you, I don't need the hassle. The money I make now; I can have any woman I want."

"How did my wife find them?" Joe repeated.

"I don't know. I got careless I guess. Andrea sent one email where the whole thread was inside it and it actually went to your real account. I'd given up on her sorry ass by then. Crazy bitch—run now, buddy, run now."

Joe rubbed his forehead, watching Andrea pull her legs up into herself and popping her fingers back in her mouth.

"You hurt her?" Joe stepped forward.

"Nah."

"Andrea does he hurt you?" She looked up slowly and shook her head. "You really thought I sent those emails?" She nodded and he felt his heart pounding in his chest. "Okay then why are you still here? If she's such a crazy bitch and you are done with her, why are you here?"

"You're engaged. I'm done."

"That doesn't answer my question. And we're not engaged!" Joe looked back to see Andrea returning to a trance. "And I think she needs help, can't you see that? Why are you here?"

"Cash."

"Cash?"

The two men stared at each other, neither backing down. Joe's mind raced to his own missing money.

"Do you know how much money I've given this bitch. Over ten years, since Toronto. Not saying it wasn't worth it. She's the best lay I've ever had—but you know that." *I don't,* Joe thought, but it wasn't worth saying out loud. "Clothes, and handbags and Jesus Christ, this house!" Dominic turned to Andrea and shook his head. "Never seen her as bad as this. Glad I'm getting out of here. Just looking for the stash, then I'm gone."

"The stash?"

"Yeah, the money she owes me. The house I'll put up for sale tomorrow. I don't give a shit anymore. I know I can't get back all the crap I gave her, but I know there's cash in here, lots of it."

Andrea pulled into a ball.

"You need to leave," Joe commanded. "She's getting more upset. Obviously she's not well and you are making it worse." Having come here to confront her, he was surprised to find himself suddenly sympathetic.

"Fine. Whatever." Dominic threw his arms up. "I'll be back, Andrea." He stormed out the door.

Joe turned back to the withering woman who jumped at the sound of the slamming door. "Andrea, can you hear me? I'm going to get you some help."

She lifted her head and the clarity returned to her eyes. "No, Joe, I'm okay."

"Does that guy hurt you?"

"No. He was my boyfriend. I mean, sometimes boyfriend. Well, we have an understanding. He buys me stuff and I do what he wants. He has lots of money. Lots and lots. He, oh Joe, can this be between us?"

"Sure."

"He steals it. Not like a robber or anything. He does it on the computer. He has millions. And I get cash sometimes too and presents. It's all upstairs. But now it seems like he wants it all back. I guess because of you and I being in love now."

Joe knew he needed to call someone. He was over his head talking to this woman in her delusional state. But he didn't. Instead he kept calmly talking to her, listening to her explaining about their love. Amazed at her stories of the small things he'd said and done that she'd taken as huge gestures. Somehow, in her mind, him being a kind partner at the law firm, an occasional smile, a friendly wave, had turned into her vision of love, and something within her had snapped. He should have been afraid. But he didn't feel any fear as she slowly led him up to her bedroom closet, opened a latch in the wall and pulled out a safe. He watched her bat her eyelids as she slowly counted the cash and handed it to him with a small giggle. "I'm sorry," she whispered. "One night before Dom realized you and I were in love, but when I knew, I showed him into the office. I needed to pay for the wedding."

"It's okay," Joe lied, taking the sixty thousand dollars from her. He had what he'd come for. He'd go to Doug and the police. As for Andrea, she seemed peaceful as she was. He felt sorry for her and wanted to help.

Returning to the kitchen he poured her a glass of water and watched as she sipped it.

"Andrea. I really do think you need some help. Do you have family here or a friend I could call maybe?"

"You're my family, Joe." She smiled.

"Okay, well, in that case, I think we should give your doctor a call. I can take you over," he said as a text came through on his phone. He was late for his meeting with Chase.

"Who is that?" Andrea asked, clear voiced again, like the woman who had worked for him.

"Margot. I have a client now."

"Go."

"No, I think we need to wait. Actually, I'll call an ambulance."

"I'll call my mother. She'll come right over." With that Andrea picked up her phone and after a moment Joe heard her speaking and arranging the visit. She hung up. "Mom's on her way. She's just five minutes away, even in the snow she'll be right here. You can go."

Hesitant, Joe gathered the cash under his jacket, pacing the foyer a few times hoping to see the car arrive.

"Seriously Joe, I'm fine. Part of that was an act to get rid of him."

"Promise me you'll go to the doctor?"

She nodded.

He looked her square in the eye. "Andrea, you know we aren't getting married, right?"

She nodded.

"And that guy, he's a criminal. I'm going back to the office and once I talk to Doug, I'm calling the cops."

"Okay."

"Lock your door until your mom comes."

"She'll be right here," she said.

Joe opened the front door and stepped out on the porch, searching for Andrea's mother's car. He opened his trunk and pulled the zipper on his gym bag, pulling out some sweaty clothes from the morning before to make room for the cash and finding the screwdriver from Maddie's room at the bottom. After packing the cash into the gym bag, he re-zipped it and dropped it into the trunk, gathered up his clothes and the screwdriver and slammed the trunk firmly closed.

As he opened the car door, Margot texted again, asking how long he'd be. Tossing the bundle of clothes and hardware into the back seat, he tapped out a quick reply, took one last look at Andrea in the window and drove out, just as a small red Accord with an older woman driver passed him on the narrow crescent. He nodded to the woman who nodded back.

Back at the office, Joe immediately met with Chase, then requested a meeting with Doug. But Doug, tied up in court, never returned to the office. *First thing in the morning then,* Joe thought. *I'll call him and we can meet up before I head to Chase's trial. Then we'll call the police together.*

Andrea stood at the window watching Joe drive away. She was pleased that Joe's strong words had finally put Dominic in his place. And faking calling her mother had sent Joe calmly on his way. She'd take a nap now; the meeting had been a lot to take in. And when she woke up Meg would be here and they could talk more about the wedding.

CHAPTER 45

"She needs to rest and, I think, Taryn, how do you feel about a short walk once you've rested? Perhaps next time you need the bathroom?" The pear-shaped nurse spoke like a kindergarten teacher, causing Ryan and Taryn to share a sibling smirk.

"Yeah, I'll get going." Ryan stood up and kissed Taryn on the non-bandaged side of her face. "Get some sleep."

"Any word?" she whispered, another tear from the endless supply trickled past her lips.

"No. But both Doug and Margot have my number, they'll text okay? And the police are here, back and forth. It won't be long now." He stroked her hand.

"Perhaps another sedative?" The nurse smiled. "I can go grab one."

"No, I'm okay." Taryn's words caught in a cough as she smiled and leaned back on her pillows. "Go home and see the kids." She winked at her brother who agreed, promising to be back later and to call if he had any news, as did the hospital staff.

The nurse lowered the light and tiptoed out, leaving the door ajar. Taryn closed her eyes as the same image kept pushing into the forefront of her mind. Joe. Driving along Old Country's Edge highway, his left hand on the steering wheel, his right hand in hers, grasping it tightly every few minutes as they wound along, laughing that their intention of seeing their favourite views was defeated by the storm. It wasn't that they hadn't known that it would be so, it was just that driving this route held such memories. It was a drive they'd taken a thousand times and, tonight, after reconciling and sipping wine and making love into the wee hours of the morning, it seemed like it solidified everything. There were faster ways to their farmhouse, safer ways. But hindsight was everything. If only she could have seen what lay ahead. But, in the spirit of sentiment, she'd suggested it. "Let's take Old Country," she'd smiled as she'd gotten into the car, Joe insisting she get in and be warm while he brushed away the inches of snow that had accumulated. She'd watched him out of the half-cleared windshield, a skip in his step, the devilish smile as he'd pretended to throw snow at her with his thickly gloved hand.

When he'd gotten into the driver's seat he was completely salted in snowflakes, despite having tried to brush them off. But he'd leaned over and kissed her, again. "Old Country?" he'd asked. It had been her chance to say no, to rewind this tragedy. They could have taken the main highway, or even the winding back roads of Highway 21. But no, she'd wanted Old Country. She wanted to feel it again, like the time they drove it after a date early on in their relationship, or the day they found the farmhouse. She wanted to drive back to their house her favourite way.

His voice. He'd said it a few times: "I'm not sure; the steering feels weird, loose. Maybe it got cold or something? Remind me to call Hank's and get it checked out." Taryn had agreed, and then told him she'd take care of it herself. He had too much on his mind today with the trial. She felt a bit guilty keeping him up so late, it was after two in the morning, but when she mentioned it, he'd just smiled and told her their night had been a sign—that he now knew he'd win in court.

All those things he'd told her as they'd lingered on the sofa, the things he'd found out about Andrea. Taryn felt a chill go down her spine. Was Andrea really dangerous? Perhaps she should mention it to someone now. Perhaps that skinny detective, Flannery, was still here. It might be a good idea to talk to him.

Wide awake now, she thought of another idea. The nurse had told her it was time to start walking. Perhaps she was strong enough. She'd just stroll down to the nursing station and see if Flannery was there.

She tested herself, swinging her legs over the side of the bed to see if she felt woozy. One foot went down to the floor, then the other. Other than the pain in her head, she felt perfectly fine. Surprisingly fine. She stood up and reached for the housecoat that Ryan had brought earlier and tied it around her waist. Using the side of the bed to reassure her balance, she stepped into her slippers. One foot timidly in front of the other, she walked forward, feeling a sense of weakness every once in a while, and knowing it did not come from her injury. Where could Joe have gone? If only she could remember something, anything, but her last clear memory was holding his hand and the clear sound of her own screams.

The hospital ward was eerily quiet and Taryn stood in her doorway a few minutes, gaining her orientation. To her right, about six rooms down, was a wide, rounded desk with several chairs, computer monitors and binders. It wound around out of her sight and she thought she heard the faint murmur of people whispering from beyond her line of vision. A man in a tweed coat emerged then from the room across from hers. He stepped into the hallway, pulling the door shut quietly, and offered her a nod before heading towards the nearby elevator.

Looking to her left, she noticed that the ward she was on came to an abrupt end. This must be the construction zone that Ryan was talking about earlier. Part of the hospital was being renovated and he'd asked her if there'd been any noise during the day but she couldn't recall, being in and out of drug-induced sleep. Curious, she stared a moment at the dark corridor, blocked by a wall of thick, overlapping transparent plastic panels that could be parted and pushed through as a doorway. Then she turned to her right to venture down to the nursing station.

She grasped the railing and glided down the hall, making an accomplishment out of passing each patient room, occasionally peering inside out of curiosity and hearing only breathing sounds in the dim, ailing light. Approaching the nurses' station, she saw a few of them gathered in a room beyond the desk. Through the window she could see the nurse who had been taking care of her that day, reading to the others from a tablet and nodding.

Faintly she heard the ding of the elevator from down by her room but turning back was more difficult than she'd anticipated, her attempt to turn her head ineffective against the thick bandages and sudden dizziness. Taking the railing by both hands now, she managed to look back but saw only the flash of a coat, entering the elevator again as the doors closed. Fearful that the dizziness could recur with greater intensity she decided to make her way back. She had already walked too far anyway.

Andrea checked the name scrawled on the whiteboard beside the door then stepped in to the room, gripping the looped ends of the scissors between her two fingers inside the deep coat pocket. The room was intended for two patients, but the second bed lay tidy and made. It was obvious that Taryn had just left the tousled bed nearest the door. Andrea poked her head into the bathroom, expecting to find the little slut standing there, looking at herself in the mirror.

Those things Joe had said to her yesterday. He was so mixed up because of Taryn, thinking she still cared about him. Thinking she'd ever really cared about him. Poor Joe, he was so easily convinced of things. If only he'd seen things clearly from the beginning. She should have been angry with him, changing his mind about things and even denying their wedding. But how could she be angry with him, the love of her life, her prince?

She needed to do what had to be done to make it clear for him, clear that she was the only woman in the world who was truly good for him. Once and for all, get rid of Taryn's horrible influence so he could see the truth. As soon as they found him, he'd come back to her. He'd say those things again like he'd said in the emails. Poor Dominic, pretending he'd sent them, trying so desperately to keep her in his grip when now she had Joe. And their dream wedding, just like the one in her childhood dreams, would all come true, with or without Meg.

But the bathroom was empty. Andrea stood a moment assessing her own reflection. My God her hair was a mess. She leaned in to the glass, stroking her skin. It was so dry from neglect the last couple of days. She'd have to dash back home and do herself up better, for surely the search parties would have found him by now. He was probably just hiding to get away from Taryn.

Turning back towards the room, Andrea seethed at the seven different flower arrangements and row of get well cards. This woman was unbelievable. Andrea took one of the cards from the shelf, sneering at the fat bear in bed with an ice pack on its head then laughing out loud at the shaky printing of "we love you Auntie Tarry" in orange crayon. She shook her head and tossed the card to the floor. This woman, this fraud, had to be stopped if she and Joe were to ever find true happiness.

The iPhone on the bedside table buzzed, startling Andrea. Andrea looked over at the screen as it flashed "Margot calling". Heat rose through her spine. That other cruel bitch who ruined everything. Spitting, she reached for another greeting card.

"I can't reach her. As soon as Joe's here, I'll run upstairs. I can't believe we beat them," Margot said. At word that Joe had been found, Margot had joined Doug in his car, surprised to find a young woman sitting in the passenger seat. Doug introduced her as Meg Vaillancourt, Andrea's sister, and went on to explain that Meg had been at his office when word had arrived that they'd found Joe. "There's a lot to tell you," he'd continued as they'd sped to the hospital. "I asked Meg to come with me because I know Flannery is at the hospital and she needs to speak with him and the police, but not now, let's focus on Joe now. Flannery's meeting us there."

229

Now the three stood in the main entrance of Highlands Hospital Emergency, awaiting the ambulance. "He was far out. The crash was far out, almost at the farmhouse, so a good forty-five minutes' drive. The nurse says they've radioed and they're almost here," Doug reassured her.

"Did they say how he is?" she asked him again, hoping that now that they were in Emergency there'd be more news.

Doug shook his head. "Just that he's alive."

"Can I go and get you some coffee?" Meg asked, desperate for an excuse to leave their intimate moment. "Or perhaps I should just wait in the car?"

Margot looked at the young woman then to Doug who signaled with his eyes to be patient and he'd explain. "No thanks," she said.

Doug turned to Meg. "No, it's okay. I want you to talk to Flannery."

"Doug?" Margot started then interrupted herself. "There, there they are!" she exclaimed, running towards the doors where the ambulance was pulling up. "He's here! Joe's here!"

The three watched as the paramedics pulled the stretcher through the doors, and then raced towards him. Behind them a news van pulled up.

"Joe! Joe! It's Margot!" She turned to the paramedics, "How is he?"

Joe lay back with his head propped on pillows and smiled while the paramedics reported his injuries to the medical team who took over and whisked him into a bay. Doug and Margot followed, Joe telling the team that he wanted them there with him as a silver blanket was whisked off his mangled, bloody leg and intravenous fluids were started.

"Where's Taryn?" he asked. "Is she ...?"

"She's okay. Joe, she's okay," Doug reassured him, placing his hand on Joe's shoulder. "She was in intensive care but they've moved her up to a ward. She's going to be fine."

With that, Joe's shoulders fell and he began to sob. "Take me to her," he said.

"Soon, Joe," the nurse in charge said, wrapping a blood pressure cuff around his arm.

"We need some images right away," the doctor commanded.

"Try her again," Doug said to Margot, remembering that Taryn hadn't answered earlier. "Maybe they can bring her down here. Or maybe someone at the desk can call up?"

Taryn regretted venturing so far down the hallway and considered turning back or calling to get the attention of the young clerk who had appeared at the desk. But she barely had any voice from her ordeal in the cold and then being intubated for a day in the ICU. Throughout the day, her raw throat and swollen vocal chords had gotten worse, to the point where she'd spoken to Ryan in only a whisper. But now she was more than halfway back to her room and had paused a moment to take in some deep breaths, it really didn't seem that far. She'd walk along the wall until she got to her bed, then curl up and wish for Joe as she'd been doing all day.

Looking in the room beside hers, she saw a man mesmerized by the flickering glow of his television. Taryn paused a moment, recognizing the familiar squares of the *Jeopardy* board, a show her mother used to enjoy, and wondering if her head could handle the flashing light of television. Perhaps she'd watch the game to kill some time and keep her mind off the fact that a long, worrisome night was upon her.

Faintly she heard the ward telephone ring and looked back, finding the young clerk was no longer at the desk. It rang several more times, and as she listened, Taryn couldn't help but think it was news about Joe.

Slowly, she padded her way to the door of her own room, reaching for the doorframe to guide herself, she brought her hand to her mouth in shock as a wave of electricity shot through her body. For although she had her back to the door, the blonde woman was definitely Andrea Vaillancourt. Taryn could hear smacking noises emerging from the woman's lips as one by one she threw Taryn's greeting cards and flowers to the floor with her left hand, her right hand firmly inside of her pocket. Walking backwards, without the aid of the doorframe, Taryn stepped, using a surge of adrenaline to find the strength to run to the nurses' station, she turned that direction but was suddenly overcome as the ceiling seemed to fly to the floor and the walls spun around her. She felt herself falling but managed to catch herself just as Andrea came running towards her.

Silent and staring, Andrea stepped forward and pulled a pair of gleaming silver scissors from her pocket. With her other hand she grabbed Taryn's wrist. Taryn felt one of her slippers slide off as she sank down onto her knees.

"HELP!" Taryn screamed, looking up and noticing the security mirror by the elevator but seeing no one. She heard only the whisper of the H, followed by an overwhelming need to cough. She pulled back and slid her arm out of Andrea's grasp. Scurrying backwards on all fours, she slid out of her housecoat and threw it at Andrea who flung herself towards her. With all her strength, Taryn reached for the scissors that pointed directly at her chest and twisted, releasing them from Andrea's grip and tossing them away from her. They skimmed across the tile floor as Andrea shrieked. Panting with her mouth gaping open like an animal, Andrea turned to get them.

Finding the strength to stand up again, Taryn kicked off her remaining slipper and ran as fast as she could away from Andrea, suddenly finding herself against the plastic construction panels and turning her small frame to slip between them.

Stuart Flannery sat next to Meg on the olive green waiting room chairs as she relayed the incredible story of her sister's wedding delusion and sipped vending machine coffee. A few reporters sat a couple of rows over. Flannery purposely kept their conversation to a whisper.

"It's just crazy," she said. "Mr. Forester thought I should talk to you and I guess the police. I mean, if she's sick, I'm just so afraid. I want to get her some help."

"Where is she now?"

"She's at home. I had to leave. She was so upset."

Flannery took the last gulp of coffee grinds, causing his face to grimace as he looked up to see Doug and Margot, followed by Joe Sinclair laid out on a stretcher.

"He's managed to piss off the doctors," Margot reported with a smile. "He needs surgery but he's refusing until he sees Taryn. So we're all heading up to her room."

"It's not like another fifteen minutes will do any more damage to my leg than walking on it for the past, well, however long I've been walking on it?" Joe grinned, realizing he had no idea how long he'd been missing.

The orderly pushing the stretcher frowned and shook his head. "Joe, they're booking the OR now. We'll go up to the fifth floor so you can see your wife, but then we're going right to the second floor for surgery, okay?"

"Joe." Flannery reached forward to shake Joe's hand. "It's been a while."

Joe smiled, thinking of their first meeting so many years ago, but also of all the work they'd done together over the years since then. "You always see me at my worst, Stu." Joe laughed, then noticed Meg, who stood back from the group.

Doug turned to her, "You and Flannery come up too."

"Oh, no," Meg whispered stepping back.

"Please come." Flannery reached out his hand. "Stay with me. The police are on their way and meeting us up on the fifth floor."

"Let's go!" Joe demanded, and with that the group piled into the elevator. A reporter tried to follow but the orderly pushed him away as the doors glided shut.

Taryn cursed at being forced into this wing of the hospital. Had she gone the other way she'd have been safely with other patients and staff. Silently, she tried her best to tiptoe in her bare feet against the cold floor to the opposite end where an exit sign illuminated red against the darkness. She could hear Andrea coming, her high heeled boots stomping against the floor and her voice almost cackling against the wooden construction beams. Doing her best to keep her balance and not turn too quickly, she felt her head pounding. The pain medication was wearing off and her racing heart was flooding her brain with pressure.

"Taryn Sinclair—not Sinclair for long. You stupid, stupid, little girl," she muttered. "Where the fuck are you? Come on, let's get this over with."

Taryn slid back into what used to be a patient room where some light from the parking garage shone through the window. She leaned against a small broken counter and stained sink, smelling rust from a slowly dripping faucet. How could she get out of here? She had to either dash towards the exit stairs and fly down the five stories to the outside, or turn back to the nursing unit, past Andrea and scream for their attention. She had to get past this woman, this woman who had come into their lives, ruined their lives. Why hadn't she believed Joe? Thank God she believed him now and had told him so. And those things he told her before the accident. Oh Joe, where are you? She felt herself weakening then snapped back. No! *This isn't going to end this way.* She slid her body down the wall, hiding next to the sink.

Tink. Tink. Tink. The faucet dripped and she held her breath, listening for any other sound. She shivered from the cold entering the opening in the back of her hospital gown.

"Auntie Tarry," Andrea laughed and Taryn could tell she was closer now, just outside the door of this old patient room. "Where are you Auntie Tarry?"

Doug wanted to tell him so much as the elevator glided up the five stories. Chase McGill was innocent and the trial would be cancelled. And Andrea. Who knew, as Meg's memories returned and she'd begun thinking more about Gary Avery dating her mother and the blood on Andrea's dress. The long unsolved mystery of Lauren's murder, with every unravelled thread of emotion, uncertainty and distrust, was finally weaving together. But as his mind raced, ready to explode, he bit his lip and remained silent, watching his friend, his protégée, lie on the stretcher with his eyes closed awaiting the moment he'd see Taryn.

When the elevator chimed and the doors opened, Margot took charge, telling the orderly which room was Taryn's and practically running towards it, only to stop dead as before them lay an empty room, a crumpled house coat and two slippers on opposite sides of the hallway.

"What?" The orderly let go of the stretcher and ran towards the nurses' station from which several nurses came running. "Where's Mrs. Sinclair?"

"She was out walking. I saw her," the young clerk explained. "I saw her walk back to her room."

"Her flowers are all smashed!" Margot cried, emerging from the room. "Where is she? What's happened?"

"Call security!" Flannery commanded and the clerk sped to the phone.

"Where are the police? There were police here earlier!" Margot screamed.

"They're coming," Flannery said. "GET THEM!" he shouted to one of the nurses.

Joe pushed up on his arms trying to get off the stretcher but Doug pushed him back. "What's going on?"

"I think. We think. It's Andrea, Joe. She's, she's not right in the head," Doug said.

Joe nodded. "Yeah, I know. I think I know more than you do."

The two men stared at each other a moment, wondering what the other meant. Suddenly Joe snapped to attention. "What? You think she's got Taryn?"

Meg, who'd stayed back by the elevator door, felt her eyes fill with tears. How could her sister be causing so much panic? She turned her head from the commotion towards her right and saw a flash of something beyond the plastic construction partitions. Amid the confusion and yelling, she slipped between the panels.

"Search the floor! There's a woman who may be here. She's dangerous!" Flannery yelled as the security guards arrived, two of them heading room by room down the populated wing of the hospital while one of them entered the abandoned construction wing.

Taryn felt the dryness of her mouth and stood up to look through the darkness into the dusty mirror at her bandage, bringing her hand to touch it as a wave of nausea overtook her and a piercing pain shot behind her eye.

"You can't have him."

She looked up to see Andrea standing behind her, calmer now, still grasping the large scissors like a dagger.

"Andrea," Taryn whispered, turning around and trying hard to make her voice work. "I, I don't know what you're doing, what you're thinking."

"You bitch. Joe and I were happy until the other day. We were getting married in a few weeks, New Year's Eve."

"What? No, Andrea, you aren't thinking straight. Please. Just put the scissors down and we can talk." Taryn coughed, subconsciously putting her hand to her throat. She thought she saw Andrea's expression change very slightly and rethought her approach. "Okay, okay. You're right," she lied and saw Andrea smile. "Yes, you were getting married. Joe told me all about it."

"At the yacht club," Andrea stated.

"Yes, Andrea, at the yacht club."

Andrea paused a moment and Taryn watched her looking up towards the top of the door. Then she returned her gaze to Taryn and stepped forward. "Until YOU RUINED IT!" she screamed. "YOU stole him and then he disappeared!" She flung her body over Taryn's, lunging the scissors upward. You're just like Lauren!"

Taryn's muddled head struggled to understand. "Lauren?"

"STOP!" Meg leapt in the air, grabbing Andrea's wrists until the scissors fell into the sink with a clank. "Stop it, Andrea. Stop it!"

Releasing Taryn, Andrea spun back towards her sister. "Meggie, let go!" She shoved Meg against the wall as Taryn eased back, wanting to flee but wanting to help the young woman who'd rescued her. Reaching in the sink, Taryn grabbed the scissors with shaking hands.

"Stop it, Andrea!" Meg cried. "You're hurting me."

Andrea grabbed her again, reaching for her throat and pushing her sister back out the door where the two fell in a heap. Straddling her younger sister, Andrea squeezed tightly until Meg could only gasp.

"YOU. RUIN. EVERYTHING!" Andrea lifted Meg by the neck and slammed her head against the floor with a *thunk.*

"No," Taryn sobbed. "Let her go." Taryn reached around Andrea's waist, using all her strength to pull her off her sister before the two fell backwards into the wall with Taryn underneath. Andrea rose then, spinning around and backing up as Taryn, trembling in her hospital gown, stepped forward with the scissors, knowing that what she had to do next was inevitable.

"No Taryn. You don't have it in you." Andrea took two steps back towards the structure of the door of another partially framed room. Taryn looked down at Meg still lying on the floor. She raised the scissors and took a step forward, then froze.

As the bullet from Stuart Flannery's gun hit Andrea's chest, she spun and fell forward, landing face down on a nail-clad beam. Meg shrieked in horror and scurried over to collapse on her sister's legs.

"You have to let us go back there!" Joe yelled at the remaining security guard who blocked Taryn's room where he, Doug and Margot remained. He swung his good leg over the stretcher. "That was a gunshot!"

"Flannery," Doug said. "He carries a gun."

Margot gasped and the guard put up his hand. "Please, wait here," he said and left to join the two other guards who had followed Flannery into the construction wing. Doug and Margot followed as

Joe got down off the stretcher and hobbled to the door. Excruciating pain shot through the injured leg now that he'd been off of it for a while and Joe hopped on one foot out into the hallway.

From behind the panels, Meg emerged, holding a security guard's arm. She looked at Doug and slowly walked towards him, collapsing into his embrace. Joe watched, confused, turning his head from the entrance, to his partner and the young woman and back again.

"Andrea's dead," Joe heard the woman cry, and then felt the tender touch of Margot's arm around him.

Then the sway of a flashlight beam caught their eyes from behind the plastic and he heard Margot whisper in his ear, "There she is!" Before them, Taryn walked under Flannery's arm, his suit jacket draped over her shoulders.

"Joe!" Taryn's scratchy voice whispered as she let go of Flannery and staggered towards him. Standing on one leg, Joe reached for her and pulled her in close.

CHAPTER 46

TARYN POURED THE LAST DROP OF EGGNOG into a glass and handed it to Doug. Together they walked into the living room to join the others gathered by the fire. Doug sat himself on the edge of the armchair next to Marlena, bringing her hand to his lips.

"Did Meg get off okay?" Margot leaned towards the coffee table, taking a moment to peruse the selection of hot appetizers laid out before them.

"She stayed until today to get her mother through the funeral and then make sure she was okay. But she seemed in decent spirits, in spite of it all," Doug answered.

"So much to go through," Margot said.

"Wasn't just finding out how sick Andrea was and then losing her. Meg had repressed a lot of memories from her childhood. I think she knew Andrea had killed someone but never pieced it all together—that it was Lauren."

"Did Andrea's mother know about Lauren?"

Doug followed Margot's gaze across the room to where Joe sat listening in sheltered silence.

"I don't think so, just that her daughter needed help. Andrea'd tried to stab the mother though, Meg now remembers, so the mother tried to get her help but I guess it wasn't enough. Meg knew Andrea'd gone away to a hospital but never fully understood. Flannery had Meg talk to someone here yesterday, some therapist the police use, and she's going to get some help out west too, just to get through it all. I dropped her off at the airport this morning."

"That was very kind of you," Margot said, finally selecting a stuffed mushroom then beaming a smile to Dorothy Sinclair. "Delicious."

Dorothy smiled back. "Well, it's a bit of a makeshift Christmas, but what can you do?"

"You've done a lot, Mom." Joe stood up and reached for his mother with the arm that wasn't supporting his crutches. She set down another tray, this time assorted cheeses. "And all I can smell is that turkey." He kissed her cheek, cringing ever so slightly at bending down with his still broken ribs. She hugged him gently, lost in wordless excuses for her husband's absence that no longer bore any need. Together they stayed standing, watching over the family and friends.

"Yes, Mom, thank you so much for your help. Thank you all," Taryn whispered, her once black and blue face now a brownish purple with a yellow hue. Her hair was pulled back in a paisley scarf to cover the areas the hospital had shaved away. "Joe and I could never have pulled off hosting Christmas in our shape. Let alone with the entire house still all packed up."

"That's what paper plates and fake trees are for," Ryan joked, pointing to the half-naked small plastic tree he'd purchased the day before. "Next year we'll do it a bit better." He turned to his wife who smiled and rubbed her hand along his leg.

"It's perfect," Taryn said to her brother, feeling tears welling in her eyes as his children sat mesmerized by a board game. "But this time we'll clean up after ourselves and throw the paper plates away." She winked towards Margot.

"It is wonderful," Flannery said, "and here I thought I'd be dining at O'Reilly's again this year." He popped another mushroom into his mouth and sat down next to Margot.

"And what's the latest on that guy? Dominic?" Taryn asked.

"Dominic Larenta," Flannery replied. "We can't find him yet, elusive fella. RCMP's after him now. Won't be long, but he sure knew how to cover his tracks in a hurry."

"I should have called you or the cops right away. I don't know where my head was at that morning." Joe shook his head.

"Nah, they'll get him. He's been at this a long time. Now that they've dug into things, they've found he's got quite a reputation among hackers, using various names. They've linked him to a lot of stuff, mostly stealing money from corporations and routing it through all kinds of channels."

"Just like he did to us. I still can't believe someone stole from us like that," Margot's voice trailed off.

"Well, you're all protected now," Flannery reassured her. "And stealing from you folks wasn't really about the money for him. A drop in the bucket really, it was more about keeping Andrea's attention. That must have been some messed up relationship."

Joe spoke slowly, as though trying to understand it all himself. "From the little I saw, it sure was. Seems like he was some kind of stereotypical computer genius with no social skills. I guess they used each other for what they both needed. He kept her housed and set financially and she gave him," Joe paused, "sex, I guess the only way he could get it."

"It's all kind of sad," Taryn said, as those close to her smiled at her ever-extending compassion.

"Cops talked to Lauren Avery's parents too," Flannery changed the subject.

"Such a long time. They must be so relieved though, to finally know the truth. I don't think Gary Avery was ever really convinced ..." Dorothy cut herself off and pulled Joe in tight.

The doorbell chimed and despite offers from Doug and Ryan to get it, Joe hobbled along the hallway and answered it, curious since no one else was expected. Chase McGill stood before him as a running car with Chase's uncle in the driver's seat idled in the driveway. Joe stepped out onto the porch.

241

"Chase!"

"Mr. Sinclair. Joe. I'm so really sorry to bother you at home on Christmas."

"It's okay, do you want to come in?"

"No, like I said, I'm sorry. It's probably not, appropriate or whatever, for me to be here. But, with Christmas and all, and the offices being closed."

"Come in, Chase. Would your uncle like to come in too?"

"Nah, he'll wait." Chase followed Joe into the hallway. At the sound of the young man's voice, Doug and Flannery appeared. Taryn and Margot followed behind.

"I, uh, well I'm sorry. I found your address on the internet. It took some searching. I guess that wasn't really appropriate. I mean, you probably don't want people just showing up. But I didn't know how else to do this, privately ya know, without reporters and stuff."

"What is it Chase?" Joe shifted his weight on his crutch as the young man's dark eyes glossed over.

"I, I just never really got to thank you. I mean really thank you. I knew things started looking better when Mr. Forester called me after we met at the office and went to the police station. Then the next day, when Mr. Forester came by and confirmed everything was over. You just can't imagine how great that felt."

Lost for words, Joe looked at Doug, pausing a moment to share a silent smile.

"It's not me you should thank, Chase. I was holed up, stranded and then in the hospital when everything came together. It's Doug and Flannery who figured it all out. Those threatening calls we both got from those guys. And you, coming forward to tell the truth. That's what really saved you. Honestly, I was asleep most of the time." Joe laughed and watched as Chase, the young and clumsy kid, puffed his chest and stuck out a rigid hand to Flannery and then Doug.

"Thank you Mr. Flannery. Mr. Forester."

"You're welcome, kid," Flannery said with a gravelly voice.

"Glad to help, Chase." Doug smiled, shaking Chase's hand. "All that matters is the truth."

"And those idiots being put away," Margot chimed in. "A big crime ring like that here in Millerton. It makes me sick."

Chase nodded. "Yeah," he turned back to Joe. "I'm glad you are OK, Mr., Joe." His eyes glazed over further and he turned to look at Margot and Taryn. "I was really worried."

"Thanks Chase. Me too. Merry Christmas. It is nice to meet you," Taryn replied, smiling kindly.

"Merry Christmas." Chase turned to leave then turned back. "You know, my Mom's in the hospital. Uncle Jack convinced her to get some help. I'm going to keep living with him for a while."

"That's great, son." Joe heard himself say "son" and wondered where it came from.

"Yeah, I'm thinking of taking some classes. I don't want to push myself too hard but, one course at a time, ya know. I'd like to finish high school. I think I can do it."

"Of course you can," Doug said with confident assurance.

"Yeah, I think so. Then, after that, who knows?" Chase turned back and opened the door. "Thanks again. Thanks for believing me." He reached for Joe and hugged him then exited quickly, head down.

The five began walking back to the dining area where Dorothy had begun serving dinner.

"That kid'll make it," Doug said, seating himself down at the head of the table.

Flannery slid into the spot next to Margot.

"He should become a cop," Flannery said.

"I'm thinking lawyer," Doug winked.

Across the table by the window, Joe and Taryn stood with their backs to their guests, lost in their own moment, as the first flakes of a new snow began to fall.

About the Author

Kathi Nidd is the author of several short stories, novellas, and poems published in Canada and the United States. While born in Ottawa, Canada and still residing there, Kathi considers home to be anywhere she finds herself engaged in a good conversation and fine wine. Travels with her work as a healthcare consultant or during magnificent vacations with her husband have provided great inspiration for stories, settings and characters. A strong love of nature and animals and an interest in synchronicity provide common themes in most works.

A former member of The Ottawa Story Spinners, Kathi participated in five of their short story collections "The Black Lake Chronicles". In 2013, the Fuzzball short story set was created on a whim but turned into a fundraiser for animal shelters across North America. More recently, Kathi was chosen as a poetry contributor to the Canadian Poetry Institute's anthology "Island Magic", selected as a contributor to a romance short story anthology "Romancing the Story", and selected for a publication of flash fiction in Haunted Waters Press. In addition, she has contributed to short story publications in several on-line magazines.

Kathi's plan is to grow her small business, "The Writing Spot", and provide mentorship and support to writers in all stages of growth through in-person and online writing groups and workshops.

"When I am writing, and so lost in the story that I lose track of time and space, that is a true moment of joy and relaxation for me."

www.thewritingspot.ca

CPSIA information can be obtained
at www.ICGtesting.com
Printed in the USA
LVOW08s0141161116

513114LV00001B/4/P

9 781773 020976